D0205138

CHARLiE BONE
AND THE TIME TWISTER

Books by Jenny Nimmo

Midnight for Charlie Bone
Charlie Bone and the Time Twister
Charlie Bone and the Blue Boa
Charlie Bone and the Castle of Mirrors
Charlie Bone and the Hidden King
Charlie Bone and the Wilderness Wolf
Charlie Bone and the Shadow of Badlock
Charlie Bone and the Red Knight

Henry and the Guardians of the Lost

The Secret Kingdom
The Secret Kingdom: The Stones of Ravenglass
The Secret Kingdom: Leopard's Gold

The Snow Spider Trilogy

CHARLIE BONE
AND THE TIME TWISTER

JENNY NIMMO

EGMONT

EGMONT

We bring stories to life

First published in paperback in Great Britain 2016
by Egmont UK Limited
The Yellow Building, 1 Nicholas Road, London W11 4AN

Text copyright © 2002 Jenny Nimmo
Cover illustration based on original works by Scott Altmann
Endpapers © Shutterstock

The moral rights of the author and illustrator have been asserted

ISBN 978 1 4052 8093 8

www.egmont.co.uk

40632/26

A CIP catalogue record for this title is available from the British Library

Typeset by Avon DataSet Ltd, Bidford on Avon, Warwickshire
Printed and bound in Great Britain by the CPI Group

CONTENTS

Beatrice Bloor
b.1835
Witch.

Bertram Babington Bloor
b.1840
Having read Mary Shelley's Frankenstein, Bertram, a scientist-magician, tried to make a human being. He was not successful.

m.

Donatella da Vinci
b.1845
Daughter of an Italian magician. She assisted Bertram but was electrocuted during one of his experiments.

Gideon
b.1875. Mathematician. Knighted for tutoring a royal prince. Sir Gideon was not endowed or interested in magic.

m.

Gudrun Solensson
b.1876
Amateur singer.

Ezekiel
b.1902
Spoiled, cunning, flawed magician. Continued his grandfather's experiments.

m.

Hilda Hansoff
b.1902
Botanist. Fatally poisoned by a rare plant.

Bartholomew
b.1930
Unendowed. Mountaineer. Lost in the Himalayas.

m.

Mary Chance
b.1930
Dancer. Danced herself to death when Bart disappeared.

Maisie
b.1?
Wid

Note:

Charlie Bone can hear the voices of people in photographs and paintings. In certain circumstances he can meet them.

Harold
b.1955
Unendowed, but interested in his grandfather's experiments.

m.

Dorothy de Vere
b.1957
Violinist.

Manfred
b.1985
Hypnotist.

Yorath Yewbeam
b.1850
Shape-shifter.

m.

Vera Kuragina
b.1862
Hypnotist.

Grace Bloor
b.1885
Painter. Unendowed.
Lived with her son and
grandson, Paton, until
she died, aged eighty.

m.

Manley
b.1884
Soldier. Killed in 1918
in the Great War.

Yolanda
b.1900
Shape-shifter.
Inherited her father's
castle. Never married.

Henry
b.1905
Disappeared when
he was eleven.
Unendowed.

Daphne
b.1908
Clairvoyant. Died
of diphtheria in 1916.

James
b.1910
Unendowed.
Historian.

m.

Solange Sourzac
b.1912
French actress. Fell and broke
her neck in mysterious
circumstances while visiting
Yolanda's castle in 1964.

Monty Bone
b.1937
Pilot. Died 1963.

m.

Grizelda
b.1937
Unendowed.

Lucretia
b.1942
Matron.
Unendowed.

Eustacia
b.1947
Clairvoyant.

Venetia
b.1952
Designer
of magic
clothes.

Paton
b.1957
Power-
booster.

Amy Jones
b.1967
Store assistant.

m.

Lyell
b.1962
Pianist.
Disappeared in
1994.

Note:

When James Yewbeam's
wife, Solange, died, his four
daughters went to live with
their evil great-aunt,
Yolanda, who turned them
against their father. Yolanda
also tried to steal Paton,
but James resisted her.

Charlie
b.1992
Picture
traveller.

THE ENDOWED

The endowed are all descended from the ten children of the Red King; a magician-king who left Africa in the twelfth century, accompanied by three leopards.

The Red King had already lived for several centuries and he made a marvellous glass sphere, putting into it memories of his life and travels through the world. He used the sphere to twist through time, visiting the past and the future.

In any other hands, the Time Twister is dangerous and unpredictable.

THE CHILDREN OF THE RED KING, CALLED THE ENDOWED

Manfred Bloor
: Head boy of Bloor's Academy. A hypnotiser. He is descended from Borlath, eldest son of the Red King. Borlath was a brutal and sadistic tyrant.

Asa Pike
: A were-beast. He is descended from a tribe who lived in the Northern forests and kept strange beasts. Asa can change shape at dusk.

Billy Raven
: Billy can communicate with animals. One of his ancestors conversed with ravens that sat on a gibbet where dead men hung. For this talent he was banished from his village.

Zelda Dobinski
: Descended from a long line of Polish magicians. Zelda is telekinetic. She can move objects with her mind.

Beth Strong
: Beth is also telekenetic. She comes from a family of circus performers.

Lysander Sage   Descended from an African wise man. He can call up his spirit ancestors.

Tancred Torsson   A storm-bringer. His Scandinavian ancestor was named after the thunder god, Thor. Tancred can bring rain, wind, thunder and lightning.

Gabriel Silk   Gabriel can feel scenes and emotions through the clothes of others. He comes from a line of psychics.

Emma Tolly   Emma can fly. Her surname derives from the Spanish swordsman from Toledo, whose daughter married the Red King. He is therefore an ancestor to all the endowed children.

Charlie Bone   Charlie can hear the voices of people in photographs and paintings. He is descended from the Yewbeams, a family with many magical endowments.

Bindi and Dorcas   Two endowed girls whose gifts are, as yet, undeveloped.

A GAME OF MARBLES

It was January 1916. The coldest winter in living memory.

The dark rooms in Bloor's Academy were almost as cold as the streets outside. Henry Yewbeam, hurrying down one of the icy passages, began to hum to himself. The humming cheered him up. It warmed his spirits as well as his feet.

On either side of the passage the eerie blue flames of gaslights flickered and hissed in their iron brackets. The smell was horrible. Henry wouldn't have been surprised to find something dead in one of the dark corners.

At home, in a sunny house by the sea, his sister, Daphne, was very ill with diphtheria. To avoid infection Henry and his brother, James, had been sent to stay with their mother's brother, Sir Gideon Bloor.

Sir Gideon wasn't the sort of person you would choose to spend your holidays with. There was nothing remotely fatherly about him. He was the headmaster of an ancient school and he never let anyone forget it.

Bloor's Academy had been in Sir Gideon's family for hundreds of years. It was a school for children gifted in music, drama and art. Bloor's also took children who were

1

endowed in other, very strange, ways. Just thinking about them made Henry shudder.

He had reached his cousin Zeke's room. Zeke was Sir Gideon's only child and a more unpleasant cousin Henry couldn't imagine. Zeke was one of the endowed children, but Henry guessed that Zeke's gift was probably nasty.

Henry opened the door and peeped inside. A row of glass jars stood on the windowsill. Inside the jars, strange things writhed gently in a clear liquid. Henry was sure it couldn't be water. The things were pale and shapeless. One was blue.

'What do you think you are doing?'

Aunt Gudrun came marching down the passage, her long black skirt drowning her footfalls with a sinister hiss. She was a very tall woman with a great amount of yellow hair piled into a bun on the back of her head. A real Viking of a person (she was, in fact, Norwegian), with an enormous chest and lungs to match.

Henry said, 'Erm . . .'

'Erm is not good enough, Henry Yewbeam. You were spying in my Zeke's room, were you not?'

'No, not at all,' said Henry.

'You shouldn't be lurking in passages, boy. Come down to the sitting-room.' Lady Bloor beckoned with her little finger, and Henry had no choice but to follow her.

His aunt led him back past the mysterious locked doors that, only a few moments ago, Henry had been vainly trying to open. He was an inquisitive boy and easily bored. A huge sigh escaped him as he trundled down a creaking staircase to the first floor.

The Bloor family lived in the west wing of the academy, but they only occupied the rooms above the ground floor, which was almost entirely taken up by a draughty grand hall, a chapel and several assembly halls and classrooms. Henry had already explored some of these rooms and found them very disappointing. All they contained were rows of battered desks and chairs, and shelves of dusty-looking books.

'Here we are!' Lady Bloor opened a door and thrust Henry into the room beyond.

A small boy, who had been kneeling in the window seat, leapt down and rushed across to Henry. 'Where've you been?' he cried.

'Just exploring,' said Henry.

'I thought you'd gone home.'

'Home is miles and miles away, Jamie.' Henry plonked himself in a deep leather chair beside the fire. The logs in the big iron grate smouldered with strange images. When Henry half-closed his eyes he could almost see the cosy sitting-room at home. He sighed again.

Aunt Gudrun frowned at Henry and said, 'Behave yourselves, boys.' She went out closing the door behind her.

When she had gone James came and sat on the arm of Henry's chair. 'Zeke's been doing funny things,' he whispered.

Henry hadn't noticed Zeke, but now he became aware of his strange cousin, enclosed in a gloomy silence at the other end of the room. He was sitting at a table, absorbed in something laid out before him. His pale, bony face was frozen in an attitude of intense concentration. Not a muscle twitched, not a breath escaped him.

'I was scared,' James said quietly.

'Why? What did he do?' Henry asked in a hushed voice.

'Well, he was doing a puzzle. There were pieces all over the table. Then Zeke stared at them and they all crawled together. Well, most of them. They made a picture. He showed it to me. It was a ship, but some of the pieces wouldn't fit.'

'It's rude to whisper,' said Zeke without taking his eyes off the puzzle.

Henry pulled himself out of the chair and strolled over to his cousin. He glanced at the twelve pieces lying beside the puzzle and then at the picture of the ship. It took less than a minute for him to see exactly where each piece fitted.

'Hm,' said Henry, and without another word he picked up the single pieces, one by one, and deftly placed them into the picture; two in the sky, three in the ship's hull, two in the rigging and four in the sea.

For a moment, Zeke watched Henry's hands in fascination. It was only when Henry was putting the last piece in place, that Zeke suddenly leapt up, crying, 'Who asked you? I could have done it. I could!'

'Sorry,' said Henry, stepping back. 'I thought you wanted some help.'

'Henry's good at puzzles,' said James.

'Well I'm good at *other* things,' snarled Zeke.

James was too small to see the danger signs. The angry glitter in Zeke's black eyes went straight over his head. 'Magic doesn't always work,' the little boy said blithely. 'Henry's cleverer than you are, Zeke.'

With that remark poor James Yewbeam sealed his brother's fate and, of course, his own.

'Get out!' cried Zeke. 'Both of you. Hateful Yewbeams. Go, now. I can't stand the sight of you!'

Henry and James ran for the door. There was a violent gleam in their cousin's pale face, and they didn't want to wait around for him to do something nasty.

'Where are we going?' panted James as he tore down the passages after his brother.

'We'll go to the big hall, Jamie. We can play marbles there.' Henry pulled a small leather bag out of his pocket and waved it at his brother.

It wasn't to be. Before they could go any further there was a shout from Aunt Gudrun.

'James, bedtime.' James pretended not to hear her. 'Now, this minute.'

'Better go,' said Henry gently. 'She'll punish you, if you don't.'

'But I want to play marbles,' said James.

Henry shook his head. 'Sorry, Jamie. Not now. Tomorrow. But I'll come and read to you later.'

'Promise? Will you finish the story of the Wallypug?'

'James, come here,' shouted Aunt Gudrun.

'I promise,' said Henry, and he meant to keep his promise. But Zeke had other plans for him.

Hanging his head, James trailed back towards the tall figure at the end of the passage.

'And you, Henry!' called Aunt Gudrun. 'You keep out of trouble.'

'Yes, Aunt,' said Henry.

He was about to descend the rather grand staircase down to the hall when he had an idea. It was already so chilly he could see his own breath, billowing away from him in little grey clouds. The great hall would be even colder. He might freeze to death.

Henry retraced his steps until he found the door to a room he had already investigated. It was a huge storeroom, full of clothes left behind by past students of the academy. There were rows of coloured capes: blue, green and purple; shelves of hats and suits, and boxes of ancient leather boots.

Henry selected a warm blue cape and put it on. It reached well over his knees, a perfect length for a draughty hall. He would be able to kneel on it without feeling the cold stone floor.

Henry descended into the hall. His hoard of marbles was the envy of all his friends. Henry's father travelled extensively and never came home without at least one precious new marble for his son's collection. Henry's leather bag held onyx stones, polished agate, glass, limestone, quartz and even spheres of painted china.

There were no lights in the hall but an early moon

sparkled through the long, frosted windows, giving the grey flagstones a soft pearly glow.

Henry decided to play Ring Taw, his favourite game. Deprived of an opponent, he would try to improve his skill by playing alone. With a piece of chalk, kept handy in his pocket, Henry drew a large ring in the centre of the hall. He then chalked a smaller ring inside the first. Selecting thirteen marbles from his bag, he placed them in a cross inside the smaller circle.

Now Henry had to kneel on the icy floor, just outside the large ring. Already his hands were blue with cold and he could hardly stop his teeth from rattling. Tucking the blue cape under his knees, he took out his favourite marble; it was a clear blue with a silvery glint inside it, like starlight. This was always his taw, or shooter.

Placing the knuckles of his right hand, palm outwards, on the floor, Henry put the blue taw on the tip of his first finger and flicked it with his thumb towards the marble cross. With a sharp clink it hit an orange marble right out of the two circles.

'Bravo!' Henry shouted.

There was a light creak from behind him. Henry squinted into the deep shadows on the oak-panelled walls. Was he imagining it, or did a long tapestry shiver slightly? On the other side of the tapestry a small door led into the west wing. Henry preferred the main staircase, for the passage behind the door was dark and creepy.

A cold draught swept past his knees and the tapestry

billowed again. A flurry of hailstones clattered against the windows, and the wind gave a sudden moan as it rushed round the snowy courtyard.

'Wind.' Henry shivered and drew his cape closer. For good measure he even pulled the hood over his head.

In the passage behind the tapestry, Ezekiel Bloor stood with a lantern in one hand, and in the other – a glowing glass sphere. Dazzling colours swirled out of the glass; a rainbow laced with gold and silver; sunshine and moonlight, one after the other. Zeke knew he mustn't look at them. He held one of the oldest marbles in the world.

On her deathbed, Zeke's great-aunt Beatrice, a witch if ever there was one, had pressed the marble into his hand. 'The Time Twister,' she said in her cracked, dying voice. 'For journeys through time. Do not look on it, Ezekiel, unless you want to travel.'

Ezekiel didn't want to travel. He thrived in the great gloomy building that was his home and could seldom be persuaded to leave it. However, he longed to know what would happen if someone *did* look into the Time Twister. No one, in Zeke's opinion, was more deserving of a shove through time, than his wretched cousin Henry Yewbeam.

Henry had by now knocked another three marbles out of the small chalked ring. He hadn't missed once, in spite of his freezing fingers. He was just stepping back to his place outside the circle when a glass ball came rolling towards him. It was slightly larger than Henry's blue taw, and tiny points of coloured light danced and shimmered all around it.

'Oh, my,' breathed Henry. He stood where he was while the strange marble rolled on until it reached his foot.

Henry picked it up. He gazed into the bright depths within the glass. He saw domes of gold, cities in sunlight, cloudless skies and much, much more. But even as he watched the scenes taking place before his eyes, Henry became aware that a change was taking place within his body, and he knew that he shouldn't have looked upon those unbelievable and breathtaking scenes.

The oak-panelled walls were breaking up. The frosted moonlight was fading. Henry's head whirled and his feet began to float. Far, far away, a cat began to mew. And then another cat, and another.

Henry thought of his small brother. Would there be time to reach him before he faded away completely? And if he did, and James saw a brother disappearing before his eyes, might he not be so frightened he would have nightmares forever? Henry decided to leave a message.

While he still had the strength, he took the chalk from his pocket and with his left hand (the right was still clamped round the Time Twister), he wrote on the stone floor, 'SORRY, JAMES. THE MARBLES . . .'

It was all Henry had time for. The next moment he had left the year of his eleventh birthday and was travelling forwards, very fast, to a year when most of the people he knew would be dead.

*

In a small, chilly room at the top of the west wing, James waited for his brother. He was so cold he had put his coat on over his flannel nightshirt. On the table beside him the flame from his candle quivered in a draught from the door. Where was Henry? Why was he taking so long?

James rubbed his eyes. He was very tired but too cold to sleep. He drew the bedcovers up to his chin and listened to the patter of freezing sleet against the windowpane. And then his candle went out.

James sat rigid in his bed, too frightened to call out. Aunt Gudrun would be cross and Cousin Zeke would tease him for being a baby. Only Henry would understand.

'Henry! Henry, where are you?' James closed his eyes and sobbed into his pillow.

Before he had completely run out of tears, James stopped shivering. The room was getting warmer. He opened his eyes and found that he could see his pillow, his hand, the window. A soft glow had spread across the ceiling. When James looked to see where it was coming from, he was amazed to find that three cats were silently pacing round his bed. One was orange, another yellow and the third a bright coppery colour.

As soon as the cats knew they had been observed, they jumped up and rubbed their heads against the boy's cold hands, his neck and his cheek. Their gleaming fur was as warm as sunlight, and as James stroked them, his fear began to leave him. He decided to go and look for Henry. Hardly had this thought entered his head than the cats leapt off the bed and ran to the door. They waited, mewing anxiously, as James pulled on his socks and his small leather boots.

With light sparkling on their silver whiskers and bright fur-tips, the cats led the way down the dark passages and narrow steps, while James hurried after them. At last he came to the wide staircase leading down into the hall. Here the cats' worried mewing became loud and urgent, and James hesitated before he descended into the vast moonlit room.

Henry was not there. His marbles lay scattered on the stone floor, winking in the bright frosted light from the windows. As James moved slowly down the stairs, the cats ran before him, wailing and growling.

James reached the bottom step and walked to the chalked circle. He could see that Henry had been playing Ring Taw, his favourite game.

'Henry!' James called. 'Henry, where have you gone?'

Never had a place appeared so vast and empty to small James Yewbeam. Never had his brother's absence seemed so utterly complete. He wouldn't try to call again. It was quite clear that Henry was gone. And he hadn't even said goodbye.

Before the tears could fall again, the three cats pounced into the white circle, drawing the boy's attention to four words chalked on the floor. A message? If only James could read. Henry had been patiently trying to teach him for weeks but, so far, James hadn't managed a single word.

Perhaps he hadn't really tried. Now, when it was a serious matter . . .

'S . . . s . . . s . . .' murmured James as the cats paced along the row of letters.

Next came an 'o' and then two 'r's, and further on his own name. And all at once James found he could understand the words his brother had left for him.

'SORRY, JAMES,' he read, 'THE MARBLES . . .' There the message ended.

Obviously Henry wanted his brother to keep the marbles safe for him. James picked up the leather bag but before he could reach the blue taw, the orange cat tapped it playfully and it sped across the hall. The yellow cat raced after it while the copper cat swept another three marbles out of the ring.

Now the great hall was alive with the sound of clinking glass and joyful purring. James was surrounded by dancing, glistening spheres of colour. The cats were playing a game and, as he watched them, a big smile broke over the boy's face.

'Stay with me,' James begged the cats.

The cats would stay. For as long as he was in that cold, dreary building, they would keep James Yewbeam as warm and safe as any small boy had a right to expect.

GRANDMA SLAMS A DOOR

Winter held the city in an iron fist. Roofs, trees, chimneys and even things that moved, were covered in a thick crust of frozen snow.

Charlie Bone had been looking forwards to an extra day of Christmas holiday. The new term surely couldn't start in this weather? But Grandma Bone had dashed his hopes.

'No shirking for you,' she said in her usual sneering way. 'Bloor's Academy opens come rain, wind or snow. The snowploughs have cleared the main road, and the school bus will stop at the top of Filbert Street on Monday morning at eight o'clock sharp.' Her lips made a nasty backfiring noise as she said the last word.

Charlie was a weekly boarder at Bloor's Academy and on Sunday nights he had to pack a bag for five days away from home. On this particular Sunday, Charlie was paying more attention to the snowflakes brushing his window than his packing.

'Pyjamas, toothbrush, pants,' Charlie muttered to himself. 'Socks, clean shirts . . .' He scratched his head. He was supposed to wear a blue cape to school but he

13

hated putting it on before he got to the academy. The other children in Filbert Street sniggered at him. Bloor's was a rather unusual school. Only children who were talented in music, art or drama could get in. Charlie had none of these talents. He was one of the twelve endowed children who were there because of unique other gifts. In his case, it was a gift he often thought he would rather be without. He could hear photographs, or rather the people in them. As soon as Grandma Bone and her three nasty sisters found out they had packed him off to Bloor's. Theirs was a family of clairvoyants, hypnotisers, werewolves, witches and worse. They were descended from a mysterious Red King, a magician of amazing powers and, like all endowed children, Charlie must be watched, his talent nurtured.

The doorbell rang and Charlie ran downstairs, eager to escape the dreary packing. As soon as he opened the door, his friend Benjamin's dog, Runner Bean, pushed past Charlie and began to shake wet snow off his back. His feathery tail sent sprays of water flying across the hall, straight into the path of Charlie's other grandma, Maisie Jones.

'You'd better dry that dog in here,' said Maisie cheerfully, as she stepped back into the kitchen. 'I'll fetch his towel.' She kept a special towel for Runner Bean, who was a frequent visitor.

The big yellow dog bounded after her while Charlie took Benjamin's coat and hung it on the hall stand.

'Are you on for building a snowman tomorrow?' Benjamin asked Charlie. 'Our school definitely won't open.'

14

'Mine will,' said Charlie gloomily. 'Sorry, Ben.'

'Aw!' Benjamin's face fell. He was a small straw-haired boy with a permanently anxious expression. 'Couldn't you pretend to be ill or something?'

'No chance,' said Charlie. 'You know what Grandma and the aunts are like.'

Benjamin knew only too well. Charlie's aunt, Eustacia, had once been Benjamin's minder. It was the worst two days of his life: disgusting food, early bedtimes and no dogs in bedrooms. Benjamin shuddered at the memory. 'OK,' he said sadly. 'I guess I can make a snowman on my own.'

A door opened on the landing above them and a voice called out, 'Is that you, Benjamin Brown? I can smell dog.'

'Yes, it's me, Mrs Bone,' said Benjamin with a sigh.

Grandma Bone appeared at the top of the stairs. Dressed all in black and with her white hair piled high on her head, she looked more like the wicked queen from a legend than someone's grandmother.

'I hope you don't intend to stay more than ten minutes,' said Grandma Bone. 'Charlie has to have an early night. It's school tomorrow.'

'Mum says I can have another hour,' Charlie shouted up to his grandmother.

'Oh? Oh, well, if that's the case, why should I bother to take an interest in your welfare. I'm clearly wasting my time.' Grandma Bone swept back into her room, slamming the door behind her.

Whether it was this door-slamming or a minor earth

15

tremor, Charlie would never know, but something caused a small picture to fall from its hook in the hall.

Charlie had never studied the faded old photographs that adorned the walls of the dark hallway. In fact, since he had discovered his unwelcome talent, he had positively avoided them; he didn't want to hear what a group of crusty-looking forebears had to say.

'Well!' exclaimed Benjamin. 'How did that happen?'

Charlie realised this was a photograph he wouldn't be able to avoid. As he picked it up and turned it over, he felt a strange fluttering in his stomach.

'Let's see!' said Benjamin.

Charlie held out the black-framed picture. It was one of those faded sepia-coloured photographs. The glass was cracked but hadn't fallen out, and through the cracks the boys could make out a family of five, grouped together in a garden. Behind them, the yellowed wall of a cottage could be glimpsed, and on the other side of the photo, beyond a stone wall, a small sailing boat sat on a velvety sea.

'Are you OK?' Benjamin glanced at Charlie.

'No,' muttered Charlie. 'You know why. Oops, here we go.' Already a thin buzz of voices was coming through to him.

It was the mother who spoke first. *Henry, stand still. You'll spoil the picture.* She was a pretty woman in a lacy frock with a high collar. A brooch, like a star, was pinned just beneath her chin. A boy of about four sat on her lap, and a girl of perhaps six or seven leaned against her knee.

Beside the woman stood a man in a soldier's uniform. He had such a merry face Charlie couldn't imagine him with the fierce and solemn look a soldier was supposed to have. But it was the boy, standing in front of the soldier, who held Charlie's gaze.

I can't breathe, muttered the boy.

'Hey, Charlie, he looks a bit like you!' Benjamin pointed a grubby finger at the older boy.

'Mm!' Charlie agreed. 'Same age as me too.'

A stiff white collar seemed to be giving the boy called Henry some trouble. It was clamped round his neck above a tightly-buttoned jacket, and almost brushed his chin. He wore knee-length breeches, long, black socks and shiny black boots.

Ouch! muttered Henry.

His mother sighed. *Is it too much to ask you to stand still?*

I think there's a fly under my collar, said Henry.

At this, the soldier burst out laughing, and Henry's brother and sister dissolved into helpless giggles.

Really, said the serious mother. *I'm sure our poor photographer doesn't find it amusing. Are you all right, Mr Caldicott?*

There was a mumbled, *Yes, thank you, madam*, and then something fell over. Charlie couldn't be sure if it was Mr Caldicott or the camera. The figures in the photograph swung all over the place, making Charlie feel quite dizzy.

'You look green,' Benjamin remarked. He led the rather

shaken Charlie into the kitchen, where Maisie was rubbing Runner Bean with a towel.

'Oh dear,' said Maisie, taking in the situation at a glance. 'Have you had one of your thingies, Charlie?'

'He has,' said Benjamin.

There was a loud sizzle as Charlie's mother, Amy, dropped an exotic-looking vegetable into a frying pan. 'What was it this time, love?' she asked.

Charlie put the photograph on the kitchen table. 'This fell off the wall when Grandma Bone slammed her door.'

'It's a wonder there are any doors left hanging in this house, the way that woman slams them,' said Maisie, emptying the cracked glass into a newspaper. 'What with the slamming and your Uncle Paton's light bulbs, and your mum's rotten vegetables. I sometimes think I'd be better off in a Home for the elderly.'

Everyone ignored this remark. They'd all heard it so often. Maisie wasn't old enough to be in a Home, and she'd been told a hundred times that her family couldn't live without her.

'So do you know who these people are?' Charlie pointed to the family in the black frame. Without the cracked glass, the soldier and his family could be seen more clearly.

Charlie's mother came and looked over his shoulder. 'They must be Yewbeams,' she said, 'Grandma Bone's relations. You'd better ask her.'

'No way,' said Charlie. 'I'll ask Uncle Paton before I go to bed. Come on, Ben.'

Tucking the black frame under his arm, Charlie led Benjamin and Runner Bean up to his room. An hour playing computer games passed very quickly, and then Grandma Bone was hammering on Charlie's door and telling him, 'Get that dog off your bed.' How did she guess? But then a lot of the Yewbeams had powers.

The boys trailed downstairs with Runner Bean behind them, and Charlie let Benjamin and his dog out of the front door.

He stood in the hall a moment, staring at the rectangle of pale wallpaper where the framed photograph had hung. What had caused that photo to fall? Could it really have been a door being slammed? In this house, the force at work was bound to be more mysterious.

'Perhaps Uncle Paton will know,' Charlie murmured. He ran upstairs.

Uncle Paton was Grandma Bone's brother, but he was twenty years younger, and had a good sense of humour. He also had a talent for exploding light bulbs when he got near them, so he spent most of the day in his room and only went out after dark. Even in the daytime, lights were on in shop windows. At night he was not so easily seen.

Charlie retrieved the photograph from his room, and knocked on his uncle's door, ignoring the permanent DO NOT DISTURB sign.

There was no response to his first knock, but his second drew an irritated, 'What is it?'

'It's about a photo, Uncle Paton.'

'Are you hearing voices again?'

''Fraid so.'

'Come in then.' This was said in a weary tone.

An extremely tall man with a great amount of untidy black hair looked up from a desk by the window. As he moved, his elbow sent a stack of books toppling to the floor.

'Bother,' said the tall man, 'and other more rude things.'

Paton was writing a history of his family, the Yewbeams, and he needed a great many books to help him do it.

'Where's the photo then? Come on, show, show!' Paton clicked his fingers impatiently.

Charlie laid the photo in front of his uncle. 'Who are they?'

Paton squinted at the family group. 'Ah, that's my father.' He pointed to the small boy sitting on his mother's knee. 'And that,' putting an ink-stained finger beside the girl, 'that's poor Daphne who died of diphtheria. The soldier is my grandfather, Colonel Manley Yewbeam – a very merry man. He was on leave from the army. There was a war on, you know. And that's my grandmother, Grace. She was an artist – a very good one.'

'And the other boy?'

'That's . . . good lord, Charlie, he looks rather like you. I never realised that before.'

'His hair is different. But I suppose he could have had it squashed down with something.' No amount of squashing would keep Charlie's thick, springy hair flat.

'Hm. Poor Henry,' muttered Paton. 'He disappeared.'

20

'How?' Charlie was amazed.

'They were staying at Bloor's, Henry and James, while their sister Daphne was dying. It was the coldest winter for a century – my father has never forgotten it. One day, in the middle of a game of marbles, Henry just vanished.' Paton stroked his chin. 'My poor father. Suddenly, he was an only child. He idolised his brother.'

'Vanished,' murmured Charlie.

'My father always suspected his cousin, Ezekiel, had something to do with it. He was jealous of Henry. Ezekiel was a rotten magician, but Henry was just naturally clever.'

'Is that the Ezekiel who's . . .?'

'Yes. Dr Bloor's grandfather. He's still there, festering away somewhere in the academy, surrounded by gas lamps and bad magic.'

'Wow! So he's about a hundred years old.'

'At least,' said Paton. He leaned forwards. 'Tell me, Charlie, these voices you hear, do they ever say anything that isn't directly connected to that moment in time when they were being photographed?'

'Erm, no,' said Charlie. 'Not yet. I don't like looking at them for too long.'

'Mm, pity,' said Paton. 'Could be interesting. Here you are then.' He held out the photograph.

'No thanks,' said Charlie. 'You keep it.'

Paton looked disappointed. 'My father would be so happy to know a little more.'

'Is he still alive, then?' Charlie was surprised. He'd never seen his great-grandfather. In fact, he'd never heard anyone speak of him.

'He's a grand old fellow,' said Paton. 'He's in his nineties now, but he still lives in that very same cottage by the sea.' He tapped the photograph. 'I visit him every month. If I start at midnight I can be there before sun-up.'

'What about Grandma and the aunts. They're his daughters, aren't they?'

Uncle Paton made one of his here-comes-a-bit-of-scandal expressions. His thin lips compressed and his long black eyebrows arched up towards his hairline. 'There was a rift, Charlie. A terrible quarrel. Long, long ago. I can hardly remember what caused it. For them, our father doesn't exist.'

'That's awful!' But somehow Charlie wasn't surprised. After all, Grandma Bone wouldn't even speak of Lyell, her only son and Charlie's father. When he vanished, she had simply sliced him out of her heart.

Charlie said goodnight to his uncle and went to bed. But as he lay awake, trying to imagine his first day back at Bloor's, Henry Yewbeam's mischievous face kept breaking into his thoughts. How had he disappeared? And where did he go?

A TREE FALLS

The temperature dropped several degrees during the night. On Monday morning, an icy wind sent clouds of sleet whipping down Filbert Street, blinding anyone brave enough to venture out.

'I can't believe I've got to go to school in this,' Charlie muttered as he struggled through the wind.

'You'd better believe it, Charlie, there's the bus! Good luck!' Amy Bone blew Charlie a kiss then turned into a side street and made her way towards the greengrocer's. Charlie ran up to the top of Filbert Street where a blue bus was waiting to collect Music students for Bloor's Academy.

Charlie'd been put in Music only because his father had been in it. His friend, Fidelio, on the other hand was brilliant. Fidelio had saved a seat for Charlie on the bus, and as soon as Charlie saw his friend's bright mop of hair and beaming face, he felt better.

'This term's going to seem very boring,' sighed Fidelio, 'after all that excitement.'

'I don't think I mind a bit of boringness,' said Charlie. 'I'm certainly not going in the ruined castle again.'

The bus parked at one end of a cobbled square with a fountain of stone swans in the centre. As the children left the bus, they noticed that icicles hung from the swans' beaks and their wings were laced with frost. They appeared to be swimming on a frozen pool.

'Look at that,' Charlie exclaimed as he passed the fountain.

'The dormitory's going to be like a fridge,' Fidelio said grimly.

Charlie wished he'd packed a hot water bottle.

Another bus had pulled up in the square. This one was purple and a crowd of children in purple capes came leaping down the steps.

'Here she comes!' said Fidelio, as a girl with indigo-coloured hair came flying towards them.

'Hi, Olivia!' called Charlie.

Olivia Vertigo clutched Charlie's arm. 'Charlie, good to see you alive. You too, Fido!'

'It's good to *be* alive,' said Fidelio. 'What's with the Fido?'

'I decided to change your name,' said Olivia. 'Fidelio's such a mouthful and Fido's really cool. Don't you like it?'

'It's a dog's name,' said Fidelio. 'But I'll think about it.'

Children in green capes had now joined the crowd. The Art pupils were not as noisy as the Drama students and not so flamboyant, and yet when their green capes flew open, a glimpse of a sequinned scarf, or gold threaded into a black sweater, made one suspect that more serious rules would be broken by these quiet children than by those wearing blue or purple.

The tall grey walls of Bloor's Academy now loomed before them. On either side of the imposing arched entrance, there was a tower with a pointed roof and, as Charlie approached the wide steps up to the arch, he found his gaze drawn to the window at the top of one of the towers. His mother said she had felt someone watching her from that window, and now Charlie had the same sensation. He shivered slightly and hurried to catch up with his friends.

They had crossed a paved courtyard and were now climbing another flight of steps. At the top, two massive bronze-studded doors stood open to receive the throng of children.

Charlie's stomach gave a lurch as he passed through the doors. He had enemies in Bloor's Academy and, as yet, he wasn't quite sure why. Why were they trying to get rid of him? Permanently.

A door beneath two crossed trumpets led to the Music department. Olivia waved and disappeared through a door under two masks, while the children in green made their way to the end of the hall where a pencil crossed with a paintbrush indicated the Art department.

Charlie and Fidelio went first to the blue cloakroom and then on to the assembly room.

As one of the smallest boys, Charlie had to stand in the front row beside the smallest of all, a white-haired albino called Billy Raven. Charlie asked him if he had enjoyed

25

Christmas but Billy ignored him. He was an orphan and Charlie hoped he hadn't had to spend his holiday at Bloor's. A fate worse than death in Charlie's opinion. He noticed that Billy was wearing a pair of smart fur-lined boots. A Christmas present, no doubt.

They were only halfway through the first hymn when there was a shout from the stage.

'Stop!'

The orchestra ground to a halt. The singing died.

Dr Saltweather, head of Music, paced across the stage, arms folded across his chest. He was a big man with a lot of white, wiry hair. The row of music teachers standing behind him looked apprehensive. Dr Saltweather was just as likely to shout at them as the children.

'Do you call that singing?' roared Dr Saltweather. 'It's a horrible moan. It's a disgraceful whine. You're musicians, for goodness sake. Sing in tune, give it some life! Now – back to the beginning, please!' He nodded to the small orchestra at the side of the stage and raised his baton.

Charlie cleared his throat. He couldn't sing at the best of times, but today the assembly room was so cold he couldn't stop his jaw from shaking. The temperature had affected the other children as well, even the best singers were hunched and shivering under their blue capes.

They started up again, and this time Dr Saltweather couldn't complain. The old panelled walls vibrated with sound. Even the teachers were doing their best. Merry Mr O'Connor threw back his head and sang heartily, Miss

Chrystal and Mrs Dance smiled and swayed, while old Mr Paltry frowned with concentration. The piano teacher, Mr Pilgrim, however, did not even open his mouth.

Charlie realised that Mr Pilgrim was not standing up. He was next to Mrs Dance, who was extremely small, and being very tall himself, it was not immediately apparent that he was still sitting down. What was wrong with him? He never looked you in the eye, never spoke, never walked in the grounds like other teachers. He seemed to be completely unaware of his surroundings, and his pale face never showed the slightest flicker of emotion.

Until now.

Mr Pilgrim was staring at Charlie and Charlie had the oddest sensation that the teacher knew him, not as a student, but someone else. It was as if the dark, silent man was trying to recognise him.

There was a sudden, violent crack from beyond the window. It was so loud they could hear it above their boisterous singing. Even Dr Saltweather paused in his conducting. Another crack resounded over the snow outside, and then a tremendous thump shook the walls and windows.

Dr Saltweather put down his baton and strode to one of the long windows. When some of the children followed he didn't bother to stop them.

'Good lord!' exclaimed Dr Saltweather. 'Snow's done for the old cedar!'

The huge tree now lay halfway across the garden; its branches broken and its tangled roots pulled clear of the ground. There was another crack as a long branch supporting the crown of the tree finally broke and, with a dreadful groan, the trunk sank into the snow.

So many games had been played under its sweeping branches, so many whispered secrets kept safe by its wide shadow. Now it was gone, and in its place there was only a wide expanse of snow and an unbroken view to the ramparts of the ruined castle. Snow encrusted the top of the walls and clung to the uneven surfaces, but the blood red of the great stones stood out ominously in the white landscape.

As Charlie stared at the castle walls, something happened. It could have been a trick of the light, but he was sure another tree, smaller than the cedar, appeared in the arched entrance to the castle. Its leaves were red and gold and yet other trees had lost their autumn colours.

'Did you see that?' Charlie whispered to Fidelio.

'What?'

'A tree moved,' said Charlie. 'Look, now it's standing by the castle wall. Can't you see it?'

Fidelio frowned and shook his head.

Charlie tried to blink the tree away. But when he looked again, it was still there. No one else appeared to have seen it. Charlie had a familiar fluttery feeling in his stomach. It always happened when he heard the voices, but this time there had been no voices.

A bang from the stage made him look back. Mr Pilgrim had got to his feet, very suddenly, knocking over his chair. He gazed over the heads of the children, into the garden beyond the window. He could have been looking at the fallen tree, but Charlie was sure he was staring past to the red walls of the castle. Had he seen the strange, moving tree?

Dr Saltweather swung away from the window. 'Next hymn, children,' he said as he marched back to the stage. 'You'll never get to your classes at this rate.'

After assembly, Charlie had his lesson with Mr Paltry – Wind. Mr Paltry was an impatient, elderly flautist. Teaching Charlie Bone to play the recorder was like trying to fill a bucket with a hole in it, he complained. The old man sighed frequently, polished his glasses, and wasn't above whacking the recorder while Charlie was in mid-blow. Charlie reckoned that if Mr Paltry continued attacking him in this way, he would eventually lose his teeth and then perhaps he would be released from his horrible music lessons.

'Go, Bone, go!' Mr Paltry grunted after forty minutes of mutual torture.

Charlie went, very happily. Next it was on with the wellingtons and out into the snowy garden. In cold weather the children were allowed to wear their capes outside; in summer, capes had to be left in the cloakroom.

Fidelio was late arriving from his violin lesson, so when the two boys finally ran outside, the snow had already been trampled by three hundred children. Snowmen were being built, snowball fights were in progress, and Mr Weedon, the gardener, was trying to shoo children away from the fallen tree.

'I want to see something by the castle,' Charlie told Fidelio.

'You said you didn't want to go near it,' his friend reminded him.

'No, but . . . it's like I said, I saw something. I want to know if there are any footprints.'

'OK.' Fidelio gave a good-natured shrug.

As they ran past the fallen cedar, Billy Raven called out, 'Where are you going, you two?'

Almost without thinking, Charlie shouted, 'None of your business.'

The albino scowled and shrank against the dark branches of the tree. His ruby-coloured eyes flashed behind the thick lenses of his glasses.

'Why did you say that?' Fidelio asked as they hurried on.

'I couldn't help it,' said Charlie. 'There's something wrong with Billy Raven. I don't trust him.'

They had reached the entrance to the ruined castle. The snow beneath the huge arch was clear and smooth. No one had been in or out of the ruin.

Charlie frowned. 'I saw it,' he murmured.

'Let's go in,' said Fidelio.

Charlie hesitated.

'It doesn't look so bad in daylight,' said Fidelio, peering through the arch. He bounded in and Charlie followed. They tramped across a courtyard and took one of the five passages that led deeper into the ruin.

After several minutes of shuffling through the dark, they

emerged into another courtyard. That's where they saw the blood. Or something like it. A few deep red flecks lay in the snow beside a patch of red-gold leaves.

'The beast!' cried Charlie. 'Let's get out.'

It was only when they were standing safely outside the walls again that Fidelio said, 'It might not have been the beast.'

'There was blood,' said Charlie. 'And it *was* the beast. It's killed something. Or wounded it.'

'But there were no other marks, Charlie. No sign of a fight, or footprints . . . or . . .'

Charlie didn't wait to hear the rest of his friend's very reasonable doubts. He raced away from the ruin as if he were re-living the long night when a yellow-eyed beast had chased him through the endless passages and cold echoing chambers. When he reached the fallen tree, he waited for Fidelio to catch up with him.

'Clear off, you!' said a deep voice behind him.

Already nervous, Charlie jumped and swung round. Mr Weedon's red face appeared through the mesh of broken branches. He was wearing a shiny black helmet and Charlie caught the glint of a saw, held in the big man's black gauntlet.

'This tree's dangerous,' said Mr Weedon. 'I've told you kids not to play here.'

'I wasn't playing,' said Charlie. Fidelio had caught up with him and he felt a little more confident.

'Oh, no. Not you, Charlie Bone. You never play, do ya? A very serious boy, aren't cha?'

'You don't know anything about me,' Charlie said angrily. 'You can't . . .'

There was a loud roar followed by a grinding noise as Mr Weedon made his way through the tangle of branches towards Charlie. Twigs flew in all directions as the saw bit through wood and foliage.

'Come on!' Fidelio pulled at Charlie's cape. 'Let's get out of here.'

'That man's dangerous,' Charlie muttered as they ran away from the tree. 'How does he know who I am?'

'You're famous,' said Fidelio breathlessly. They were now far enough from Mr Weedon to take a rest. 'Getting lost in that old ruin last term was quite an event. Everyone knows who you are.'

Charlie wished it wasn't so.

The sound of a hunting horn rang out across the grounds, a signal for the end of break.

The temperature was still falling. After supper, the twelve endowed children went, as usual, to the King's Room, to do their homework. It was there that a very nasty row broke out between two great friends: Tancred Torsson and Lysander, the African.

Lysander was feeling the cold more than most, but being a good-humoured person his complaints were made in a friendly, almost jokey, way. What he actually said to Tancred was, 'Tanc, what have you done to the weather?'

'Not you too!' Tancred jumped up and stamped his foot. 'I can't change the temperature. Storms are my thing, but

I don't use my talent frivolously. I thought that you, of all people, would know better.'

Before Lysander could reply, Manfred Bloor spoke up. 'Come on, Tancred! Spare a thought for our African friend here. You're freezing him to death.'

'I'm not!' screeched Tancred, tearing at his crackling hair.

'He's only joking, Tanc,' said Lysander with a smile.

By this time some of the children were beginning to feel uncomfortable. Charlie was particularly concerned. Lysander and Tancred had saved him from the ruin. Together they were a powerful force against the darker powers that lurked in Bloor's Academy. He couldn't bear to see them quarrelling.

'Are you on his side now?' Tancred demanded, glaring at his old ally.

'Everyone's on my side,' sniggered Manfred.

Lysander silently shook his head, but unfortunately Zelda Dobinski chose that moment to show off her particularly nasty gift for moving things. She was staring at a huge reference book on the shelves behind Tancred. The book launched itself across the room and caught Tancred in the back just as he whirled towards the door.

'Owww!' roared Tancred.

Six children burst into wild laughter, while five looked on in horror.

Tancred didn't notice the sympathetic faces. He was only aware of the mocking laughter. Wind rushed furiously round the room as the stormy boy swept through the door, leaving it banging violently against the wall.

Charlie couldn't stop himself. 'Wait!' he cried, leaping after Tancred.

'And where do you think you're going, Bone?' said Manfred.

'I've left my pens in the cloakroom,' lied Charlie.

A scrawny, red-haired boy looked up and sneered, 'Always forgetting things, aren't you, Bone?'

'Not always, Asa.' Charlie was scared of Asa Pike. He was Manfred's sidekick and could change his shape at dusk.

'Close the door,' said Asa, as Charlie stepped outside.

Charlie pulled the door shut behind him. The passage outside was deserted. Charlie decided to try the hall.

As he descended the wide staircase, a blast of arctic air almost rocked him off his feet. He stepped down into the stone-flagged hall and stood very still. Something was happening to his eyes. He was seeing things that should not be there. A cloud of sparkling particles swirled in the very centre of the long room. Was it an ice storm?

Gradually the pale fragments grew more vivid. Now they were forming a blurred shape, blue with a touch of black beneath it. Before Charlie's astonished gaze, a figure in a blue hooded cape was materialising.

Charlie had no doubt that he was seeing a ghost. But when the figure turned to face him, he found, to his horror, that he was looking at . . . himself?

HIDING HENRY

It was the other Charlie who spoke first.

'What a joke,' said the boy. 'I haven't travelled very far at all.'

He had such a normal sort of voice that Charlie was reassured. This wasn't a ghost. But if not a ghost, what was it? Clearing his throat, he asked, 'Where have you come from exactly?'

'Here,' said the boy. 'Just now I was here, but,' he shaded his eyes with his hand and gazed up at the row of electric lights illuminating the hall, 'it wasn't like this. How did it get so bright?'

'Electricity,' said Charlie. He was beginning to recognise the boy. 'Are you . . .?' he began. 'I mean, have you . . . well, the thing is, I've seen you in a photo. Are you Henry Yewbeam?'

'That's me,' said Henry, beaming. 'I think I've seen you too. Somewhere. Who are you?'

'I'm your . . . erm . . . sort of cousin, Charlie Bone.'

'No! This is very good news. A cousin, well, well.' Henry

35

marched over and shook Charlie's hand. 'Very glad to meet you, Charlie Bone.'

'The news isn't that good,' said Charlie. 'What was the date when you . . . just now?'

'January 12th, 1916,' said Henry. 'I always know the date.'

'I'm afraid it isn't that now.'

'No?' Henry's smile began to fade. 'So . . .?'

'You're almost ninety years ahead of where you were,' said Charlie.

Henry's mouth opened but no words came out. Instead, there was a sharp ping as something dropped out of his hand and hit the floor.

Charlie saw a large glass marble rolling across the hall. 'Wow!' he exclaimed, but before he could pick it up, Henry shouted, 'Careful, Charlie. Don't look at it.'

'Why?'

'It's what brought me here.'

Charlie stood back from the shining glass marble. 'You mean it brought you through time?'

Henry nodded. 'It's a time twister. My mama told me about it, but I'd never seen it until just now. I should have guessed what it was. I knew Zeke would try and punish me.'

'Zeke?'

'My cousin, Ezekiel Bloor.' Henry suddenly grinned. 'I say, he's probably dead by now.' And then a sad and solemn expression crossed his face. 'They're probably all dead: Mother, Father, my sister, and even my brother, James. There's no one left.'

36

'There's me,' said Charlie, 'and I think your brother is . . .'

At that moment, a dreadful howl came from the stairs above them. The boys looked up to see a squat, ugly-looking dog standing at the top of the stairs. It howled again, raising its long nose towards the roof, while folds of almost hairless skin shook beneath its whiskery chin.

'What an ugly beast,' Henry whispered.

'It's Cook's dog, Blessed.' Charlie didn't wait for the dog to howl again. 'Quick,' he said, grabbing Henry's arm. 'You've got to hide. This isn't a good place for you to be right now. There are people here who might – do something nasty, if they find out who you are.'

'Why?' asked Henry, his eyes widening.

'Just a feeling,' said Charlie. 'Come on.' He dragged Henry towards the door into the west wing.

'Where are we going?' said Henry, scooping up the Time Twister and slipping it into his pocket.

For a moment Charlie had no idea why he was taking Henry into the west wing. He turned the heavy brass ring in the door and pushed his new friend into the dark passage beyond.

'I know this place,' whispered Henry. 'I never liked it.'

'Nor me,' said Charlie. 'But we have to go this way to find somewhere safe.' He closed the door behind him just as Blessed gave another mournful howl.

The two boys made their way along the passage until they reached an empty, circular room. A dim light, hanging from the ceiling, showed an ancient wooden door and, opposite the door, a flight of stone steps.

'The tower?' Henry looked at the steps and pulled a face.

It was then that Charlie realised why he had brought Henry to this place. 'You'll be safe at the top,' he said.

'Will I?' Henry looked doubtful.

'Trust me,' said Charlie.

As Henry began to mount the steps, Charlie noticed his peculiar tweed breeches. They reached only to the knee, where a button held them in place over loose grey socks.

Henry's boots looked distinctly feminine: black and shiny, they were neatly laced just above the ankle.

'We'd better find you some more clothes,' Charlie muttered as they reached a second circular room. A door led off this room into the west wing, but Charlie urged Henry up a second flight of steps. 'The Bloors live through there,' he said.

'Interesting,' said Henry. 'Some things haven't changed then.'

They kept climbing upwards but long before they reached the top of the tower, the sound of a piano could be heard, echoing down the narrow stairwell.

Henry stopped. 'There's someone up there.'

'It's the piano teacher, Mr Pilgrim,' said Charlie. 'No one else comes up here, and Mr Pilgrim doesn't really notice things. He won't be a problem, promise!'

Another two sets of stairs brought them to the small room at the top of the tower. Sheets of music lay scattered on the floor and the shelves that ran from floor to ceiling were crammed with huge leather-bound albums, and thick dog-eared scores.

'It'll be warm here,' said Charlie, moving a few piles away from the bookcase. 'You see, if we put some paper on the floor like this,' he spread several sheets of music between the bookcase and a wall of piled scores, 'it'll make a sort of bed, and you can hide here till morning.'

'And then what?' asked Henry.

'Well . . .' Charlie scratched his head. 'Then I'll find a way to get you some breakfast, and maybe some new clothes.'

'What's wrong with my clothes?' Henry gave an anxious frown.

'They're just different. We don't wear that kind of stuff now.'

Henry glanced at Charlie's long grey trousers and thick-soled shoes. 'No. So I see,' he said.

'I'd better be getting back,' said Charlie. 'The head boy, Manfred Bloor, will be after me, and I don't want to get on the wrong side of him. He hypnotises.'

'Oh. One of those.' Henry had heard about the hypnotisers in his family. 'Are you one of *them*?' he asked Charlie. 'The endowed?'

''Fraid so,' said Charlie. 'That's how I knew you.'

'What about him?' Henry pointed to the door behind which the piano music flowed on.

'He won't bother you,' said Charlie. ''Bye now.' He gave a wave and backed out of the small room feeling inexplicably guilty.

In the King's Room, a boy with a long, sad face glanced anxiously at Charlie's empty seat. The boy's name was Gabriel Silk, and he worried about Charlie. He should have gone after Tancred, not let Charlie go. Charlie was younger and likely to land in some sort of trouble. He was the kind of boy unfortunate things happened to.

And then the howling began. At first they all tried to ignore it, but in the end Manfred flung down his pen and exclaimed, 'Bloody dog! Billy, go and shut it up.'

'I'll go,' Gabriel offered.

'I said Billy.' Manfred gave Gabriel one of his horrible stares and then turned his piercing black gaze on Billy. 'Go on,' he said. 'You can talk to the wretched thing. Ask it if it's got a bellyache.'

'Yes, Manfred.' Billy scuttled to the door.

As he ran down the chilly stairwells and dark corridors, he talked to himself. He hated it when everyone else was shut away doing homework. He was afraid of meeting the ghosts. He knew they were there – gliding about in the dark. Billy never went home. He had no home to go to. Sometimes he stayed with an aunt. But not often.

He had reached the wide landing where a grand staircase led down into the hall. Blessed was sitting at the top of the stairs, still howling.

Billy sat beside the dog and put one hand on its plump back. 'What's the matter, Blessed?' The words came out in a series of little grunts and sniffs. A language that Blessed could understand.

The old dog stopped howling. 'Boy came,' he said. 'Bad thing. Wrong.'

'What boy? Why was it wrong?' asked Billy.

Blessed considered this question. He seemed to be having some difficulty with his reply. At last he grunted, 'Boy came from nowhere. With ball, very small. Shiny. Blessed not like this ball. It bad magic.'

Billy was perplexed. 'Was it Tancred?' he asked. 'Boy with lots of yellow hair?'

'No. Boy was like that one.' Blessed stared down the hall. Following the dog's gaze, Billy was surprised to see Charlie Bone quietly closing the door into the west wing.

'Where've you been?' Billy called.

Charlie looked up, startled. 'Nowhere,' he said. 'Just looking for Tancred.'

'Blessed said another boy was here; a boy like you.'

'Blessed's got a vivid imagination.' Charlie began to cross the hall.

'He says there was a ball. It was small and shiny and he didn't like it.'

'I think Blessed was dreaming,' said Charlie, climbing the stairs towards Billy.

Billy looked at the old dog. 'Blessed doesn't lie,' he said. 'Dogs can't.'

'They can dream, can't they? Come on, Billy. We'd better

get back to our homework or we'll get detention.'

'Go back to Cook,' Billy told the dog. 'Go on, Blessed. No more howling.'

Blessed gave a sullen grunt and began to flop down the stairs, while Billy and Charlie ran back to the King's Room.

When homework was over, Charlie had half a mind to go and visit Henry. He didn't like leaving him alone in the tower, nearly a hundred years from where he was supposed to be. Of course, he wasn't quite alone, but Mr Pilgrim hardly counted. Charlie badly needed to confide in someone.

When he reached the dormitory, he found Fidelio filling his cupboard with the clothes from his bag. There were two boys from Drama in the room and Charlie couldn't risk being overheard. 'I want to ask you something,' he whispered to his friend. 'Can we go somewhere else?'

'The art room,' Fidelio said softly.

As they came out of the dormitory, they walked straight into Billy Raven.

'Billy gives me the creeps these days,' Fidelio whispered as they sped down the corridor. 'I used to feel sorry for him, but I don't like the way he watches people.'

'Someone's got to him,' said Charlie. 'I don't know who it is, but they're making him spy for them. I don't think Billy can help it.'

They had reached the art room.

'Light's still on,' Charlie commented. 'But no one's here.'

'Mr Boldova might come back,' warned Fidelio. 'We'd better hide over there.'

A large painting of trees had been propped against two easels near the wall, and the boys managed to squeeze behind it and squat on the floor. In a hushed voice, Charlie began to tell his friend about the sudden appearance of Henry, the boy with the Time Twister, who had vanished nearly a hundred years ago. However, as soon as he mentioned the voices in the photograph, Fidelio clutched his arm.

'Hold on,' he said. 'D'you mean you can *hear* what's going on in photos?'

Charlie nodded. He had never told Fidelio about his peculiar talent. 'I don't like people to know,' he muttered.

'I don't think I would either,' said Fidelio. 'Don't worry. I won't tell a soul. Go on about Henry. Where is he now?'

'I took him up to the top of the music tower. I couldn't think of anywhere else.'

'What about Mr Pilgrim?'

'He won't even notice Henry, and if he does . . .' Charlie hesitated, 'I don't think he'll harm him.'

'Hm. I wonder! You can't tell with Mr Pilgrim,' murmured Fidelio. 'So, what are you going to do with this long-lost great-great-uncle?'

'I thought I'd try and smuggle him home at the weekend. But first I've got to get some food to him.'

'Lunch break would be best,' said Fidelio. 'He can have my meat – if it's not mince; and you can sneak up to the tower while I . . .' He broke off suddenly, as a face appeared at the top of the tree painting.

'What are you doing?' asked Emma Tolly.

43

Charlie was tempted to tell her; she was, after all, a friend, as well as endowed, but something held him back. 'We're just talking,' he said. 'Can't get any peace in the dorm.'

'I know,' Emma sighed. 'I came to finish a drawing.'

'We were just going,' said Fidelio.

The two boys wriggled out from behind the painting.

Just as they were leaving the art room, Charlie caught sight of a large sketch book, lying open on a table. He stared at it, and moved closer.

'It's mine,' said Emma. 'Just sketches, nothing special.'

But they were special. Both pages of the open book were covered with pictures of birds: birds in flight; swooping, hovering, soaring and diving. They were so real, Charlie felt that if he touched them he would feel real feathers.

'They're brilliant,' he murmured.

'Brilliant,' Fidelio repeated.

'Thank you!' Emma gave one of her shy smiles.

All at once, the door behind them opened, and a voice said, 'What's going on in here?'

Mr Boldova appeared. You could tell he was an art teacher because his clothes were covered in splashes of paint. Even his green cape, which he often forgot to wear, had little flecks of colour on the sleeves. Mr Boldova always looked as if he had just been on holiday. He had bright hazel eyes, a very healthy complexion, and long brown hair tied in a ponytail.

'I was showing my work to Charlie and Fidelio,' Emma said confidently. 'We were just going.'

44

'That's all right, Emma.' The art teacher beamed at them all.

It was impossible to be afraid of Mr Boldova. He never gave detention, never punished pupils for untidiness, forgetfulness or even being late. The only thing that made him angry was bad art. He gave Charlie a searching look and said, 'Ah, Charlie Bone.'

'Yes, sir,' said Charlie. 'Goodnight, sir.'

The three children slipped past him and ran for their dormitories. It was already five minutes to lights out. Matron would be on the warpath, and Matron was not an understanding person. She was, in fact, Charlie's great-aunt, Lucretia Yewbeam.

As they dashed into their dormitory, the boys heard Miss Yewbeam shouting at some poor girl who had lost her slippers.

'We'll just make it before she gets here,' said Fidelio, rushing to the bathroom.

Billy Raven was sitting up in bed. 'Where've you been?' he asked Charlie.

'Had some extra work to do,' said Charlie. He pulled on his pyjamas and jumped into bed, just as Matron poked her long face round the door.

'Lights out!' she barked, flicking the light switch.

Out went the bare bulb hanging in the centre of the room.

'That was a close one,' murmured Gabriel Silk from the bed next to Charlie.

Just before Charlie finally drifted off, he thought of the

boy in the tower; cold, hungry, and probably frightened. What was to be done with Henry Yewbeam?

Unable to sleep, Henry Yewbeam was staring out across the city. There was a small, round window in the wall between the bookcases and Henry, anxious to know if the world had changed in ninety years, had climbed on to a stool to find out.

The world had, indeed, changed. The sky above the horizon seemed to be on fire. It had a terrifying orange glow. Could it be the rows of street lights leading into the distance? Pinpricks of radiance shone out from the dark blocks of houses and, below the tower, pairs of shining lights, some red, some white, swept across Henry's field of vision, like earthly shooting stars.

'Motor cars,' murmured Henry, as one came closer. 'So many.'

'So many,' said a voice, like an echo.

Henry became aware that a man was standing in the darkness beside him. The piano music coming from the room next door had stopped. Henry was relieved; he didn't have much of an ear for music.

'Are you Mr Pilgrim?' Henry asked.

There was no reply to his question. In the soft light coming through the window, Henry could make out a pale face and very black hair. The man's expression was solemn and faraway.

'I'm Henry Yewbeam,' said Henry.

Still no reply.

It was like talking to someone who wasn't really there. Perhaps it wouldn't matter if Henry told him the truth.

'I'm very old,' he said. 'Or at least I should be.'

In the distance a clock began to strike. The deep chimes of the cathedral pealed out across the city. Mr Pilgrim turned to Henry. His eyes held a strange glitter.

Henry had just counted the twelfth stroke when Mr Pilgrim said, 'Are you cold?'

'Yes,' said Henry.

The piano teacher took off his blue cape and wrapped it round the boy's shoulders.

'Thank you,' said Henry, stepping off the stool.

Mr Pilgrim smiled. He stretched up to a high shelf and pulled a tin from a row of books. Lifting the lid, he offered the tin to Henry. 'Oatcakes,' he said. 'You see, I live up here practically. And one gets hungry.'

'One does,' Henry agreed, politely taking only one oatcake.

Mr Pilgrim didn't offer him any more. He put the tin on the stool and said, 'Help yourself.' The faraway look had come back into his eyes. He seemed to be trying to remember something. Frowning, he murmured, 'Goodnight.'

And then he was gone, slipping away down the stone steps with hardly a sound.

Henry would have liked the strange man to stay. He was grateful for the extra cape but, to tell the truth, it was not as cold as it had been. In fact, the temperature was

47

rising rapidly. The icicles hanging outside the window were beginning to melt.

All around the tower there was a steady drip, drip, drip of ice turning to water. It was a sound that filled Henry with foreboding. He had just worked out that his sudden twist through time must have had something to do with the cold. He had arrived in Bloor's when the temperature had reached exactly the same degree as when he had left, in 1916. A change in the weather could make a difference to time travel.

'I won't be able to get home,' Henry said to himself. 'I'll never see my family again.' And suddenly his situation seemed almost too grim to bear. 'But I must!' he murmured.

OLIVIA MAKES A MESS

Billy Raven lay wide awake. For two weeks he had slept alone in the long dormitory. Now he must get used to the grunts and snores, the heavy breathing and tiny whimpers of other boys. It wasn't easy. Billy had always been a light sleeper.

Tonight he was feeling excited. He had something to tell old Ezekiel Bloor. Perhaps he would be rewarded. When he was quite sure the other boys were asleep, Billy swung his feet into his slippers and pulled on his dressing gown. The floorboards gave only the slightest creak as he crossed the room and slipped out of the dormitory.

Manfred Bloor had given Billy a present for Christmas: a long black torch with a very powerful beam. Billy hadn't expected a gift from the head boy of all people, but when Manfred bent down and whispered, 'We must keep our spies happy,' Billy had understood.

He switched on the torch and a brilliant shaft of light swept right to the end of the passage. Billy began his long journey to the upper regions of the west wing. He usually waited for Blessed to lead him. But tonight he couldn't wait.

As Billy made his way closer to the old man's room, he had to navigate a gloomy realm that never changed. It was one of the few places where Ezekiel's flawed magic had worked as he wished. So Billy's slippered feet made no prints in the thick dust, and the cobwebs he walked through wove themselves together as soon as he had passed. If it were not for the occasional hiss from a gaslight, you would have thought the creaking steps and shadowy passages had been deserted for a hundred years.

Billy had reached a black door, the paint scarred by years of dog scratchings. He knocked twice and a voice croaked, 'Who is there?'

'Billy Raven,' said Billy.

'Enter, Billy Raven,' said the voice.

Billy walked in.

Ezekiel Bloor sat in his wheelchair beside a blazing fire. A sheepskin rug was draped round his shoulders, and his ancient skull-like face poked from beneath a black woolly hat. A pile of faded velvet cushions were propped behind his back, and he wore a black velvet jacket studded with gold buttons. For all his finery, though, Billy couldn't help thinking the old man looked a bit like a dead sheep.

Without being invited, the small boy sat down heavily in the chair opposite Ezekiel. The sudden change in atmosphere made him feel dizzy.

'Where's the dog?' asked the old man.

'I don't know. I couldn't wait for him. I wanted to tell you something.' Billy's glasses had misted up in the steamy atmosphere. He took them off and rubbed the lenses with his thumb.

'Ah good. Something about Charlie?' The old man leaned forwards eagerly.

'Sort of,' said Billy.

'Come on, then. Tell, tell.'

'Well, it was Blessed really. He saw it.'

'*It*?' wheezed the old man. 'It? What "it" was this? And the dog's name is Percy. How many times do I have to tell you!'

'Sorry. But *he* thinks he's Blessed.'

'Yes, yes. Never mind. Go on!' Ezekiel waved his hand impatiently.

Billy put his glasses back on, and then wished he hadn't. The old man's wizened face loomed unpleasantly close. Billy could see every wart and bristle in vivid detail.

'The dog was howling and Manfred sent me to sort him out, knowing I could understand dog-talk, and all that.'

'Wish I could understand the wretched dog.' Ezekiel shook his head. 'So what did he say?'

'Said he'd seen a boy, come from nowhere. And this boy had a ball, very small and shiny. He said it was bad . . .'

'WHAT?' The old man clapped a hand over his mouth. 'What? A boy and . . . and was it glass, this ball?'

'Could be,' said Billy, amazed by the excitement his news had caused.

'No, no, it can't be.' Ezekiel stood up, but his useless legs

51

let him down, and he sank back into his cocoon of sheep's wool and velvet.

'And then I noticed Charlie Bone in the hall, and Blessed said he looked like the appearing boy.' Billy smiled and waited for the effect these words would have. He wasn't disappointed.

'Charlie Bone,' breathed Ezekiel. 'Yes, yes, of course. He *was* a bit like Charlie Bone. No wonder I can't stand the boy. Find him, Billy. Bring him here.'

'Who? Charlie?'

'No, you fool. The other one. My cousin, Henry.'

'Your cousin?' said Billy, confused. 'How? I don't know where he is?'

'You've just told me he's in the building. It can't be that difficult.'

'You mean *he's* your . . .?'

'My cousin, yes. I sent him packing years ago. Never thought I'd see the wretch again.' The old man's voice dropped to a low mumble. 'Must be the weather – co-ordinating temperatures. Mm, hmm . . . Time Twister works that way . . . Ho hum.' He drummed his fingers on the arm of his wheelchair.

Billy was intrigued. 'What's a time twister?'

Ezekiel looked up. His small black eyes seemed to be staring right through Billy. 'It's a marvellous thing,' he murmured. 'A crystal ball, hardly bigger than a marble. It can twist you through the years. No wonder the dog didn't like it. Never look at it, unless you want to travel, that's what my aunt told me. Ask the dog where that boy is. Percy knows everything. Now get out and close the door.'

Billy was very disappointed. He'd expected to be rewarded with a cup of cocoa at the very least. 'Er . . . you know what you said about my parents . . .' he began.

'Parents? You haven't got any,' said Ezekiel. Clearly his mind was on other things.

'No, but you said someone wanted to adopt me,' Billy said hopefully.

'Did I? Can't remember. We'll see about them when you've found the boy. And don't forget the Twister.' Ezekiel dismissed Billy with a wave of his bony hand.

Billy slipped out of his chair and made for the door. Then he turned to the old man and said, 'Thanks for the boots. My chilblains are much better.'

Ezekiel grunted. He wasn't listening to the boy. When Billy had gone, the old man stared into the flames and uttered a stream of strange words and sounds. Now and again the name 'Henry' bubbled to the surface, and then 'Time Twister'. Other recognisable words were 'Never' 'How?' 'No, no!' 'Why?' 'Impossible!' These were spat so hard into the flames they began to sizzle. The fire might have gone out altogether if the old man hadn't reached into a silver box beside him, and tossed a handful of sparkling sticks into the grate. But these small magic sticks caused such a violent explosion, clouds of black smoke billowed out into the room, and the old man was overcome by a violent fit of coughing.

'Idiots!' he croaked at the innocent silver box.

Charlie was awake, he couldn't think why. Something must have woken him. What was it?

The distant chimes of the cathedral clock began to ring out across the city. It was midnight and the back of Charlie's neck began to tingle. He felt as he always did when he heard the clock strike twelve. Afraid and elated at the same time.

A bed creaked at the end of the room and he wondered if Billy had been out and about. Even if he had, he wouldn't be punished for it. Last term Billy had won the ruin game, and he was now the proud possessor of a bronze medal, a medal that would give him extra privileges and a whole year free of detention.

'Billy, is that you?' Charlie whispered.

No answer, but there was another long creak, and Charlie was sure that it came from Billy's bed.

'Where've you been?' he asked.

'None of your business,' came the reply.

It was definitely Billy's voice. Charlie burrowed under the covers. If Billy wanted to be secretive, let him, Charlie thought. He had other things to worry about: rescuing Henry, for one thing. The whole enterprise needed very careful planning. First of all, he would have to get some food to Henry. Before he could decide how to do this, Charlie had fallen asleep.

Fidelio's dreams had been more productive. He had devised a way for Charlie to nip up the music tower after lunch. But they would need help.

Over breakfast, next morning, Fidelio outlined his plan to Charlie. 'Olivia will do it,' he murmured in Charlie's ear. Although there was a great deal of noise all round them, Fidelio didn't want their plans to be overheard.

'Olivia? How can she help?' Charlie said softly. He tried to keep his lips as rigid as possible because Billy Raven, sitting opposite, was watching him intently.

Fidelio was also aware of Billy's intense stare. He turned his head away from the table and whispered harshly, 'She can create a diversion. We need someone to stop Manfred and Asa Pike reaching the hall, when you go through the door to the tower. They both use the Drama canteen; if Olivia can hold those two up for a few minutes, you stand a chance. No one else would bother to watch us.'

'What are you whispering about?'

Charlie and Fidelio looked up to see Manfred Bloor leaning over Billy's chair. He was studying them closely. It was almost as if the younger boy had called him over.

'Well, come on, share your secret, Charlie Bone!' Manfred's black eyes glittered dangerously.

Charlie immediately lowered his head. He knew he could fight Manfred's hypnotising stare, but he didn't want to get into trouble with the head boy before Henry had been rescued.

Fidelio said quickly, 'We were just discussing Olivia Vertigo's hair.'

'Oh?' Manfred raised a thin black eyebrow.

'Yes, we thought blue looked very nice on her,' said

Charlie, 'but we didn't like to say it out loud, in case she heard us.'

'As if,' said Manfred scathingly. 'It's not exactly quiet in here, is it? Personally, I think Olivia Vertigo's hair looks ghastly.'

He shouted this last remark and, hearing her name mentioned, Olivia looked over from the table behind him. When she saw Charlie's serious face, she grimaced and returned to her attack on the lumpy porridge.

Manfred drifted away and began to shout at a small girl who was wearing her cape inside out.

'Phew!' muttered Charlie. 'Let's talk at break.'

'Good idea,' agreed Fidelio.

By the time the two boys had managed to call Olivia away from her friends, break was almost over. Olivia came bouncing across the snowy ground in bright pink lace-ups, studded with sequins.

'The snow's taking all the paint off,' she complained, holding out her left foot. The toe of her boot was a nasty grey colour.

'Olivia, we need a favour,' said Charlie, coming straight to the point.

'Oh?' Olivia put her foot back into the snow. 'What sort of favour?'

Charlie knew it was no good trying to get Olivia to do something without a proper explanation. She would have to know all about Henry Yewbeam before she agreed to help. So, as quickly as he could, Charlie told her everything.

Olivia's mouth dropped open and her large grey eyes grew even wider.

'D'you mean that he got himself, sort of, whizzed out of the past to here-and-now?'

'Yes.' Charlie looked over his shoulder. He thought he saw Billy Raven hovering behind a group of music students. 'But we want to keep it a secret until we know how to help him. I've got to get him some food.'

'And we thought Charlie could sneak my sausages up the tower at lunch break,' said Fidelio, 'if you could keep Manfred and Asa in your canteen for a few extra minutes.'

'No problem,' said Olivia. 'Leave it to me.'

A long blast from the hunting horn sent children racing in from the field, and Olivia ran off to join her friends.

'We'll just have to trust her,' said Charlie. 'She's usually reliable.'

Each department had its own canteen, and the Drama canteen was always the noisiest and most undisciplined. Manfred had done his best to stop them wearing fancy shoes and long skirts but the drama teachers were very lax with the rules. They seldom complained about their pupils' choice of clothing, in fact they rather encouraged hats with ears, unusual footwear and coloured face-paint. Mrs Marlowe, head of Drama, considered clothes a means of self-expression, the more unusual the better. All this infuriated Manfred, but there was little he could do about it, so he took it out on the children in Music and Art.

Today, the Drama canteen was a mess. Someone's

waistcoat was moulting and white fur lay all over the floor. Someone else's hat was shedding feathers and these had floated into the gravy pan. Glitter had stuck to some of the chairs, and the tables were littered with paint flakes, tinsel, and bits of false hair.

'It's disgusting,' grumbled Manfred, staring at a sequin in his custard. 'Why can't people be more conventional?' For himself, he favoured plain black with, occasionally, a purple shirt to match his cape. Even the ribbon in his ponytail was black.

Asa Pike gave a nervous snigger. The moustache he was fond of wearing had just dropped on to his plate. 'Oops,' he said. 'Forgot I was wearing it.'

Manfred shot his companion a look of contempt. 'There are times, Asa, when I would enjoy giving you a good kick.'

Asa's yellow eyes took on a nasty gleam. Manfred began to regret his words. He and Asa were not true friends. They stuck together because everyone else disliked them. Asa might fawn on Manfred, but Manfred knew quite well that Asa could be as dangerous as he was. Manfred could hypnotise, but when night fell, Asa could become something wild and deadly – a creature beyond Manfred's power.

So the two boys sat at their table, with tight lips and brooding eyes, until a sudden commotion by the door broke their disagreeable silence.

'It's Olivia Vertigo again,' said Asa, looking towards the disturbance.

Manfred stood up. 'Not her.' He strode over to the door.

Olivia had managed to tip the entire contents of a tray right in front of the door. Most of the glass and crockery had broken and now lay in jagged pieces caked with gravy and custard.

'Sorry, sorry, sorry,' said Olivia. 'I slipped.'

'Sorry's not good enough,' said Manfred. 'Go and get a cloth.'

'Yes, Manfred.' Olivia walked briskly across the canteen and into the kitchen. 'I'll give them five minutes,' she muttered, looking at her watch.

No one paid any attention to Olivia, until Cook came through a door at the back of the kitchen. She marched up to Olivia and said, 'You're the wrong side of the door, dear!'

'I came for a piece of bread,' lied Olivia.

'Didn't you have enough to eat?' asked Cook.

'I was late,' said Olivia, glancing at her watch.

'Tch! Tch! I'll see what I can do.' Cook was about to turn away when the door behind Olivia was suddenly flung open.

Manfred stood glaring at Olivia. 'Where's the cloth, you idiot? We can't get out until that mess is cleared up.'

'I er . . .' Olivia began.

'Hold your horses, Manfred Bloor,' said Cook sharply. 'Everything comes to those who wait.'

'Huh!' grunted Manfred.

Cook ambled across the kitchen and took a cloth, a bucket, and a pair of rubber gloves from under the sink.

Manfred shouted, 'For God's sake, hurry up, woman.'

Cook froze. She dropped the bucket and stared at Manfred with her hands on her hips. 'Don't you speak to me like that. Don't you dare. Don't you ever, ever use that tone with me again.'

'Yeah! Yeah!' said Manfred nervously.

'Apologise,' said Cook.

'Sorry,' mumbled Manfred, pretending to examine his fingernails.

Olivia could hardly believe it. In a few words, Cook had reduced the head boy to a jittering junior.

Cook picked up the bucket and handed it to Manfred. 'If you want a mess cleared up, do it yourself.'

'But I didn't make the mess!' cried Manfred, turning scarlet.

Cook shrugged and walked away.

Manfred gave Olivia a vicious shove through the door and, as soon as they were on the other side, handed her the bucket.

At that very moment, Charlie and Fidelio were crossing the hall. Now that the children from Drama were all trapped in their canteen, there were fewer people about, and Charlie managed to nip through the door into the west wing without being seen. Fidelio stood guard. When Charlie had completed his mission he would give two taps on the door, and if the coast was clear, Fidelio would tap back.

Charlie raced up the deep spiralling steps that led to the top of the tower. By the time he reached the music room, he was out of breath and had a stitch in his side.

Henry had gone. A large blue cape lay over the back of a chair, and there was an empty tin on a stool. Some of the books were covered in crumbs and two sweet papers had been dropped by the window.

Mr Pilgrim was playing very softly today. He kept repeating the same notes over and over again, as if he couldn't remember where the music was going.

Without knocking, Charlie opened the door and looked in. Mr Pilgrim was alone. He wasn't wearing his cape, and Charlie remembered that he'd been without it at assembly; but then, Mr Pilgrim often forgot things.

The music teacher looked over the piano and frowned at Charlie.

'Excuse me, sir,' said Charlie. 'Have you seen a boy? A boy a bit like me?'

Very much to his surprise, Mr Pilgrim answered quite clearly, 'Yes. There was a boy.'

'And do you know where he is now, sir?'

'He shouldn't have been up here alone,' said Mr Pilgrim. 'Not at night. It's too cold.'

'Yes, but – where did he go?'

'He was hungry.' Mr Pilgrim must have suddenly recalled the notes he'd been searching for, because he played two loud chords and then launched himself into a very complicated piece of music.

Charlie realised that it would be useless to ask the teacher any more questions. Besides, if he didn't get back soon, Manfred and Asa would be prowling round the hall.

'Thank you, sir.' Charlie left the room and, closing the door behind him, ran all the way down to the bottom of the tower. He descended the winding stairs so quickly, by the time he reached the ground floor he felt very wobbly on his feet.

Before he went into the dark passage that led to the hall, he stopped to listen. He could hear nothing. It was safe to enter the passage. All the same, he tiptoed over the stone floor. He had only gone a few metres when he walked straight into something; a small, thin figure that was hardly a person at all. It whimpered slightly and scuttled away, but when Charlie turned to look back at it, the person or thing turned back too. Its eyes glittered behind a thin black veil, and it whispered, 'Boy,' then it was gone.

INTO THE FREEZER

Charlie tore to the end of the passage and whizzed through the door at the end, almost knocking Fidelio off his feet.

'You forgot to tap,' said Fidelio fiercely. 'Someone's watching.'

'Who?' Charlie saw Billy Raven disappear into the cloakroom. 'Oh no,' he groaned. 'Not him.'

At that moment, Manfred and Asa appeared at the far end of the hall. Manfred looked furious. As soon as he saw the two boys, he shouted, 'Out! Out! Why aren't you two outside?'

'It's – er – wet,' said Charlie.

'Wet? Of course it's wet, you idiot. Not afraid of a bit of snow, are you?'

'We couldn't find our boots,' said Fidelio quickly.

'Then go out in your shoes!' barked Manfred.

'But . . .' began Charlie.

'So you'll have wet shoes. So what? That'll teach you to lose your boots.' Manfred had worked himself into a fine temper. His normally pale face was quite pink.

Charlie and Fidelio scuttled out into the garden without another word.

'Phew. I bet that was all due to Olivia,' said Fidelio.

'I hope she hasn't got detention,' said Charlie. 'Henry wasn't there, by the way. Now I don't know what to do.'

'We'll find him,' said Fidelio confidently. 'But we'd better get to him before Manfred. What scared you in the tower? You looked as if you'd seen a ghost?'

'I think I did,' said Charlie. 'It was horrible. All black and wispy.'

'The dark lady,' said Fidelio. 'Gabriel told me about her. She hangs around the music tower. I think she likes Mr Pilgrim's piano-playing.'

A few minutes later, Olivia joined them in the garden. 'Hi, folks, did it work?' she asked.

'It was brilliant,' said Charlie. 'You must have held them up for at least ten minutes.'

'How did you do it?' asked Fidelio.

Olivia told them about her accident with the tray. 'But now I've got detention,' she said, 'so I won't be going home till Saturday night.'

Charlie's face fell. 'I'm sorry. I should have known that would happen.'

'Oh, I don't mind,' said Olivia. 'I can do a bit of exploring. As long as someone else gets detention with me. I don't fancy being on my own.'

'Oh.' Charlie felt even worse. 'Well, if you don't mind, I think I'm going to be busy.'

'Of course. Cousin Henry,' Olivia said cheerfully. 'I understand. And I know Fido will be doing some musical thing or other.'

'Well, now that you mention it . . .' said Fidelio.

'It's OK. Don't look so guilty, both of you. I'll try Emma Tolly.' Olivia bounced off in her pink boots, and headed towards Emma who was walking round with her nose in a book.

The two boys spent the rest of break walking up and down on the flagstones outside the garden door. It was several degrees warmer and the snow was turning into a watery slush. Charlie's left shoe was leaking.

Just before the horn went for the end of break, Olivia came up to them looking very fed up. 'Guess what?' she said. 'Emma Tolly doesn't like to leave her aunt alone at weekends. I ask you! I helped to rescue her from those awful foster parents and now she won't even spend a few hours with me.'

'In that case, I'll try and get detention,' said Charlie. 'Henry can wait a bit longer.'

'No, he can't,' said Olivia. 'You get him out of here as soon as you can. It's OK. Bindi's going to stay with me.' She shook her head. 'I don't know what's got into Emma. She's so prissy these days.'

'She's never had a proper home before,' said Charlie. 'I suppose she just wants to be in it as much as she can.'

'Hm.' Olivia sauntered off.

As the two boys walked to their history lesson, Fidelio

said quietly, 'Charlie, I think you're going to have to carry out your rescue mission tonight. You won't get another chance today.'

Charlie agreed. But he had no idea where to start looking for Henry.

'Try the kitchens,' Fidelio suggested. 'He must be starving by now.'

That night, as Charlie lay in bed, he tried to remember all the stairs and passages that eventually led to the kitchens. He knew there were three kitchens, one behind each of the three canteens. They were connected by swing doors, so he would be able to creep through all three, once he had found his way to the first one.

'D'you think Cook will still be in the kitchen?' Charlie whispered to Fidelio.

'Not after midnight,' Fidelio said softly.

'Shut up, you lot!' said Damian Smerk.

'Shut up, yourself.' Fidelio threw a damp shoe in his direction. It was a good shot and grazed Damian's cheek.

'I'll get you, Fidelio Gunn, you wait!' screeched Damian.

'You're on,' said Fidelio. 'See you by the garden door, straight after breakfast.'

Damian snivelled and pulled the bedclothes over his head. He was terrified of violence, but he often made silly remarks about getting people, and then pretended he had hurt his arm, or his leg, so he could excuse himself from a fight.

Charlie was just about to speak when the door opened and the light came on.

'Who was talking?' Matron stood on the threshold.

No one answered.

'Own up!' she said.

'We were,' said Charlie.

His great-aunt swung her long nose in his direction. 'Oh? Is that a confession?'

'We all confess,' said Fidelio.

Matron stared round the room unpleasantly. 'If I have to come in again, you'll all be put in detention,' she said.

'Except me,' said Billy.

Ignoring Billy, Lucretia Yewbeam walked out and slammed the door.

'That was close,' Fidelio whispered so softly no one but Charlie could hear him. 'Do you want me to come with you tonight?'

'No,' Charlie whispered back. 'It's better if just one of us goes. Thanks anyway.'

'Good luck!' Fidelio turned over and was soon asleep.

For a few moments, Charlie lay with his eyes wide open, fighting sleep. In desperation, he threw off the bedclothes. Now he was so cold, sleep was impossible.

He waited until he heard the cathedral clock strike twelve, and then, with a mixture of fear and excitement, he quickly pulled on his dressing gown and slippers and crept out of the dormitory.

'Right, then left, then down the stairs,' Charlie murmured

to himself. The beam of light from his torch was so feeble he couldn't see much beyond his feet. By the time he'd managed to find his way down two staircases, he realised he was lost, or certainly in a place he didn't recognise. Everything looked so different in the dark.

Taking a chance, Charlie continued for several metres until he came to another set of steps. He had descended two when something bumped into his knees and sent him crashing to the floor.

'Ow! Ooo! Ouch!' Charlie muttered under his breath. No bones were broken but he felt bruised and shaken. 'Can't go back now,' he muttered.

Picking himself up, he turned a corner and found himself on the landing above the hall. The lights here were left burning all night and, with a soft whoop of relief, Charlie ran down the stairs and on into the long passage that led to the canteens.

Stumbling against chairs and tables, Charlie made his way through the blue canteen and into the kitchen. Here, counters covered in saucepans blocked his way. Machines jutted out at odd angles, mops and buckets were hidden beside cupboards. A heavy pan crashed to the floor as Charlie felt his way along a shelf. He froze for a second, and then became aware of a low light coming from the frosted glass at the top of a door beside him. Very slowly, Charlie opened the door.

He looked into a small room with walls of tall white fridges and freezers. Henry Yewbeam stood in front of the tallest.

'Henry, thank God,' breathed Charlie. 'What are you doing?'

'Hullo, Charlie,' said Henry. 'It's good to see you.'

'It's freezing in here,' said Charlie, whose teeth had begun to chatter.

'I know.' Henry smiled mysteriously. 'It's just what I want.'

'What are you talking about? Please come out of there. I think we could die of cold.'

'I don't want to die,' said Henry. 'But I think I will if I don't get home.' He stepped out of the freezing room and closed the door.

Charlie relaxed. It was warm in the kitchen and he found it easier to think. He perched himself on a counter and Henry jumped up beside him.

'I looked for you at lunch break,' Charlie said. 'I sneaked some food up to the music room. Where were you?'

'There was a lady, very small, all in black. She took me to her room. I was a bit frightened of her, but she gave me a cup of tea and some sweets.' Henry held out a sweet wrapped in silver paper. 'Have one! She gave me a handful.'

Charlie took the sweet. It was chocolate with a strawberry centre. One of his favourites. 'Yummy,' he said. 'I bumped into that woman. I thought she was a ghost.'

Henry shook his head. 'Not quite a ghost. She used to play the violin, but now her left hand doesn't work and that makes her very, very sad. You could say she was in mourning for her fingers.'

Henry had an odd way of putting things. Charlie was intrigued. 'Who is she?'

'I didn't like to ask. Mama said it was rude to pry. The lady told me to go to the kitchens at night. So here I am. But Charlie,' Henry's face lit up, 'I have found a wonderful thing.'

'What?'

'In there,' Henry pointed to the cold room, 'a cupboard that's full of ice.'

'A freezer,' said Charlie.

'A freezer?' Henry repeated. 'Well, I never. It hums in a very comforting way. Charlie, I think it will take me home.'

'What d'you mean?' said Charlie anxiously.

'I have come to the conclusion that I arrived in this new century because the weather was right. When I left 1916, it was the coldest day for many, many years. And when I got here it was exactly the same. But now it's getting warmer and if I use the Time Twister, I could end up anywhere.'

'You'd be crazy to use it,' Charlie agreed.

'Not if I go into the freezer,' said Henry earnestly.

'What? You'd freeze to death.'

'You could help me, Charlie. Just open the freezer door, now and again, to make sure I'm breathing. Once I hit the right temperature, I'll be gone.' Henry leaned forward. 'Please help me. I want to go home so much. I want to get back to 1916 and see my family. I'll never survive in this new world. I don't belong.'

Charlie had only known his new relation for a day, but

already he had begun to like him a lot. He would miss him, he realised. 'It's a bit dodgy,' he said evasively. 'I mean, you could end up back in the ice age, with mammoths and things.'

'I've considered that, but I want to take a chance. If I think hard about Mama and Papa, and my brother and sister, I'm sure I'll get back.' He grinned encouragingly at Charlie. 'What d'you say?'

'OK,' said Charlie reluctantly. 'Let's give it a go. But if you turn blue, I'm pulling you out of there.'

'Thank you, Charlie.'

The two boys swung themselves off the counter and went into the cold room. For a moment, Henry stood looking at the tall, white freezer and then he took the Time Twister out of his pocket. Charlie caught a glimpse of sparkling light in Henry's hand and he looked away quickly. But the light was reflected on the low ceiling, and through a mist of swirling colours, Charlie could make out a city of dazzling golden domes, and then a range of snow-clad mountains. The snow became a forest, and the trees turned into the crashing green waves of a mighty sea. And then a river of glass swept beneath the bluest sky Charlie had ever seen.

Mesmerised by the amazing world above him, Charlie felt himself being drawn towards it. When his feet began to slide from under him, he tore his gaze away from the ceiling, but he was too late to see his cousin step into the freezer. Henry had already disappeared.

Charlie stared at the tall white door. How long should

he wait? He didn't want to ruin Henry's chances, but what if he should freeze to death before the Time Twister did its work? He closed his eyes and slowly counted to ten. Then, seizing the freezer door, he pulled.

The door wouldn't open. Charlie pulled again. He put both hands on the handle, braced himself, and tugged with all his might. The freezer door was stuck fast. Either it was ice, or some tremendous force inside the freezer was holding the door shut.

Charlie tried again. He banged on the freezer, he twisted, pulled, had a short rest and then tried again. 'Henry! Henry!' he called, pummelling the door.

'And what d'you think you're doing, Charlie Bone?'

Charlie whirled round to see Cook standing in the doorway.

'I . . . I . . .' Charlie began. 'Cook, there's a boy in the freezer. I don't know if he's dead or . . . or gone. You see he might've, but I've got to know . . .'

'Lord save us,' cried Cook, almost knocking Charlie off his feet as she charged at the freezer.

With one mighty heave, she pulled open the door.

Henry was crouched at the bottom, under a huge frozen carcase. His face was blue and his hair and cape were covered in frost.

'Heavens above!' exclaimed Cook as she pulled Henry out of the freezer.

He was cold and stiff, but Charlie was relieved to hear him give a small groan as Cook gathered him into her arms.

'Follow me, Charlie Bone,' she commanded. 'You'd better tell me what all this is about.'

Cook crashed her way through the door, across the kitchen, and into what started out as a broom cupboard, but ended up being a long, softly-lit corridor. Even though she was carrying Henry, Cook walked so fast, Charlie found it hard to keep up with her.

At the end of the corridor, several steps led down to another small cupboard and this opened into one of the cosiest places Charlie had ever seen. Bright pictures hung all round the room, from just beneath the very low ceiling, almost to the floor. The chairs looked old and soft, and a gleaming ancient dresser had been filled with gold-patterned cups and plates. In a deep alcove there was a large black stove; a kettle boiled on the top, while bright coals flickered in a window at the bottom. They filled the room with a warm, glowing light.

Cook laid Henry in a large armchair beside the stove and began to rub his hands. As she did this, Henry's stiff fingers relaxed and the Time Twister dropped to the floor.

'What's that?' said Cook.

'It's er . . . um . . . a time twister,' said Charlie.

'Huh!' grunted Cook, not at all surprised. 'I might have known. It always causes trouble. Put it in that red mug on the dresser. But *don't* look at it.'

'I won't,' said Charlie. He picked up the shining marble and dropped it into the mug. Vivid colours spun and twisted inside the mug, and Charlie was tempted to wait and see what sort of picture they would make.

'Don't look, Charlie!' Cook warned again.

'No, no. I won't.' Charlie stepped away from the dresser.

Cook continued to rub Henry's fingers, but he didn't stir or make a sound. She looked back at Charlie and said, 'You stupid boy. You of all people, Charlie Bone. What were you thinking of?'

'I was trying to help,' whispered Charlie.

'Help? Help? Murder more like,' Cook said coldly.

'No, no, I didn't . . .'

'Who is this boy?'

It took Charlie a few seconds to remember his exact relationship to Henry. Very slowly he said, 'He's my Great-Great-Uncle Henry, I think. But I just call him a cousin. He came from 1916.'

'And the Time Twister's responsible, I presume.'

'Yes, poor Henry's come a long way. I mean, he's come from a long time away.'

'I'll say,' said Cook. 'Get my dressing gown.' She nodded at a large red garment lying over a chair.

Charlie brought it to her.

'Now, take off this poor boy's cape.'

Cook gently lifted Henry out of the chair, while Charlie took off the frost-covered cape. On Cook's instructions, he wrapped his cousin in the big red dressing gown, but still Henry showed no sign of life.

Cook felt the frozen boy's pulse, shook her head and then put her ear to his heart. 'Something,' she murmured. 'Something there.'

Charlie felt terrible. He sank into a chair and covered his face with his hands.

'All's not lost,' said Cook. 'They're here.'

Charlie heard a faint mewing above his head. He looked up to see a skylight of small green glass panes. Peering through the glass were three cats with glowing yellow eyes.

'The Flames,' breathed Charlie.

'Yes, the Flames. Mind out, Charlie.'

Charlie jumped out of the chair as Cook came towards him. She climbed on the chair and opened the skylight. A blast of cold air and a shower of snow brought one of the cats sliding down on to the back of the chair. He was a handsome creature with deep copper-coloured fur.

'Aries!' said Charlie.

The cat gave a long, welcoming miaow.

'You know these creatures then?' said Cook, as an orange cat, and then a yellow, followed Aries. They landed either side of him and greeted Charlie with loud purring voices.

'Leo and Sagittarius,' said Charlie. 'Yes, I know the Flames. And I think I know what they're going to do.'

The three cats leapt down from the chair and ran over to Henry. Charlie could hear the crackle of tiny flames as the cats rubbed their heads against the red dressing gown. They began to circle the chair where Henry's blue-tinged face rested on a faded cushion. Cook closed the skylight and stepped off the chair.

'They saved my friend's dog,' Charlie told Cook. 'And I think they've saved a lot of people. But I can't understand how they know when they're needed.'

'Sixth sense,' said Cook. 'Now hush. Let them do their work.'

Charlie sank into a chair opposite Henry. Already he could feel the heat from the cats as they ran round the frozen boy. Soon all Charlie could see was a bright golden-red streak circling Henry's chair.

Charlie yawned. His head drooped and his eyes closed. In a few minutes he had drifted off to sleep.

When he woke up, Henry, still wearing the red dressing gown, was sitting up and smiling at him. He held a mug of something steamy and sweet-smelling.

'Hullo again, Charlie!' said Henry.

Charlie blinked and rubbed his eyes. 'I'm sorry, Henry,' he said. 'It didn't work, did it? I tried to get you out but something, I don't know what, it seemed to be fighting me.'

Henry nodded. 'I'm going to stay here with Cook,' he said. 'No one knows about this room, so I'll be safe, until we can decide what to do next.'

Cook was bustling round the stove. She took a tray of small cakes out of the oven and shook them on to a plate. 'Take one of these,' she said, offering the cakes to Charlie, 'and then I think you'd better creep off back to bed.'

'Thanks!' Charlie took a cake and bit into it. It was delicious. 'Very good,' he said quietly.

'It wasn't your fault, Charlie,' said Cook guessing Charlie's thoughts. 'I shouldn't have been so quick to blame you. You of all people.'

'Why d'you keep saying that?' asked Charlie. 'Me of all people. What d'you mean?'

'I'll tell you another time.'

Charlie looked up at Cook. For a moment he glimpsed another face behind Cook's lined, worn features; a face that was young and beautiful. He would have liked to hold the moment for a long time. He had never felt as warm and safe as he did now, sitting in Cook's wide shadow, with the glowing room behind her, the humming of the stove and the deep contented purring of the three cats, as they sipped a bowl of milk before the fire.

'Who are you?' he asked Cook.

'Me?' She smiled. 'I'm the lodestone of the house. I keep you all from flying off into the dark.'

'But your name?'

'Another time.'

'Can I come back tomorrow?' asked Charlie. He wanted to know so much.

'Better not,' said Cook. 'Wait a while. Certain persons will be watching you. And not just persons.' She nodded at a fat form that had appeared in the shadows at the back of the room.

Blessed waddled into the light. It was obvious that he wanted to sit in front of the stove, but the three cats gave warning growls and the old dog retreated.

'I've seen him before,' exclaimed Henry. 'He's very old, isn't he?'

'He's a spy,' said Cook. 'So if *you've* seen *him*, *he*'s already told someone about *you*. Charlie Bone, you'd better go back now. *Someone* might have noticed your bed's empty.'

Charlie swallowed the last of his cake and said goodnight to his cousin. Then he followed Cook through the labyrinth of cupboards and passages that led to the hall. Here, Cook took a small torch from her pocket and gave it to Charlie.

'It has a good light,' she said. 'Off you go now. And don't tell anyone about tonight. And I mean "anyone".'

'My best friends already know about Henry.'

Cook shook her head. 'Can't be helped, I suppose. But the fewer people who know about this place, the better.'

'OK. I promise I won't tell anyone where he is.'

Cook watched Charlie cross the hall and begin to mount the stairs. She gave him a quick wave and walked speedily back to her room beneath the city.

She was pleased to see that Henry Yewbeam had fallen into a deep untroubled sleep. Taking the empty mug out of his warm hand, she replaced it on the dresser. The three cats had finished their milk and were looking at her expectantly, so she stepped on to the chair beneath the skylight and opened it once more.

The Flames ran to the chair, jumped up on to the back, and from there leapt out through the skylight.

'Thank you, my dears,' called Cook. She fastened the skylight and stepped off the chair.

'Now for you,' she said to the fat dog that had moved into his favourite place before the stove.

'I know what you are,' Cook said to Blessed, 'but you've

been a good boy up to now and kept my room secret, even from your friend Billy Raven.'

Blessed looked at Cook and whined softly.

'Now, listen. Don't you dare tell that friend of yours about this boy.' She pointed to Henry asleep in the big armchair.

Blessed stared at Cook with sad brown eyes. Although she didn't speak his language, he knew her well enough to understand exactly what she was saying.

'If you give the game away, there'll be no more of Cook's chops. No more bed by the stove, or walks in the park. You'll be out on your ear, for you're of no use to me, you lazy lump of lard. I've only mothered you out of the goodness of my heart.' She wagged a finger at him. 'Are we clear about this?'

Blessed grunted and heaved himself into his basket. He knew when he was well off.

THE BLACK GLOVE

Cook's torch was unusual. Although the beam wasn't very bright, it lit the way ahead in such a way that Charlie could see details that he'd never noticed before. In fact, some of the things he passed were definitely different.

For instance, there was a row of paintings along the entire length of a wall beside one of the staircases. There was a pair of man-sized boots outside a door, and a pair of satin shoes outside another. On one of the landings, a tall plant grew in a blue china pot, and ivy trailed out of a large brass urn.

'*That* wasn't there,' muttered Charlie.

In spite of these small changes, it was easy for Charlie to find his way back. However, he had only taken a few paces down the passage to his dormitory, when a narrow beam of brilliant light almost blinded him. Instinctively, he turned off Cook's torch and waited, hardly daring to breathe.

The blinding light went out. Whoever stood at the other end of the passage was waiting to see what Charlie would do. Charlie cautiously felt his way along the wall. He knew his door was the second on his left. He passed the first door and stopped, listening intently for footsteps. Hearing nothing, he made a rush for his door and ran straight into a body.

Charlie gasped. At the same time the body squeaked, 'Ouch! You're standing on my foot.'

'Is that you, Billy?' whispered Charlie.

'What if it is?'

'Don't be silly. It was just a question.' Charlie turned on his torch.

Billy Raven blinked up at him. He had a large blob of chocolate on his chin. 'Where've you been?' he asked Charlie.

'Where've *you* been?' said Charlie, lowering Cook's torch.

Billy didn't answer.

'I just popped out to the toilet,' said Charlie. 'I can tell you've been to see someone who had a bit of chocolate to spare.'

'It's cocoa, actually,' said Billy. 'And the toilet isn't down there, it's the other way.'

'I just missed it in the dark,' said Charlie.

Billy stared at him suspiciously, then he pushed past Charlie and went into the dormitory. Charlie followed and crept over to his bed. He heard a soft rustling as Billy burrowed under the bedclothes, and then there was silence.

Charlie wondered who had been giving Billy cocoa in the middle of the night. Was it a reward for spying? Blessed had seen Henry in Cook's room, and Billy could understand the old dog's language. So, before long, the person who was supplying Billy with cocoa, would know about Henry. Charlie was too tired to wrestle with the problem any more. Somehow he would have to find a way to warn Cook.

Next morning, something extraordinary happened, and Charlie's worries about Henry were temporarily forgotten.

Breakfast was almost over when a violent gust of wind came howling down the passage to the dining hall. The doors flew open and the wind roared into the room, sending cups and plates, spoons and knives, spinning off the tables. There were shrieks of terror as sharp pieces of cutlery came zooming through the air. Most of the children pulled their hoods over their heads and ducked under the tables.

Charlie and Fidelio met Olivia crawling behind one of the benches.

'What's going on?' cried Charlie.

'I reckon it's one of Tancred's storms,' shouted Olivia. 'I heard he had a terrible row with Lysander last night.'

'Tancred? I'd better try and get to him,' said Charlie.

'Why? What can you do? It's happened before, you know.' Fidelio tugged Charlie's sleeve. 'Just leave him to calm down.'

'No. I must see him.' Charlie couldn't explain why he suddenly had an overpowering need to reach Tancred. Tancred had helped to save him, when he was trapped in the ruin, and Charlie felt he must at least try to calm him down.

Holding his hood firmly over his head, Charlie crawled

to the open door, and then out into the windy passage. The force of Tancred's anger was amazing. Charlie guessed a ninety-mile-an-hour gale was blowing towards him. His nose and mouth were soon full of dust, and the portraits that had been hanging on the walls kept flying off and whirling into his path. Occasionally, the sharp corner of a frame whacked his head, or caught the hand that was shielding his face.

Charlie gritted his teeth and kept going. He saw two figures crawling in front of him. Their capes billowed above them like angry purple clouds.

Manfred and Asa, thought Charlie.

The race to reach Tancred was now even more critical. He was likely to be hypnotised if Manfred got to him first, and not just for a few minutes. Tancred might be taken by surprise. Before he knew it, he would be lost – put to sleep, like Emma Tolly had been. Her sleep had lasted for eight years.

As Charlie emerged into the hall, he could see Manfred and Asa clinging to pieces of furniture. The handle of an oak chest suddenly came off in Asa's hand, and he slid across the floor with a howl of surprise. Manfred had been more successful. His arms were wrapped round the newel post at the bottom of the stairs.

Charlie didn't know how he could stop himself from being blown into the wall. Tancred's furious energy filled every space in the hall. Chairs were tumbling about like matchsticks. As he raised his head, he saw Tancred standing in front of the huge doors leading to the outside world. His blond hair was standing up like a stiff, sparkling brush. A few metres behind him, Dr Bloor, bent double, was shouting into the wind.

'Tancred Torsson, calm down. Come away from those doors. Immediately!'

Tancred took not the slightest notice. Indeed, Dr Bloor's voice was almost drowned by the noise.

All at once, Manfred let go of the newel post and began to crawl across the floor towards Tancred.

Charlie knew it was no use shouting a warning. Tancred would never have heard him.

Manfred had almost reached the stormy boy, when Tancred wheeled round and, seeing Manfred, let loose such a fierce bolt of electricity, that the head boy was sent sprawling away from him. At the same time, the massive doors cracked down the middle and, with a loud splintering sound, they flew open.

Tancred turned and marched out, taking his stormy power with him.

Dr Bloor rushed to close the doors, but they were so badly cracked it was impossible to lock them. The big key Dr Bloor always carried with him, clicked uselessly in the lock.

'Bring the chest,' he ordered, waving at Manfred and Asa.

As the two boys pushed the heavy chest across the hall, Charlie got to his feet. The floor was littered with debris. It was incredible how much hidden rubbish Tancred's storm had drawn out of the shadowy corners in the hall.

Lying at Charlie's feet was a black leather glove and, almost without thinking, he picked it up and put it in his pocket.

Manfred and Asa gave the big chest a final shove, and it came to rest in front of the doors.

'That'll do for now,' said Dr Bloor. 'I'll have to get Weedon to fix it. We don't want anyone else escaping.'

It makes this place sound like a prison, thought Charlie.

Some of the other children were peering cautiously into the hall, but it was Charlie whom Manfred saw first.

'Charlie Bone, what are you doing here?' shouted the head boy.

'I'm trying to get to assembly,' said Charlie.

Manfred could hardly quarrel with that. 'Get moving then,' he said irritably.

Fidelio rushed across the hall and caught up with Charlie just as he was going into the blue cloakroom.

'What about that?' whispered Fidelio. 'It was practically a hurricane.'

In all the excitement, many of the children behind them had forgotten the rule of silence.

They were immediately given detention and then despatched to the kitchens, to fetch brooms and dustpans.

'Olivia won't be lonely on Saturday,' said Fidelio. 'I heard at least six people get detention.'

Charlie sat on one of the benches and began to pick off the bits of dust and rubbish that clung to his cloak.

A great weariness stole over him, and he slumped back against the wall.

'What's up, Charlie?' said Fidelio. 'You look done in.'

'I wish Tancred hadn't gone,' Charlie murmured. 'We've got to get him back.'

'Why?'

'I can't explain. He helped me once, and now he's gone. Suppose he's expelled?'

'He won't be,' said Fidelio confidently. 'The endowed are never expelled. Sooner or later he'll calm down and come back.'

'I hope it's sooner,' muttered Charlie. He wasn't mistaken. Without Tancred there was something definitely amiss.

That night Charlie was the first to reach the King's Room with his homework. Gabriel came in a few seconds later. He looked ill at ease. Carefully placing his books beside Charlie's he said, 'Something's wrong.'

'It's Tancred, isn't it?' said Charlie. 'I feel sort of unbalanced.'

'Me too,' said Gabriel. 'We've got to get him back. Will you come with me at the weekend, Charlie?'

'To Tancred's house?'

Gabriel nodded. 'It's not far from where I live. But it's a pretty stormy place. They call it Thunder House.'

'Does anyone else in his family have a – er – weather talent?' asked Charlie.

'I'll say. His dad's really turbulent.'

'Oh.' Charlie wasn't sure if he was looking forwards to this mission.

'Where on earth is everyone else?' muttered Gabriel. 'They're ten minutes late. Manfred's nearly always here first.'

Lysander walked into the King's Room clutching a pile of sketches. His usually cheerful face looked troubled and confused. 'I thought I was late,' he said. 'Where's everyone else?'

Charlie shrugged. 'They've all disappeared – like Tancred.' He immediately regretted his words because Lysander looked even more depressed.

'What went on between you two?' Gabriel asked Lysander.

'It was a misunderstanding,' muttered Lysander. 'Manfred's fault. He asked if Tancred had made it warmer just for me. Tancred shouted that it was nothing to do with him, and I said, "Don't get upset, Tanc, I'm really grateful."'

'But Tancred doesn't do temperature, right?' said Gabriel.

'Too right.' Lysander slumped in his chair. 'And he's so touchy about things like that, he hit the roof. I forgot, you see. He's my best friend and I forgot. You know I think Manfred *made* me forget. He didn't exactly hypnotise me, but he was staring at me in a funny way. I was sort of disabled.'

'We're going up to Thunder House on Saturday,' said Gabriel. 'Come with us. He's more likely to listen to you.'

'Don't know about that,' said Lysander glumly. 'But sure I'll come.'

The three boys sat in gloomy silence for a while and then, because there didn't seem anything better to do, Charlie brought the black glove out of his pocket. He laid it on the table saying, 'I found this in the hall, when Tancred had gone.'

'It's not Tanc's,' said Lysander. 'Probably some old thing that's been lying under a cupboard for years.'

The glove was made of very soft leather. The fingers were long and narrow, and there was an opening at the wrist, with four small leather buttons on one side, and four neat holes on the other.

Gabriel frowned at the glove. He stretched out his hand. Charlie found himself crying, 'Don't, Gabriel!'

But it was too late. Gabriel had pulled the glove on to his left hand. His face suddenly creased with pain and he let out a terrible moan.

Charlie reached out to pull off the glove, but Gabriel fell forwards, his head crashing on to the table.

'He's fainted,' cried Lysander. 'What's going on?'

'It's the glove. You know Gabriel's gift. He can feel what happened to the people who wore things before him.'

'The owner of that glove must've been hurt pretty badly,' said Lysander. He touched Gabriel's head. 'He's gone cold.'

'Gabriel! Gabriel, wake up!' cried Charlie. He tried to pull the glove off Gabriel's hand but it was stuck fast.

Gabriel turned his head. 'My hand! Oooo, my hand,' he groaned.

'It's the glove,' Charlie told him. 'I can't get it off you.'

'Ooooow!' Gabriel sat up and began to tear at the glove with his right hand. 'My fingers are broken. Help! Help, someone!'

Charlie tugged the fingers of the glove while Lysander tried to peel it away from Gabriel's wrist. It was no use. Gabriel was now panting heavily. Between small grunts of pain, he said, 'She put her fingers on the door and he slammed it.'

'Who?' asked Charlie. 'Who slammed it?'

'A woman, I think. Yes, a woman. She was trying to get out, and she was shaking her head like she wouldn't do what they wanted.' Gabriel gave another moan. 'But the boy, I think it was Manfred, he slammed the door and pushed and pushed until he crushed her fingers. Ooooow. Oooh! It *is* Manfred but he's smaller. Ooow!' Gabriel's head fell forwards again.

At that moment, there was a tap on the door and Olivia looked in. 'There you are,' she said. 'Fidelio sent me to look for you. He couldn't get away because he's in the front row.'

'Front row?' said Charlie.

'Don't tell me you all forgot,' said Olivia. 'There's a concert in the theatre tonight. What's wrong with Gabriel?'

'He's not well,' said Lysander.

'I can see that, but you'd better get him to the theatre quickly if you don't want detention.'

'Gabriel, can you walk?' Lysander asked gently.

Gabriel moaned. 'If I have to.'

'Come on then. Charlie, help me!'

Lysander pulled the stricken boy upright, and putting Gabriel's arm round his shoulders, clutched him by the waist. Charlie did the same. He got the arm with the glove on it, and it worried him to see how limp and crushed Gabriel's left hand looked.

'I'd better go ahead and make sure there are three seats at the back for you.' Olivia rushed off.

By the time the three boys had staggered into the dark theatre, the concert had begun.

'You'll have to manage on your own for a bit,' Lysander whispered to Gabriel.

'Uh!' Gabriel grunted.

Charlie pulled the sleeve of Gabriel's cape over the black glove, and helped Lysander to manoeuvre him into a seat. Olivia had been as good as her word and there were three empty seats waiting for them at the back of the auditorium.

Unfortunately, Dr Saltweather saw the boys come in late. He frowned at them and shook his head, then turned his attention back to the stage. Dr Bloor was making a speech about music, and it soon became clear that he was describing the life and work of the other man on the stage: Mr Albert Tuccini.

Behind Dr Bloor, a man with a deep tan sat at a grand piano. He had brown curly hair and a rather morose expression. His arms were folded across his chest and he occasionally glanced at the red velvet curtains at the back of the stage.

Dr Bloor came to the end of his speech. The audience

clapped enthusiastically. Albert Tuccini swivelled round to face the piano and his long fingers pounced on the keys.

Gabriel was a pianist himself, and he listened intently to the complicated chords that Albert Tuccini rung out of the piano. Gradually, his hard breathing eased, he forgot the pain in his fingers and managed to enjoy the music.

The pianist's second piece seemed familiar to Charlie. But he couldn't remember where he had heard it before. A memory was buried at the back of his mind. Far, far back. Could it have been the music his father played? He began to nod off. And then he was asleep and dreaming. He dreamed of a room Grandma Bone had described to him. A white room, with pale curtains at the long windows. A room empty of everything except Lyell, his father, and a grand piano. But he couldn't see his father's face. He didn't even know what he looked like. Grandma Bone had hidden or destroyed every photo of her only son.

'Charlie, wake up!' Gabriel was nudging his arm.

Charlie opened his eyes. The lights were on in the auditorium and children were moving up the aisles towards the exit doors. The stage was empty.

'How long have you been asleep?' asked Gabriel.

'Don't know,' Charlie murmured. 'Most of the time, I think.' He dragged himself out of his seat.

Lysander left the theatre with them, but then he had to get to his own dormitory. 'Are you going to be OK?' he asked Gabriel before he parted from them on the landing.

'I'll live,' said Gabriel, grinning.

'We'll have another go at getting that glove off,' said Charlie, who was feeling more awake.

In the dormitory, Charlie told Fidelio what had happened and they spent several minutes trying to tug the glove off Gabriel's hand. It was impossible. Gabriel went to the bathroom and tried soap and water but the glove clung even tighter. He came back and sat on the edge of his bed. 'Poor woman,' he murmured. 'She must have broken all her fingers.'

'Do you know who she was?' asked Charlie.

'Is,' said Gabriel. 'She's still here. I've seen her. It's the dark lady from the tower. I used to think she was a ghost, but she isn't. She's just sort of useless and alone.'

Billy Raven had crept up behind them. He stared at the black glove on Gabriel's hand. 'What's that?' he asked.

'What does it look like?' said Fidelio.

'A glove. Why are you wearing one glove, Gabriel?'

Gabriel sighed. 'Because I can't get it off, that's why.'

Billy frowned. He didn't ask any more questions, but wandered back to his bed with a thoughtful expression.

Charlie and Fidelio made one more attempt to prise the glove off Gabriel's hand, but the water had made it cling like a second skin.

'It's no use, guys,' sighed Gabriel. 'I'll just have to sleep with it on. Maybe it'll come off when it's dried out.' He yawned. 'I'm so tired, nothing will keep me awake tonight.'

Gabriel was right. He fell asleep almost as soon as he got into bed. But while he slept, his dreams became nightmares, and he moaned with pain as he tossed and turned in his bed.

Gabriel made so much noise, Charlie couldn't sleep a wink. The other boys woke up too. Damian Smerk threw his pillow at the moaning boy, but it didn't wake him. He was buried deep in his troubled sleep.

The next night, Charlie and Fidelio tried, once again, to pull off the clinging black glove, but now it had shrunk. It wouldn't even peel away at the wrist. Gabriel's hand hung uselessly at his side. He couldn't even feel his fingers, he said.

They didn't know what to do. Telling Matron was out of the question. Charlie had an idea. After lights out, he leaned close to Gabriel's bed and whispered, 'I know someone who can help.'

'Who?'

'Someone who lives behind the kitchens. We'll have to wait till after midnight though.'

'Wake me up, when it's time to go,' said Gabriel.

'OK.'

Charlie had promised Cook that he wouldn't tell anyone where Henry was hiding. But that wasn't quite the same as taking someone to her secret room. Besides, this was an emergency.

YOU CAN'T GO BACK!

At five minutes past midnight, Billy Raven left the dormitory. Charlie wondered if he could get Gabriel down to Cook's room and back, before Billy returned.

'Gabriel,' he whispered, shaking Gabriel's shoulder. 'Wake up! It's time to go.'

Gabriel dragged himself out of bed and fumbled with his dressing gown. 'Ready!' he murmured.

Charlie grabbed his arm and led him out of the dormitory. Only then did he turn on Cook's torch. Its soft light illuminated every tiny detail of the long corridor.

'Wow,' said Gabriel. 'That's impressive.'

'Follow me,' Charlie whispered.

He began to jog, as quietly as he could, while behind him Gabriel floundered and tripped in his badly-fitting slippers.

By the time Charlie had found his way to Cook's cupboard entrance, Gabriel looked exhausted. The fingers on his left hand had begun to throb again, and the pain made him ache all over.

Charlie didn't like to burst in on Cook unannounced, so he knocked politely on the cupboard door.

There was a shuffling noise behind the door and then it was opened, just a crack.

'Shoot me,' said Cook, peering out at Charlie. 'What are you doing here?'

'I'm sorry, Cook,' said Charlie. 'But . . .'

Behind him, Gabriel gave a low moan.

Cook opened the door a little wider. She was wearing her red dressing gown. 'Shivering cats,' she said. 'Who on earth is this?'

'Gabriel Silk,' Charlie told her. 'He's had a sort of accident with a glove.'

'Tch! Tch! You'd better come in.'

Charlie led his friend through the cupboard and Gabriel looked round Cook's secret room in amazement. 'What a lovely place,' he said.

Cook made him sit down and examined his gloved hand, while Charlie told her how he'd found the glove, and how poor Gabriel had an unfortunate talent for experiencing other people's feelings, when he wore their clothes.

'Hm,' muttered Cook. 'That's Dorothy's glove.'

'Dorothy's?' said Charlie.

'It's the dark lady's,' said Gabriel. 'She haunts the music tower. I've seen her. She had her fingers broken in a door.'

Cook nodded. 'That's what you call her, do you? The dark lady. Well, I'll have you know that the dark lady is Mrs Bloor.'

'What? Manfred's mother?' said Charlie. 'I thought she was – well, dead.'

'So do most people,' said Cook. 'Poor thing. She lives a terrible half-life. When Manfred crushed her fingers she gave up. Faded away, so to speak. She comes down to my little room, now and again, and we talk. But she's a sad, sad creature.'

'Too right she is,' said Gabriel. 'This glove makes me feel so miserable I could do myself in.'

'Now then, we'll have none of that talk,' Cook said sternly. 'We'll have that glove off you in no time. Mind you, the only person who can do it is the owner of the glove.'

'Why's that?' asked Charlie.

'It's just the way it is. Musician's hands are very special. There's a lot of feeling in that glove, and I can see that it's really made itself at home on your skin, Gabriel.'

'I'd rather not lose any skin, if you don't mind,' said Gabriel. 'I'm a bit squeamish.'

'Endowed children were a lot more stoical in my day,' Cook remarked as she ambled across the room. 'I'll fetch Dorothy.' She opened the door of a small corner cupboard and the boys caught sight of a narrow stairway, before Cook squeezed herself into the cupboard and closed the door.

They heard the soft tap of footsteps behind the wall, and then over their heads. For a plump person, Cook was surprisingly light-footed.

'What a place,' Gabriel murmured, gazing round at the bright pictures and gleaming antique furniture. 'You'd never guess that all this was right under that gloomy old building.'

'Never,' agreed Charlie. 'Mind you, I think part of it

must be under the city. You can see the sky through that window.' He nodded at the small window in the ceiling.

Gabriel turned to look at the skylight. 'So what's up there?' he said.

Charlie shrugged. 'Who knows? Someone's garden. A road.' He was wondering what had happened to Henry. Had Cook sent him back through time? Had he run away?

Soft footfalls overhead told them that Cook was returning with someone who walked with a peculiar shuffling sound.

A few moments later, the door in the cupboard opened and Cook came in, followed by a small woman in a long, shapeless black dress. A dark shawl covered her head so her face could hardly be seen; she walked with her head bent as though she were searching the ground.

'Now, Dorothy, you sit here, dear!' Cook pushed a chair close to Gabriel's. 'This is Gabriel, and he seems to have got himself stuck into your glove.'

Dorothy looked at Gabriel's limp hand, and then she stared round at Charlie. Her shawl fell to her shoulders, revealing long grey hair and a pale face with two grey eyes in deep dark sockets. 'And who is this?' she asked in a tiny voice.

'I'm Charlie Bone,' said Charlie. 'Pleased to meet you, Mrs Bloor.'

'Oh?' said the faint little voice. 'So *you're* Charlie. I know . . . I knew . . .'

Mrs Bloor appeared to have forgotten what she knew, or had known, for she turned her attention back to Gabriel and said, 'Poor boy. You play the piano, don't you? I like to listen. I'll do my best for you, but I can only use one of my hands. The other has been cursed, you see. And it gets into the glove, and on to my towels, and I have to keep washing and washing it away.'

The boys gasped in horror.

'Who cursed you?' breathed Charlie.

Mrs Bloor just shook her head. With her right hand, she began to peel the leather glove away from Gabriel's wrist. It took a long time, and after a while, in a light trembling voice, Mrs Bloor began to tell them her story.

Dorothy de Vere had been a very talented violinist. Soon after she inherited a large fortune from her aunt, Dr Harold Bloor had courted her. They were married within a year and Dorothy gave him half her fortune. And then her troubles began. Her son Manfred hated all forms of music. He screamed when she picked up her violin. She only dared to play in a room where no one could hear her. Old Ezekiel Bloor demanded that she hand over the rest of her fortune. She refused. On her father's advice, she had put it in a secret bank account in Switzerland. Nothing would make her hand it over. She was deeply unhappy in the gloomy academy and planned to leave it.

'They did terrible things to people,' she murmured, 'and I couldn't stand it. One day, one wild, stormy day . . .' Her voice grew so faint they couldn't hear it, and then she stopped altogether, and it was Cook who told them what had happened. There was a violent thunderstorm and hoping the noise would cover the sound of her departure, Dorothy had packed her bag.

She had been about to leave her room, when Manfred looked in. 'You can't go,' he had snarled. 'We won't let you. Not until you've signed over the money.'

Once again, Dorothy had refused. Manfred said he'd lock her in her room. Dorothy put her hand on the doorframe to stop him, and he slammed the door – crack – on her fingers.

Mrs Bloor's head drooped. She shuddered. 'Tell them, tell them,' she murmured. 'Tell Charlie Bone.'

'She fainted, poor thing,' Cook went on. 'When she came to, she was on her bed. Old Ezekiel was sitting beside her. He'd soaked her injured fingers in one of his vile potions. He told her she'd never play her violin again. Never leave here. As far as they were concerned, she didn't exist, so she might as well give them the money.'

'But I didn't,' whispered Dorothy. 'I never will.' She had peeled the glove back, so that Gabriel's fingers could now be seen. With a light tug, she pulled it right off.

'Phew!' said Gabriel, shaking his hand. 'It feels OK. It really does. Thanks!'

'I'm glad, so glad,' murmured Mrs Bloor.

Charlie was relieved but anxious to get back to the dormitory before Billy. 'I think we'd better go now,' he said. 'But Cook, where's – you know who?'

'Fast asleep,' said Cook.

Charlie looked round the room. There was no sign of a bed.

Cook laughed. 'I have other rooms,' she said, 'and I've

got a very nice bathroom and toilet, but I'm not showing you round tonight. Off you go, both of you.'

'But I'll be going home tomorrow,' said Charlie. 'How am I going to get Henry out?'

'I'm afraid there won't be a chance,' said Cook. 'And perhaps it's better that those Yewbeam sisters don't see him. We'll have to have a good long think about Henry's future.'

She seemed to know a lot about Charlie's family.

Charlie and Gabriel said goodnight to the two women and, before they left, Gabriel did something rather surprising. He seized Mrs Bloor's injured hand and kissed it. Mrs Bloor smiled for the first time that night. It changed her face completely.

Charlie turned away in embarrassment. Gabriel really was a most peculiar person. 'By the way,' he said to Cook, 'the torch you gave me – it's magic or something, isn't it? It showed me things I've never seen before.'

'That was you, Charlie, as well as the torch. And there'll be more.'

As the boys made their way back to the dormitory, Gabriel asked, 'Who is this mysterious Henry?'

In a deep whisper, Charlie told the amazed Gabriel about Henry and the Time Twister. He knew he could trust him.

They reached the dormitory without any mishaps and, luckily, just a few minutes before Billy Raven came back from his midnight ramble.

In the morning, Gabriel handed Charlie a slip of paper. 'It's my address,' he said. 'Don't forget we're going to

Thunder House to see Tancred.'

Charlie showed the paper to Fidelio. 'D'you want to come?' he asked.

'Hail Road, the Heights,' said Fidelio, reading the address. 'How are we going to get there?'

'I'll think of something,' said Charlie.

He spent the rest of the day trying to get a message to his cousin before the weekend. Twice Manfred found him hovering outside the canteens. The second time, he threatened Charlie with detention, and though Charlie was tempted to chance it, he knew Tancred's problem was more urgent. The stormy boy's absence was having a strange effect. In the King's Room, the empty seat next to Lysander was like a cold, airless hole. It stole their energy and made some of the endowed children shiver. They lost their appetites and couldn't think straight. This happened to Charlie, Lysander, and Gabriel. Even Emma complained that she felt ill.

Manfred, Asa, and Zelda, and even Billy Raven, sailed through their homework and bounced their way to meals and lessons with energy and enthusiasm.

Something had to be done.

At the end of the day, as everyone trooped out through the main doors, Charlie caught sight of Olivia and Bindi on the stairs. He gave them a guilty wave, but Olivia was looking very excited. He hoped she wouldn't do anything too dangerous.

The blue bus dropped Charlie off at the top of Filbert Street and, as he made his way to number nine, Benjamin and Runner Bean came rushing up to greet him.

'It's been such a boring week,' sighed Benjamin. 'What did you do?'

As they walked home together, Charlie told Benjamin everything that had happened.

'You lead a very interesting life, Charlie,' Benjamin commented, 'but I think I'd rather be me.'

'I don't have a choice,' said Charlie. 'I've just got to do the best I can to survive it all.'

The front door opened before he'd had time to ring the bell, and Maisie pulled him inside with a violent hug. 'Tea's ready,' she said, dragging him towards the kitchen, 'all your favourites. Yours too, Benjamin. Come along. And I've got a nice bone for Runner Bean.'

The boys had just sat down to enjoy Maisie's wonderful spread when Grandma Bone walked in. You could tell right away that she was going to spoil Charlie's appetite.

'What's this?' she said, slamming the photo of Henry beside Charlie's plate.

'An old photo,' said Charlie. Grandma Bone had evidently been snooping in Uncle Paton's room.

'And what happened to it?' she demanded.

'It fell off the wall when you slammed your door.'

This was the wrong thing to have said to his grandmother.

'*I* slammed the door? *Me*? *You* broke the glass, Charlie Bone, and you didn't confess.'

'He brought it straight in here,' said Maisie hotly. 'And it wasn't his fault.'

'It was *my* frame, *my* glass,' said Grandma Bone. 'I should have been told. But let that pass. It's this boy I'm interested in.' She planted a bony finger on Henry's face. 'You've seen him, haven't you?'

'Course I haven't,' said Charlie. 'That photo's ancient. He must be a hundred years old.'

Benjamin was tucking into a plate of ham sandwiches. He kept his head well down, not daring to look at Charlie.

'I have it on good authority that Henry Yewbeam is about again,' Grandma Bone said in a chilly voice, 'and that you have seen him.'

So the dog has told Billy, thought Charlie. And Billy has passed on the news to Grandma's sister, Matron Yewbeam, or to Manfred.

'You're being silly, Grizelda,' said Maisie. 'Charlie's been locked away in that horrible old academy all week. How could he have seen the fellow, unless he was a ghost, of course.'

'Keep your nose out of this!' barked Grandma Bone.

'And you keep your nose out of Charlie's tea,' Maisie shouted, rolling up her sleeves.

Arguments at number nine nearly always started this way. The pattern was familiar to Charlie. He just wished it hadn't happened quite so soon after he'd come home. He followed Benjamin's example and grabbed a sandwich. Benjamin grinned at Charlie across the table, and Charlie grimaced back. They managed to get quite a lot of food inside themselves while the grandmas insulted each other over their heads. Runner Bean added to the noise with long anxious howls. He hated arguments.

When the shouting match was over, Grandma Bone, shaking with fury, said, 'Don't think I'm going to let this matter rest.' She marched out of the kitchen, slamming the door behind her.

'Well,' said Maisie. 'That was fun, wasn't it?'

'I wouldn't say it was fun exactly,' said Charlie. 'I've had a rather tiring week.'

'Grandma Bone is going potty,' grumbled Maisie. 'As if you'd seen a boy who must be a hundred years old.'

'Not quite a hundred,' Charlie said, without thinking.

'Oh?' The truth dawned on Maisie. 'I see. You've had peculiar things happening to you, have you?'

'It happened to Henry, not me,' said Charlie, reaching for a slice of cake.

'This is a great meal, Mrs Jones,' Benjamin said quickly.

'It's all right,' said Maisie. 'My lips are sealed, certainly where your other grandma is concerned.'

The two boys managed to finish their tea in peace, and then went up to Charlie's room. Runner Bean came bounding after them. Grandma Bone had been so angry, she'd forgotten to remind Charlie that dogs weren't allowed in bedrooms.

When Benjamin had helped Charlie unpack his bag, the boys sat on the bed while Runner squeezed in behind them. Charlie told Benjamin of the plan to visit Thunder House.

He wondered if Benjamin's mum would take them up there.

Benjamin shook his head. 'Mum's working on an important case at the moment. A really gruesome murder. She'll be out till late on Saturday. So will Dad.'

Benjamin's parents were private detectives. They worked very odd hours and Benjamin often had to cook his own meals.

'I thought your mum promised to stay home a bit more often,' said Charlie.

'She has,' said Benjamin. 'She's been at home all week, but then yesterday this case came up and it was so interesting, she just couldn't refuse it.'

'Hm. I'll have to think of someone else then,' said Charlie. 'There's always Uncle Paton.'

'But he wouldn't take us till it was dark, would he?' said Benjamin. 'I don't fancy going up to the Heights in the dark. Specially to a place where you might get struck by lightning or something.'

Charlie had to agree. Still, it was worth a chance. When Benjamin had gone home, Charlie knocked on his uncle's door.

There was no answer. Charlie wondered if his uncle had gone out. It was now very dark. At that moment, his mother came in and Charlie ran down to greet her. She'd brought a bag of mouldy aubergines home with her.

Maisie was very pleased. 'They're only half mouldy,' she said, spreading the aubergines across the kitchen table. 'We'll make a nice ratathingy.'

Charlie hope she didn't mean anything that had rats in it. With Maisie, anything was possible. He decided he'd rather not know. 'Have you seen Uncle Paton lately?' he asked.

'Very little,' said his mum. 'Poor Uncle Paton. He was getting very fond of Julia Ingledew, and now she has no time for him at all. She spends the whole week preparing for Emma to come home, and then devotes her entire weekend to the girl. They visit museums and castles and talk a great deal about books, apparently. She's shut poor Paton out altogether.'

'That's tough,' said Charlie. 'So he's in, right now?'

Charlie went upstairs and tapped on his uncle's door again.

'What?' said an angry voice.

Charlie opened the door and looked in. The mess in his uncle's room was even worse than usual. There was also a very bad smell. Perhaps Paton had hidden a few unfinished meals under his bed.

'Can I talk to you?' asked Charlie, meekly.

'If you must,' murmured Paton. He was studying a book and didn't look up.

When he'd managed to reach Paton's desk, without knocking anything over, Charlie said, 'I've met that boy. The one in the photo. Your dad's brother.'

'What?' Paton's head shot up. 'Tell me more.'

Charlie told him about the Time Twister and Henry's strange arrival. When he began to describe his part in the freezer experiment, however, Paton roared, 'You did *what*?'

106

'He wanted to go back,' said Charlie, 'and I had to help him.'

'You stupid, stupid boy!' thundered his uncle. 'People can't go back. You can't change history. Think about it! When my father was five years old, he lost his brother. It changed his life. He became an only child, grew up as an only child. All his memories are of being an only one. You can't change that now, can you?'

'No,' Charlie said quickly. 'I'm sorry.'

His uncle hadn't finished. 'Henry's parents mourned him, just as they mourned poor little Daphne. James was their only child and, as a result, he was probably spoiled. His father died in the war and his mother left everything to him, including her lovely cottage by the sea. You can't change that, can you?'

Charlie sighed. 'No,' he said. And then he had an idea. 'Would your father like to see Henry again?'

Paton's angry expression gradually changed. Charlie could almost see thoughts chasing each other across his uncle's face.

'Now there's a thought,' said Paton, as if he'd suddenly found the right one.

'So what d'you think?' asked Charlie.

'I don't think anything yet,' said Paton. 'You'll have to leave me to ponder.'

Charlie judged that now would be the right time to ask his uncle a favour. But when he mentioned going up to the Heights to visit Thunder House, he didn't get the answer he'd hoped for.

'Huh!' said Paton. 'I'm not going anywhere near those storm people. It's useless to meddle with them when they're in a mood. I strongly advise you not to try.'

Charlie began to explain how urgent it was to get Tancred back to the academy, but his uncle wouldn't listen. It was obviously going to take Paton a long time to become the brave and helpful uncle that he had once been.

'We've *got* to get there somehow,' Charlie said desperately.

'I don't go out in daylight,' snapped Paton. 'You'll have to find someone else.'

THUNDER HOUSE

Henry Yewbeam was bored. Cook's underground rooms were cosy and interesting, but Henry had explored every inch of them. He wished Charlie would come and talk to him. But Cook said Charlie had gone home for the weekend.

Cook seemed to be very busy, even on a Saturday. She had found a pair of old pyjamas for Henry, and some modern-looking clothes: long trousers, black shoes and grey socks. And she had persuaded him to exchange his warm Norfolk jacket for a blue jumper. Henry found this wasn't as warm as his jacket, but at least he still had the blue cape he was wearing when he came twisting through time.

Cook had hidden the Time Twister. 'I don't want you trying anything silly again,' she said, wagging her finger at Henry. 'You're here for good now. Thing is, what to do with you?'

Henry hadn't given up hope. There had to be a way back to 1916, otherwise what would become of him? He didn't want to return to Bloor's, of course. But if he could just get to the right year, he would eventually reach his happy home beside the sea.

But I'll have to go through that other world first, he said to himself. The world in the Time Twister.

When Henry had travelled through time, he'd briefly glimpsed the world of the Red King. His mother, who was a Bloor, had told him once that he was descended from this mysterious Red King.

'Some of the king's descendants have inherited a part of his magic,' Grace Bloor had said. 'But as far as I can tell, none of us have.' And she had looked round at her family and laughed in her playful comforting way, and added, 'Thank goodness!' Henry wished he could hear her laughter again.

Charlie's got some of that magic, he said to himself.

Perhaps he could live with Charlie? That wouldn't be so bad. Charlie could teach him to use all the new-fangled things Cook had told him about: televisions, videos, computers and other amazing things.

He'd been told that Cook would be back to give him his lunch at half past twelve. But, according to the little clock beside Henry's bed, it was still only ten o'clock.

'More than two hours of nothing,' sighed Henry.

He had an idea. Now that he was dressed like all the other boys at Bloor's, surely he could do some exploring. He had always wanted to go in the ruin, but Sir Gideon had forbidden it. Now was Henry's chance.

He tiptoed out of Cook's room, carefully closing the cupboard door behind him. After several more cupboards, he found himself outside the canteen and running towards a loud noise that was coming from the hall. He looked in and saw a big man with a shaven head, hammering something into the main door.

Without stopping his work, the big man said, 'Who might you be?'

'I'm – er – Henry,' said Henry nervously.

'Henry what?'

'Er – er – Bone.' Henry didn't know why he'd said Bone. He just thought it might be a bad idea to say Yewbeam.

'Don't seem very sure, do ya?' The man continued hammering.

'I'm quite sure, thank you,' said Henry.

'We've got another Bone here. A real terror of a Bone.'

'He's my cousin.'

'I s'pose you're one of them endowed kids. Troublemakers, all of them.' The man delivered a really savage blow to the door. 'Broke the door, that's what the stormy one done, blast him!'

'Oh!' Henry continued on his way to the garden.

'Taking the dog for a walk, are ya?' said the man.

'What?' Henry increased his stride.

'The dog. Miserable beast.'

Henry looked down to find Blessed panting at his feet. 'Oh, yes. Come along,' he said and walked briskly to the garden door.

Once outside, Henry stopped to catch his breath.

Blessed looked as nervous as he did.

'What's the matter?' said Henry. He bent down and patted the old dog's head. Blessed was very ugly but there was something so sad about his solemn, wrinkled face, Henry couldn't help feeling sorry for him.

There were four boys playing football in the snowy slush just ahead of them. They paid no attention to Henry and Blessed as they walked past. A huge tree had been sawn into logs in the centre of the field and Henry was tempted to climb up on them, but time was precious and he had to see the ruin.

When they reached the great red walls, Henry felt very excited. The place smelled of age and danger. He imagined knights in armour scrambling over the walls, battle-horses charging through the entrance and arrows whizzing overhead. He was about to walk through the huge arched entrance, when a voice said, 'You boy, come here!'

Henry turned to see two older boys marching towards him. They both wore purple capes and had grim, unfriendly faces.

'Who are you?' shouted the taller boy.

Henry plunged into the ruin. He found himself in a square courtyard with five passages leading out of it. Henry took the middle one.

He could hear the other boys murmuring behind him. Henry ran as fast as he could. The passage opened into another open courtyard. Henry ran across it and stumbled down a flight of steep stone steps. He was now in a grassy glade, ringed with headless statues. In the centre of the glade, two girls in purple capes sat on a large stone tomb. One was very small and very dark, with a long black pigtail and gold-rimmed glasses. The other had a bright, healthy-looking face and amazing blue hair.

'Hello,' said Henry breathlessly. 'I'm er . . .'

'You're Henry, aren't you?' said the girl with blue hair. 'Charlie told me about you. They're looking for you, you know. The place was in a turmoil this morning. Manfred threw loads of music books out of the tower; he was in such a fury. I'm Olivia and this is Bindi.'

'I'm very glad to meet you.' Henry went to shake their hands. 'How do you do.'

'You *are* polite,' said Olivia. 'I expect that comes of being old.'

'Old? I suppose people would consider me to be old. But, actually, I only feel about eleven.'

'Me too,' said Olivia. 'But then I am. We wouldn't normally be here on Saturday, but we've got detention.'

There was a shout from the courtyard above them and Blessed came stumbling down the steps.

'They must have followed the dog,' muttered Henry. 'Two boys chased me in here. One was very tall and wore his hair like a girl.'

'A ponytail,' said Olivia. 'That's Manfred Bloor, the head boy.'

'We can't let *him* find you,' said Bindi. 'Quick, get in here.'

With surprising speed, the two girls leapt off the tomb and slid back the top. Henry stared into the dark gap. The inside of the tomb smelled of mildew and decomposing things.

'Go on,' said Olivia. 'You can breathe in there. We've tried it.'

Another shout from above made Henry climb into the tomb. The girls pushed back the lid, leaving a tiny gap for air. They swung themselves back on to the top just as Manfred and Asa came rushing down the steps.

'Have you seen a strange boy?' said Manfred.

'We've seen Daniel Robottom,' said Olivia, choosing a boy about the same size as Henry, who also wore a blue cloak. He went that way!' She pointed to an arched entrance in one of the walls.

'Daniel Robottom? Are you sure?' Asa's yellow eyes narrowed suspiciously.

'Course we're sure,' said Bindi. 'He was humming. Daniel always hums.'

Manfred and Asa rushed through the arch.

There was a tap from inside the tomb.

'Ssh!' hissed Olivia. 'You can't come out. It's not safe yet.'

She was right. A few minutes later, Manfred and Asa came running back.

'Are you positive he went that way?' said Manfred.

'Cross my heart and hope to die,' Olivia said blithely. 'But he went back up those steps about five minutes ago. You must have missed him.'

'What's he done?' asked Bindi.

'None of your business,' said Manfred.

'We're looking for someone else,' added Asa.

Manfred shot him a look that said 'Keep quiet!'

'What's my great-grandfather's dog doing in here?' asked Manfred.

'We thought we'd take him for a walk,' Bindi told him.

The two boys turned away, but as they mounted the steps, Asa looked back and said, 'Why are you two here, anyway?'

'We came for a bit of peace,' Olivia sighed. 'The boys are so rough.'

'I wouldn't stay in the ruin too long.' Asa gave her a peculiar smile and followed Manfred up the steps.

'He gives me the shivers,' muttered Bindi.

They waited another five minutes before deciding it was safe enough to let Henry out. He scrambled over the side of the tomb and dropped on to the grass. His cloak and trousers were covered in green dust and bits of cobweb clung to his hair.

'There's a huge toad in there,' he said. 'I'm not very fond of toads.'

The girls brushed him down and then all three sat on the tomb and shared a bun that Bindi had managed to sneak out of the canteen.

Henry told the girls about his home beside the sea, and how he had come upon the Time Twister. Olivia recounted some of her famous mother's adventures while filming in the jungle. And then Bindi described how she had travelled to India to visit her grandparents.

When the horn called them in for lunch, Olivia said, 'Come with us, Henry. Stay calm. Don't look nervous, and when we reach the canteen you can slip through into the kitchen.'

Henry had only told the girls he was hiding in the kitchens. Although he trusted them, he felt it would be safer if no one knew exactly where he was.

Unfortunately, when he reached the canteen he walked straight into a dinner lady.

'What are you doing in here?' she asked.

'M . . . m . . . message for Cook,' stuttered Henry.

'She's in the cold room.' The dinner lady smiled. She was young and cheerful-looking.

Henry made his way through the kitchen. Cook wasn't in the cool room. He tried to find the cupboard he'd come out of, but he kept blundering into broom closets and cupboards full of crockery. Cook's secret entrance seemed to have disappeared.

Henry was fumbling behind a row of plastic aprons when a firm hand came down on his shoulder. Henry froze.

A voice in his ear hissed, 'Henry Yewbeam, where *have* you been?'

Henry turned to see Cook's angry red face.

'I just went for a little walk,' he explained.

'Didn't I tell you not to leave here?' she whispered harshly. 'Didn't I? Never do that again. It's dangerous out there.'

'I'm sorry,' said Henry contritely.

'Took you long enough to find the right place, didn't it?' Cook turned a handle beside the row of aprons and a door swung inwards. Without a word, she pushed Henry through the door into a stack of mops and brooms. 'You'll have to find your own way now,' she said. 'If you're lucky, you'll get lunch in half an hour.' She swiftly closed the door.

Henry made his way back to Cook's rooms. He sat beside the stove, feeling rather sorry for himself. Was he to spend the rest of his life like this? Hiding from people who wished him harm. Why was it dangerous 'out there'? He recalled something Manfred Bloor had said to the girls, 'What's my great-grandfather's dog doing in here?'

Who was Manfred's great-grandfather? Was it possible . . .? No, it couldn't be. Could it? Cousin Ezekiel would be over a hundred years old.

It *is* possible, thought Henry. He shuddered. Cousin Ezekiel is still alive, and he still wants to get rid of me, one way or another.

Henry wished the Time Twister had taken him somewhere else; Charlie Bone's house, for instance.

At that moment, Charlie would rather not have been in his house. He and Benjamin were sitting in the kitchen at number nine, wondering what to do. Frantic phone calls had been made between Charlie, Fidelio and Gabriel. But no parent could be found, or persuaded, to give them a lift up to the Heights.

'We could get a taxi,' Benjamin suggested. 'I've got three pounds.'

Charlie didn't think that was enough. His mother was out at work and Maisie was shopping. He didn't think his uncle would have any money, and he certainly couldn't ask Grandma Bone.

'We're stuck.' Charlie stared glumly out of the kitchen window.

He had hardly spoken when a luxurious car drove into view. It pulled up right in front of number nine, and Lysander jumped out of the passenger seat. He waved at the kitchen window.

Charlie scribbled a note to his mother, checked the door key in his pocket, and ran to the front door. He opened it just as Lysander was about to ring the bell.

'Hi there, Charlie!' said Lysander. 'My dad's going to give us a ride up to Gabriel's place.'

Benjamin and Runner Bean appeared behind Charlie.

'Can my friend and his dog come?' asked Charlie.

'Course. More is merrier,' said Lysander. 'Come.'

Benjamin, Charlie and Runner Bean followed Lysander down the steps to the car. Lysander got in the front, while the others climbed in the back. They found Fidelio already tucked into the deep leather seat.

'How do you do, boys,' said the very handsome black man sitting in the driver's seat.

'My dad,' said Lysander quickly. 'He's a judge, but don't let that scare you.'

'How d'you do, Judge,' said Benjamin and Charlie, slightly daunted by this imposing man.

The car purred away from the kerb, sailed down Filbert Street, round the park and then up through the city. Up and up and up. None of them noticed the yellow taxi that was following them. The car was now climbing the steep road up to the Heights. They passed several grand houses and then they were beyond the fashionable area and skirting the borders of a wild-looking wood. The judge pulled up outside a rather dilapidated building with a very muddy yard. Hens scratched in a bed of shrubs and a goat with large horns was chewing a bush.

'This is as far as I go, boys,' said the judge.

'Couldn't you take us up to the top, Dad?' asked Lysander.

'I'm not driving my new car up there,' said his father. 'Too much turbulence.'

As they got out, they could hear thunder rumbling in the distance.

'Good luck, young fellows!' The judge backed into the muddy yard, turned his car and drove down the hill.

'Will he come and fetch us?' asked Benjamin, anxiously.

'Might,' said Lysander. 'Might be Mum though.'

A little further down the hill, and out of sight of the boys, the yellow taxi had pulled up. An odd-looking creature got out; an old man in a long, dirty mackintosh. He had a white moustache but tufts of ginger hair stuck out from under his filthy tweed cap. He paid the driver and then began to run up the hill, not moving like an old man at all, but more like a school-boy.

Charlie had never been so high above the city. The view was magnificent, but there was something unsettling about such a high and windy place. The trees behind them sighed ominously, and the thunder became more persistent.

They were about to walk into the yard, when Gabriel came out of the dilapidated house. He was wearing long, muddy boots and splashed deliberately through the deepest puddles. His jeans were so dirty the mud hardly made a difference.

'Hi!' Gabriel raised his left hand. 'Look! Good as new.'

'Glad to hear it,' said Lysander. 'Are we all ready then?'

'Ready for anything,' said Fidelio.

They set off, Lysander and Gabriel leading the way. After a while the road became rough and narrow, and then it petered out altogether. They found themselves at a gate. A wooden sign, marked THUNDER HOUSE, had been nailed to the top bar. Beneath this a smaller sign read, BEWARE OF THE WEATHER!

'What does *that* mean?' said Benjamin.

'We'll soon find out,' said Fidelio.

Beyond the gate, a narrow lane led between rows of dark conifers. The tops of the trees thrashed violently in the wind that swirled overhead and twigs, stones and dead grass came bowling down the lane.

'Here goes,' said Lysander, opening the gate. 'I've been here before, but it's never been this windy.'

The others followed him through. They were immediately struck by flying debris.

'This isn't going to be easy,' muttered Charlie.

Leaning into the wind, the two leaders set off up the lane. Behind them, Fidelio, Charlie and Benjamin walked in a huddle, with Runner Bean anxiously winding round their legs.

With every step they took, the wind grew fiercer, and now sharp little bolts of hail peppered their faces. Charlie took a peek round Lysander and saw an awesome grey stone building. The roof was divided into three very steep triangles, the middle section resembling a tower. The windows were long and narrow, and the porch roof echoed the sharp angle of the centre gable. A weathervane in the shape of a hammer whirled madly at the very top of the building. Every now and again the whole building shook violently.

As they drew near to the house, the porch door opened and out came a man with frizzy blond hair and a beard to match. He must have been nearly seven feet tall because he banged his head on the top of the doorframe when he stepped through it.

'It's no use,' the big man roared, as the boys battled their way towards the house. 'I've tried to calm him down, but we've got to let this storm blow itself out.'

'We need him, Mr Torsson!' Lysander shouted through the wind.

'I know! I know, but Tancred's got this weather thing worse than I have. I can't manage him at all.'

The determined gang had now reached the shelter of the house. Not that it gave them much protection. The wind came at them from every direction, tearing their hair and making their eyes stream with tears.

Mr Torsson stood with his arms across his chest, braced against the hail that battered his broad back. 'I've tried to reason with him.' He coughed and a deep rumble echoed somewhere in his chest. 'He's locked himself in his room. Furniture's probably in smithereens by now. My wife . . .' He gave another cough, this one coinciding with a bolt of lightning that came sizzling down a nearby tree.

They all watched the tree crash to the ground, its feathery branches alight with flames. These were soon put out, however, by the deluge that suddenly poured from the sky. In a brief moment of quiet before the next clap of thunder, Mr Torsson said sadly, 'My poor wife's got a terrible headache.'

'Can we just come in and talk to Tancred?' begged Lysander.

'Not a chance,' said Mr Torsson, planting himself firmly inside the porch. 'It's too dangerous. You'll just have to come back another time. Be careful on the way back. There's something out there.'

'What . . .?' Gabriel began.

His next words were drowned by a furious crack of thunder, and they all found themselves ducking. Something hit the ground with a heavy thud right behind them.

Runner Bean howled hysterically and Benjamin shouted, 'W . . . w . . . what was that?'

'A hammer,' said Mr Torsson. He disappeared into the house and they heard the rattle of locks and bolts behind the door.

'Well, that's that, I guess,' sighed Lysander. 'Let's go back through the wood. There'll be more shelter under the trees.'

They raced to the wood but Runner Bean, barking with excitement, began to dig at the ground.

'What's the matter with him?' said Charlie.

'He's found the hammer,' said Benjamin breathlessly. 'Runner, here boy. Leave it. *Now*! *It's not a bone*!'

The wood was full of thorny bushes and brambles that scratched their faces and tore their clothes. And there was something else: a feeling of being watched.

'I don't like this,' muttered Lysander. 'Let's try and get back to the lane.'

The lane couldn't be found. They fanned out, calling to each other as they searched. 'Not this way!' 'Can't see it.' 'Help, we're lost!' 'Must be this way.' 'Not here.'

All at once, Charlie found himself alone. It had become very dark. Thunder still grumbled in the distance, but the trees were eerily still. And then he saw the terrible eyes: twin pools of light, moving closer through the undergrowth. With a yell of terror, Charlie turned and threw himself at a tangle of bushes.

'Help!' he shouted. 'Help! Where are you all?'

He could hear barking, but it was difficult to tell where it came from. 'Runner!' he shouted. 'Runner Bean, here boy!'

There was a deep snarl behind him and Charlie hurled himself away from it. He tore through the wood, banging into trees, tripping, falling, scrambling on his knees, until he saw a pale strip of road. He crawled on to it and looked up to see four boys staring at him in horror.

'Charlie! You look a real mess,' Fidelio exclaimed.

'You don't look so good yourself,' said Charlie. 'How did you find the road?'

'We'd still be in the wood if it wasn't for Runner,' said Gabriel. 'What happened to you, Charlie? We called and called.'

'Didn't hear,' said Charlie. He got to his feet and shook the twigs out of his hair. 'There was something in there. An animal.'

'I know, we heard it,' said Lysander grimly. 'Whatever it was, it didn't want us in those woods. Let's get away from here.'

They staggered back to Gabriel's house and found the inside of the ramshackle building surprisingly warm and comfortable. When the boys had cleaned themselves at the kitchen sink, they fell into their chairs and gazed at mounds of roast beef, Yorkshire pudding and vegetables, not knowing where to start.

'Charlie, your mum was on the telephone,' said Mrs Silk. 'I told her you'd gone for a walk with your friends, and would be coming back here for your tea.'

'Thanks, Mrs Silk!' Charlie wondered if his mother had got his note. He wouldn't put it past Grandma Bone to have hidden it.

Gabriel had three sisters who squeezed themselves in between the boys and kept up an endless stream of chatter. The boys were too exhausted to join in. Lysander hardly said a word throughout the meal.

'Not a very promising start to the new term, is it?' said Mrs Silk. 'What with Gabriel's hand and all.' She was a neat, pretty woman with round blue eyes and brown curly hair; not a bit like Gabriel.

It wasn't easy having an endowed child in the family, but Mrs Silk did her best. She had no idea where Gabriel's strange talent (if you could call it that) came from. She and her husband were always arguing about which side of the family was responsible for it. She had a strong suspicion that it came from the Silks, some of whom were peculiar to say the least. Gabriel could never wear second-hand clothes, and as they were not a rich family, Mrs Silk often had to buy second-hand things for the girls. They found this very unfair.

After tea Gabriel took his friends to see his famous gerbils and then, as it was getting late, Mrs Silk drove everyone to their own front doors in a battered Land Rover. 'Hope your mum wasn't worried,' she called as Charlie climbed the steps of number nine.

Maisie met him in the hall.

'The Yewbeams are here,' she muttered. 'I'm off to watch my telly. Good luck, Charlie!'

SKARPO THE SORCERER

Grandma Bone's three sisters were usually entertained in the tidy room across the hall, but today, here they were, sitting round the table and swamping the normally cosy kitchen with their dreadful dark clothes and sour faces.

They had draped their black coats across the chairs and dumped their large black bags on the dresser. There was a half-eaten cake, oozing cream, on the table and the room smelled of stale buns and old lavender.

Charlie tried to make the best of things. 'Hullo, Aunties,' he said cheerfully. 'What a surprise!'

'I'm surprised your mother lets you stay out so late,' said Aunt Lucretia. 'Where've you been?'

'Where's Mum?' said Charlie, looking round.

'Where's Mum? Where's my mummy?' said Aunt Eustacia in a silly voice.

Charlie looked at the cake. No one offered him a slice.

'Your mother is out,' said Grandma Bone.

'Where?'

'Dearie me, we are in a state about our mummy, aren't

126

we?' cooed Venetia, the youngest and most deadly of the sisters.

'I'm not in a state,' said Charlie indignantly. 'It's just that I'm surprised she's not here.'

'She's gone to the theatre,' said Grandma Bone. 'She had two free tickets to see *Divine Drums*. Naturally, she wanted to take you, but *you* weren't here, were you?'

'She didn't say anything about tickets to me,' said Charlie. 'Where did they come from?'

'We don't know everything about your mum, do we?' said Aunt Eustacia. 'She probably got them from her boyfriend.'

'She hasn't got a boyfriend,' said Charlie.

'How d'you know?' said Aunt Venetia, patting her hair, which was coiled above her head like a black serpent. 'She's still a young woman.'

'She doesn't need a boyfriend,' said Charlie, 'because my dad's still alive.'

Icy silence descended on the kitchen. The four sisters stiffened. Their mouths tightened into grim dark lines.

Grandma Bone said, 'Why do you persist in this nonsense, boy? Your father died. We had a funeral.'

'But there was no body,' said Charlie. He turned to leave but all four sisters shouted, 'STOP!'

Taken by surprise, Charlie did stop.

'You haven't told us about Henry,' said Grandma Bone.

'There's nothing to tell,' said Charlie.

'You're a very stupid boy,' said Matron Lucretia. 'D'you

127

think we don't know about the Time Twister? D'you think we haven't heard how Ezekiel Bloor sent his little cousin, Henry, spinning away through time? And now he has ended up at the academy, a few years too late for his own good.'

'Ha! Ha! Ha!' cackled Aunt Eustacia nastily.

'It's not a joke,' said Charlie angrily. 'How would you like it?'

'Got you!' snapped Grandma Bone. 'Admit you've seen him!'

Charlie stamped his foot. 'I won't admit nothing.'

'Anything,' screamed Aunt Lucretia. 'Grammar, boy! You won't admit anything!'

'Oh, yes he will!' Grandma Bone leapt to her feet. 'Where is he?' she screeched. 'We'll find him eventually, you know. But if he doesn't come out soon, old Ezekiel's going to be in such a mood, he'll send him back to the ice age.'

'He can't,' said Charlie. 'Not without the Time Twister.'

'You have no idea what Ezekiel can do,' said Aunt Venetia, in her dangerous, silky tone. 'Some of it's too horrible for words. Why won't you tell us where this wretched Henry is hiding? He doesn't deserve your loyalty. He's just a nuisance. Why can't you be a good boy, for a change? I would hate Ezekiel to hurt you, my pet.'

Charlie had no idea what to say to this. Aunt Venetia always managed to catch him off-guard by being nice. Luckily, the door opened and Uncle Paton looked in.

'What was all that noise?' said Paton. 'I can't hear myself think.'

128

'Thoughts are supposed to be silent,' said Eustacia, with a giggle.

'Don't be silly,' said Paton. 'Be so good as to turn down the volume. My work has reached a very critical stage. I can't have my concentration ruined by a gaggle of screeching geese.'

'Screeching?' screeched Aunt Lucretia.

In a more reasonable tone, Grandma Bone said, 'We're interrogating Charlie about something of vital importance.'

'Well, I need him for something *more* important,' said Paton. 'Come along, Charlie!'

Charlie sprang gratefully towards his uncle, but Grandma Bone hadn't finished.

'The boy stays here,' she said, 'until we've got the truth out of him.'

Uncle Paton sighed. He directed his gaze towards the lamp hanging over the table.

'Paton!' said Grandma Bone sharply. 'You wouldn't dare.'

'I would,' said Paton.

The next moment there was a small explosion. The four sisters leapt away from the table as a shower of broken glass fell from the lamp and settled on the cake.

'Come on, Charlie,' said Paton.

Charlie quickly followed his uncle out of the kitchen, while Grandma Bone and the aunts, twittering like birds, jumped about, looking for dishcloths, picking glass off the cake and dusting down their clothes.

'Thanks for getting me out of there, Uncle Paton,' said

Charlie, as he closed Paton's door behind him.

'Not at all, not at all. I really do need you, Charlie.' Paton seemed very excited about something. 'I've been experimenting. Look!'

He took a book from his desk, opened it and began to read. Still reading, he walked to the switch by the door and turned on the light that hung in the centre of the room.

Expecting the light to shatter, Charlie ducked. But nothing happened.

'I thought that you took all the light bulbs out of your room,' said Charlie.

'So I did, so I did,' Paton murmured, still intent on his reading, 'but I've put one back.'

'So what's going on?' said Charlie.

'Turn the light off, dear boy,' said Paton. 'I can't talk and concentrate on my book at the same time.'

Mystified, Charlie turned off the light. His uncle's room was once again bathed in the soft glow from the oil lamp on his desk.

'So, Charlie, are you surprised the light bulb didn't break?' asked Paton.

'Well, yes,' said Charlie, 'but then you don't always break them, do you? Not if you're, kind of, relaxed.'

'Exactly.' Paton gave a sigh of satisfaction. 'When my mind's switched off,' he laughed, 'if you'll excuse the pun. When my thoughts are elsewhere, as it were, I'm less prone to accidents of the electrical kind. So – I decided if I read a very engrossing book, while in the presence of an electrified light bulb, the bulb might not shatter.'

'I see,' Charlie said slowly. 'That's very interesting, Uncle Paton.'

'More than interesting, dear boy. It worked. It's a damn miracle.' Paton beamed with triumph. 'I can go out in daylight if I'm reading a book. I can walk past lighted shop windows. I can walk near traffic lights without breaking them. Perhaps, I can even enter a coffee shop – if I'm reading.'

Charlie could see drawbacks to his uncle's plan. It would be dangerous for Paton to wander through the city streets, not seeing where he was going. 'It could be a bit dodgy,' he said. 'You might get run over.'

'That's where you come in, Charlie. If you were with me, you could see the pitfalls. I thought tomorrow, we might take a walk in the direction of the cathedral, just to test my theory.'

'I take it that you mean in the direction of Ingledew's Bookshop,' said Charlie.

His uncle went pink, especially round the ears. He gave a small cough and said, 'I can't deny it. Miss Ingledew has been much in my thoughts. I feel that were she to see me, walking about in daylight, she wouldn't think me such a freak.'

'She doesn't think you're a freak, Uncle. It's just that trying to be a mum to Emma is using up all her energy.'

Paton gave a huge sigh and shook his head. 'No, Charlie. She's wary of me, and who could blame her?

'OK. Tomorrow, we'll take a walk to Ingledew's,' said

Charlie, a little reluctant to be drawn away from the things on his mind.

'Thank you, Charlie!'

The telephone in the hall began to ring.

'I wonder if that's for me,' muttered Charlie.

'Better find out,' said Paton. 'You can bet that my sisters won't pass on any messages.'

Charlie went out to the landing and looked down into the hall. He was just in time to see Grandma Bone pick up the receiver and shout, 'He's not here!' and bang it down again.

'Was that for me?' asked Charlie.

Grandma Bone glared up at him. 'Of course not,' she said. 'Who d'you think you are?'

'I live here,' said Charlie, 'and it's just possible my friends might want to talk to me.'

'Huh!' snorted Grandma Bone.

The Yewbeam aunts emerged from the kitchen. They were still brushing down their coats and patting their heads.

'There's a bit,' cried Venetia, grabbing a lock of Eustacia's grey hair.

Eustacia yelled, 'Get it out! Get it out!'

Unfortunately, Aunt Lucretia looked up and saw Charlie smiling. 'You can wipe that grin off your face,' she said. 'We haven't finished with you yet.'

The three sisters trooped out through the front door and then stood on the step, whispering to Grandma Bone.

The telephone rang again and, this time, Charlie swooped

132

down the stairs and picked up the receiver before Grandma Bone could get to it.

'Hi. Is that you, Charlie?' It was Gabriel.

'Yes,' said Charlie cautiously.

'A nasty voice told me you weren't there, but I didn't believe them.'

'My grandma,' said Charlie in the same tone.

Grandma Bone closed the front door and stood watching Charlie.

'Is she there?' asked Gabriel.

'Yes,' said Charlie, turning his back on Grandma Bone.

'Look, Charlie. I found something in the lane outside our house. Several things actually. I think you ought to see them.'

'Where shall we meet?' asked Charlie.

'Mum's delivering some stuff to the Pets' Café tomorrow afternoon,' said Gabriel. 'Meet me there.'

Charlie had never heard of the Pets' Café. 'Where's that?'

'Frog Street,' said Gabriel. 'Between Mud Lane and Water Street. Just behind the cathedral.'

This was good news. 'I'm going there with my uncle,' said Charlie. 'Can I bring him?'

'Sure. Is it your glass-breaking uncle? He's brilliant.'

'It is.'

'Great. Got to go now. See you tomorrow, about three o'clock. Ouch! Gerbil bit me. Bye!'

There was a loud clunk. It sounded as if Gabriel had dropped the phone.

When Charlie looked round, Grandma Bone had gone.

He peeped into the kitchen. She wasn't there so Charlie made himself a quick snack and sat down. The table had been cleared of broken glass but something lay where the cake had been – a small picture, placed face-down. Charlie guessed that it had been left there on purpose and, knowing his aunts, he was sure that it was a trick. But what sort of trick? He concentrated on his food, refusing to look at the picture.

And then he began to wonder if it really was a trick. Gradually, Charlie's gaze was drawn to the dark panel at the back of the picture. It looked very old; the wood was cracked and covered with tiny worm holes, the screws were rusty and the string had broken.

Charlie took a breath and flipped the frame over. He saw a small painting of a room. But what kind of room? He couldn't resist taking in the details.

On the right of the painting, a tall man in a black robe was looking at a skull that lay at his feet. The man's dark beard was threaded with silver and he wore a round black skullcap on his silver hair. In an alcove behind the man, a table covered in red cloth was piled with books, bowls, feathers, bundles of herbs, animal horns and gleaming weapons. Strange symbols had been chalked on the bare stone walls and the man was in the act of drawing another: a star with five points.

Charlie found himself staring at the skull. He tried to look away from it, but he couldn't. He began to hear sounds; a low chanting in a strange language, the scraping of chalk on stone, the rustle of heavy robes. And then, suddenly, the man turned his head and looked at Charlie, looked right into his eyes.

Charlie gasped and quickly whipped the painting over. Out in the street, a car door slammed and he heard his mother's voice. A man spoke and his mother laughed. She rarely laughed. What had the man said, and who was he?

When Mrs Bone walked into the kitchen, Charlie could still see the yellow eyes of the man in the black robe, fixing him with a glare of triumph.

'Charlie, are you all right?' said Amy Bone. 'You look very pale.'

'I er . . .' Charlie touched the back of the painting. He found that he couldn't explain what had happened to him, so he asked, 'Where were you?' There was a nasty whine in his voice that he couldn't help.

'I've been to see *Divine Drums*. I wanted you to come with us, but you weren't here, Charlie.'

'Us?' said Charlie, sounding even more sulky. 'Who's "us"?'

'Bob Davies and myself.' Mrs Bone smiled encouragingly. 'He got three tickets and you were supposed to have come. I couldn't disappoint him when I found you weren't here, could I?'

'Who's this Bob Davies?' asked Charlie, hating the whine in his voice.

'Charlie, what's come over you?' Mrs Bone pulled out a chair and sat beside him. 'Bob's just a friend, a very nice man who wanted to take us to the theatre. Why are you so grumpy?'

Charlie was ashamed. He said, 'I'm sorry, Mum. I . . . something happened to me, just now. The aunts left that.' He nodded at the painting, not wanting even to touch it.

Mrs Bone picked up the painting. 'The Sorcerer,' she said, reading the painted scrawl at the bottom of the picture.

Charlie hadn't even noticed that the painting had a title. 'I think it was a trick,' he murmured.

'What sort of trick, Charlie?'

'I don't know yet.' He carefully turned the painting over again.

'Tell you what,' said Mrs Bone, patting Charlie's shoulder. 'I'll just run upstairs and change my clothes, and then we'll have a nice cup of tea before you go to bed, shall we?'

'Yes,' said Charlie, wondering how a cup of tea could take away the memory of the sorcerer's eyes.

He noted the sparkle of sequins on his mother's dress as she began to unbutton her coat. 'Mum, Dad might not be . . .'

Mrs Bone swung round. 'Might not be what?'

'Might not be dead,' Charlie said quietly.

'Oh, Charlie, bless you. Of course he is.' She gave Charlie a peck on the cheek and hastened out. She didn't seem as sad as she usually did at the mention of his father. This worried Charlie.

Mrs Bone had only been gone a few seconds when Uncle

Paton poked his head round the door. He was holding a lighted candle. 'I feel peckish,' he said. 'Mind if I turn the light out, Charlie?'

Charlie shook his head. The lamp above the table went out and Uncle Paton walked to the fridge. He brought out a plate of cold ham and tomatoes and set the plate and a candle on the table. He was about to speak when he saw the back of the painting.

'I hope that isn't what I think it is,' said Paton.

'What d'you think it is?' asked Charlie, alarmed by his uncle's grim expression.

'I'm very much afraid that it might be . . .' He turned the painting face-up and sighed. 'Yes, I thought so. I suppose my sisters left it here.'

'Is it someone in the family?' asked Charlie.

'Indeed, yes. His name was Skarpo,' said Paton, 'and he was a very powerful sorcerer.'

'Uncle Paton, my . . . my endowment,' Charlie spoke hesitantly. 'I thought it only worked with photos.'

Paton stared at Charlie. 'D'you mean that you have heard . . .?' He pointed at the sorcerer. 'Did this man speak to you?'

'Not exactly,' said Charlie, 'I just heard . . .'

'Charlie!' Paton slammed the painting face-down on the table. 'You didn't go in, did you?'

'Go in?' said Charlie wildly. 'What d'you mean, go in? I was just looking at it when he . . . when he turned his head and stared at me.'

Paton regarded Charlie with a mixture of fear and concern. 'Then he has seen you,' he said gravely.

And as his uncle spoke, Charlie heard the moan of a chill wind. He heard the rattle of chains, a terrible cry and the shrill, dry chanting of Skarpo the sorcerer.

THE PETS' CAFÉ

For a few seconds, Charlie and his great-uncle looked at each other in complete silence. And then, Paton sat at the table and said, 'I wish I'd known about this before, but to tell the truth, Charlie, I've only just learned what your endowment could lead to.'

'I don't understand,' said Charlie. At the back of his mind he could still hear the dreadful chanting voice.

'It's like this,' said Paton. 'As you know, I've been working on a history of the Yewbeams and their ancestor, the Red King. This has entailed a great deal of research, in the course of which, I have come across several characters whose talents are very similar to yours and those of your friends. One of them, a certain Charles Pennybuck, began by hearing portraits speak – he lived long before photos had arrived on the scene – and this eventually led to his entering the portraits and conversing directly with the – how shall we say – the persons depicted in the paintings.'

'You mean, they could see him too?'

'Oh, yes,' said Paton. 'Unfortunately, poor Pennybuck came to a very sticky end. Got caught in the portrait of a really nasty character, the Count of Corbeau, if I remember rightly. Went quite mad.'

'Who?' asked Charlie. 'Pennybuck or the count?'

'Pennybuck, of course,' said Paton. 'Oh dear, I probably shouldn't have told you that, Charlie. Now, you mustn't worry. I'm sure it won't happen to you.'

'But what about Skarpo?' said Charlie anxiously. 'I mean if he's seen me . . .'

'Ah, Skarpo!' Paton went to the fridge and took out a bottle of white wine. 'Hm.' He took two glasses from a cupboard and brought them to the table.

'Skarpo,' Charlie prompted. 'You were saying?'

'Skarpo lived about five hundred years ago. This portrait is very old.' Paton tapped the back of the picture. 'He was the kind of sorcerer that Ezekiel Bloor would like to have been, but old Ezekiel could never manage anything like Skarpo.'

'Such as what?' asked Charlie.

'Better for you not to know.' Paton held up the bottle. 'Want a glass of wine, dear boy? I'm sure you could do with one.' He poured a glass for himself.

'No, thanks,' said Charlie impatiently. 'Uncle Paton, I think you might tell me a bit more about Skarpo. I mean, what's going to happen to me now that he's seen me?'

'I've no idea,' said Paton. 'Perhaps nothing will happen. And then again, perhaps you can actually make use of his power. There was a lot of it, according to my books. Just be on your guard, Charlie. If you find yourself acting strangely, then come and tell me and we'll try and figure something out.'

This wasn't very reassuring, but Charlie realised it was the best he could hope for. He decided to take a sip of Paton's wine, and then another. By the time his mother came in, he was feeling quite cheerful.

'Feasting in the dark?' said Mrs Bone, turning on the light.

'Whoops!' said Paton, averting his eyes from the lamp. 'Watch out, Amy. I've already had one accident today.'

'Sorry, Paton, I forgot.' Mrs Bone turned off the light and proceeded to make a pot of tea by candlelight.

Charlie took his mug of tea up to bed. When he left the kitchen, Paton was listening, enraptured, as Mrs Bone described every scene in *Divine Drums*. Because of his light-exploding problem, he hadn't been able to visit a theatre since he was a child, and he loved to listen to Amy Bone's animated accounts. She could be a very good storyteller, when she did something out of the ordinary.

The following afternoon, Charlie and his uncle set off for the Pets' Café. At the end of Filbert Street, they met Benjamin and Runner Bean.

'Why is your uncle reading a book?' asked Benjamin, as if Paton were not there.

Charlie's uncle was hardly aware of Benjamin, he was concentrating fiercely on the large book which he held only a few inches from his nose.

Charlie explained that it was an experiment.

'Ah,' said Benjamin, with a knowing smile. 'Can me and Runner come too? You might need extra help.'

The two boys walked either side of Paton, while Runner Bean loped ahead. It was a chilly, grey Sunday and luckily there weren't many people about. Charlie felt slightly embarrassed, walking beside a man with his nose in a large book.

There was a tricky moment when they reached the traffic lights. Paton was about to walk across a red light, when the boys shouted, 'NO!' Paton glanced up startled, and Charlie whispered urgently, 'Don't look at the lights, Uncle Paton!'

'Ahem,' murmured Paton, stepping back on to the kerb.

'Whew!' breathed Benjamin. 'That was close.'

They resumed their journey, avoiding traffic lights where they could and guiding Paton across the busiest roads. At last they found Water Street and, a little further on, a narrow alley with the sign of a frog high on the wall.

'Doesn't look like a proper sign,' Benjamin commented.

'It must be Frog Street,' said Charlie, 'because it's next to Water Street.' He didn't dare to ask his uncle for advice because there was a lighted window just below the frog sign.

Runner Bean settled the question. He ran down the alley barking excitedly and the boys had no option but to follow him. It seemed a very unlikely place for a café, but as they walked further from the main road they began to hear the barks, grunts and screechings of many creatures.

'Sounds like a zoo,' said Benjamin.

Runner Bean had disappeared round a bend at the end of the alley, and was now barking deliriously. Charlie put a hand on his uncle's arm and steered him round the corner.

And there was the Pets' Café. It appeared to have been built into an ancient wall and filled the entire end of the alley. On one side, a small green door stood open to the street and on the other, a group of dogs stood barking at Runner Bean through a huge latticed window. Above the window there was a sign covered with paintings of animals. The words THE PETS' CAFÉ could just be made out between twirling tails, paws, whiskers, wings and claws.

'This is it,' said Charlie, guiding Paton to the door.

Benjamin grabbed Runner Bean's collar and they all went in.

The crescendo of animal noises was so loud Charlie could hardly hear his own voice. 'I can see a counter right at the back,' he shouted to Benjamin.

Before they could get there, a large man with curly black hair stepped in front of them. He was wearing a long white shirt decorated with elephant heads.

'Animals?' he said.

'No,' said Charlie. 'We're human.'

'I know that,' the man said impatiently. 'Where are your companions? No one's allowed in without an animal, bird or reptile.'

'Oh.' Charlie's face fell.

'We've got a dog,' Benjamin piped up. 'He's over there, talking to a labrador.'

'One animal *each*,' said the man. 'Otherwise, out!' He pointed to the door.

Paton was finding it difficult to concentrate on his book. He held it even closer to his face in his efforts to avoid looking at the lights twinkling in the low ceiling. 'Ahem,' he muttered. And then, in a low voice, 'Smells awful. Let's go.'

Charlie was just wondering what to do next when Gabriel appeared, holding a large wooden box. He took two gerbils from the box, handed one to Charlie and popped another in Paton's top pocket.

'Er – no,' Paton objected, touching a gerbil nose. But it was too late.

The large man said, 'That's better,' and ushered them up to the counter. Here they were faced with a difficult choice. All along the counter among plates of ordinary biscuits there were bowls of coloured sausages, cakes that smelled of fish, round pellets that could have been chocolate (or might not have been) and seeds of various sizes.

'I recommend the sausages,' said Gabriel. 'They're delicious.'

'They look as if they could be for dogs,' said Charlie.

'Probably are,' said Gabriel. 'They're still delicious. The gerbils love them.'

'Biscuits and three waters, please,' said Charlie, playing safe.

The man behind the counter said, 'If it isn't Charlie Bone.'

Charlie blinked. At last he recognised Mr Onimous, the mouse-catcher. It was his pointy-toothed smile that gave him away. He looked very different in his chef's white hat and apron. The last time Charlie had seen him, he'd been wearing a fake-fur coat and a velvet waistcoat.

'What are you doing here, Mr Onimous?' Charlie asked.

'Giving my wife a helping hand,' said Mr Onimous. 'It's her café, you know. Her idea entirely. Good, isn't it?'

'Brilliant,' said Charlie. 'But do the Flame cats mind all these other visitors? I mean, they live with you, don't they?'

'The Flames?' Mr Onimous raised his whiskery eyebrows. 'They're not often here, bless 'em. Far too busy with their own particular duties. They pop in around midnight for a quick bite and a snooze, and then they're off again. Unless they need me, of course. In which case, I have to follow them.'

'I see.' Charlie paid for the food. It was very cheap.

'Good to see you, Charlie,' said Mr Onimous. 'You take care now!'

'You too, Mr Onimous.'

The queue behind Charlie was growing, so he took his tray to the table where his friends were sitting. He had to push his way through a crowd of dogs before he could reach the table. Gabriel had chosen a place right beside the window and they were able to watch the strange assortment of customers approaching the café.

At the table beside them, a tarantula crawled round a red straw hat. The woman wearing the hat seemed quite happy about the situation. Now and again she passed tit-bits up to the tarantula. Fearing the tit-bits were alive, Charlie looked away.

'What have you got to show us then?' he asked Gabriel.

Gabriel pulled a plastic bag from under the table. 'Look!' He reached into the bag and drew out an old tweed cap, and a battered mackintosh.

'Asa's disguise!' said Charlie.

'Exactly. I even found the moustache.' Gabriel held up a strip of white whiskers. 'They were lying in the lane outside our yard. I reckon the wind from Thunder House blew them there. Asa probably hid them in the wood.'

Charlie shuddered. 'You mean it was Asa in the wood? Asa as a . . . whatever he can turn into when it's getting dark?'

'Does he have to take all his clothes off,' asked Benjamin, 'before he turns into a beast?'

Gabriel frowned at him. 'This is serious, Benjamin.'

'Sorry. I just wondered.'

'Why would Asa go all the way up to the Heights?' murmured Charlie. 'Does he live there?'

'I don't know where he lives,' said Gabriel. 'But I think he was warning us off. He was trying to make sure we wouldn't go back to Thunder House.'

'But why?' asked Charlie.

Gabriel shrugged. 'Perhaps it's got something to do with your cousin, Henry. That evil old man who sent him through time knows he's come back. He's probably furious.'

'Of course,' said Charlie. 'Ezekiel has ordered Manfred and Asa to find Henry. But they know that we'll protect him – you, me, Lysander and Tancred. So they're trying to

146

split us up, weaken us. Have you told Lysander about the clothes?'

'Couldn't contact him,' said Gabriel. 'I'll see him tomorrow.'

At that moment, a body flung itself at the window. Charlie looked up to see Asa Pike glaring at them through the small glass panes. His lips were drawn back in a horrible snarl, and his yellow eyes darted round the table until he saw the bag of clothes.

'Mine,' he rasped. 'Give them here, you wretches!'

His sudden appearance caused an uproar in the café. Terrified birds fluttered, screeching, to the ceiling; dogs threw back their heads and howled; cats hissed and spat; rabbits rushed under tables, and everything else hid behind the large pot plants standing round the room.

'He's not very popular, is he?' Benjamin said in a shaky voice.

'Keep reading, Uncle Paton,' Charlie warned.

The café was already in a turmoil without his uncle breaking glass. Food was flying everywhere, plates had been smashed, drinks had been spilled, and anxious customers were tripping over frightened animals.

'Look out,' said Gabriel. 'Here he comes!'

Asa crashed through the door and walked straight into the man in the elephant shirt.

'Animal?' said the man, who was evidently a sort of bouncer.

For a moment, Charlie thought Asa was going to say he

was an animal, but he just snarled into the man's face.

'That's it!' said the bouncer. 'Out!'

He grabbed Asa by the scruff of his scrawny neck and thrust him out on to the pavement. Asa whipped round and was about to burst in again, when several large dogs rushed through the open door and set upon him.

Asa gave a high-pitched yell and ran off round the corner, followed by the pack of baying dogs. If Benjamin hadn't leapt up and grabbed Runner Bean's collar, he would have joined the chase. The big dog was very disappointed to miss the fun and whined monotonously until Mr Onimous gave him a rainbow-coloured bone to chew.

The Pets' Café was emptying rapidly. Several customers had gone racing after their dogs, and the others, having caught and calmed their pets, had decided to leave before things got worse.

Charlie and his friends stayed to help Mr Onimous and the bouncer, Norton Cross, to clear up the mess.

'That tall bloke's a bit of a lazy layabout,' Norton remarked, glancing at Paton, who was still reading his book.

'He can have – accidents,' said Charlie awkwardly. 'So it's best that he doesn't help.'

'He's special,' said Mr Onimous, winking at Charlie.

'Oh Lor'. Not one of *them*, is he? We've got more than our fair share of oddballs in this city,' grumbled Norton. 'That one the dogs chased – you could tell he was peculiar. Animals always know when something ain't right.'

Mrs Silk, who had finished her deliveries, came through

148

a door at the back of the counter. She was followed by an extremely tall woman with pale wispy hair and a very long nose. Surprisingly, this turned out to be Mrs Onoria Onimous. She was a gentle, friendly person and seemed to like children almost as much as animals.

When, at last, the café was restored to order, Mrs Silk offered the boys a lift back to Filbert Street. 'And your father too,' she said, glancing at Paton. 'If that *is* your father.'

'No, I haven't got a . . . no, that's not my father,' said Charlie, handing over Gabriel's gerbil. 'And we've got to go somewhere else, thanks all the same.'

'Righty-o, then. Cheerio, boys. Come along, Gabriel.' Mrs Silk made for the door.

Gabriel pulled his other gerbil out of Paton's pocket. Luckily, it had gone to sleep and only eaten a peppermint stuck to the bottom of the pocket. 'See you tomorrow,' said Gabriel. 'It should be interesting. I wonder if Asa's been bitten.'

He staggered after his mother with the bag of old clothes under one arm, and his box of gerbils hugged to his chest with the other.

Charlie tapped his uncle's shoulder and said, 'We can go now, Uncle Paton.'

Paton stood up, his eyes still glued to the page he was reading. Charlie steered him outside where they found Benjamin clipping a lead to Runner Bean's collar. 'Just in case he gets the urge to chase something,' Benjamin explained.

Their walk to Ingledew's Bookshop was relatively easy. No traffic lights had to be navigated, no roads crossed. As they walked round the huge cathedral, they could hear the deep-toned notes of the organ, and Charlie thought of his father. Lyell Bone had been one of the cathedral organists until one foggy night, eight years before, when he had got into his car and driven over the edge of a quarry. He had never been seen again.

'I know what you're thinking, dear boy,' Paton murmured. Lyell was his nephew and also one of his best friends.

There was a CLOSED sign on Ingledew's door, but a soft light in the window illuminated the piles of ancient-looking books.

Charlie rang the doorbell. There was no answer. He pressed the bell again. They could hear it ringing in the back of the shop, but no one came to the door.

'Didn't you say they went out at weekends?' said Benjamin. 'They could be at a museum, or the cinema, or something.'

'Of course,' said Charlie. 'I forgot.'

Paton snapped his book shut and stared despondently at the window.

'I wouldn't do that if I were you, Uncle P . . .' Charlie began.

But Paton's distress was too great. With a small pop the light in the window went out, and a shower of glass settled on the antique books.

'Damn!' muttered Paton. 'She'll know it was me.'

'No, she won't,' said Charlie. 'Miss Ingledew probably often has lights failing.'

'*Failing*, yes,' moaned Paton, 'but not bursting. She knows it's what I *do*.'

'Come on, Uncle.'

'Oh dear. Oh, damn. I'll never be able to face her again,' sighed Paton.

'Course you will. Let's go home. You won't have to read any more because it's dark.'

'*That's* true!' Paton turned away from the shop and strode towards the nearest alley.

Charlie and Benjamin had to run to keep up with him, while Runner Bean dashed ahead, hoping for a game.

They were moving rapidly down Filbert Street when Paton said, 'I don't want my sisters to hear about this little set-back.'

'Why are your sisters so mean?' asked Benjamin.

'It goes back a long way,' said Paton.

'They always do whatever Ezekiel Bloor wants,' said Charlie. 'It's like they're afraid of him.'

'They are,' said Paton. 'He's a cousin and, at the moment, he holds the power. They admire that.'

'I'm glad I haven't got any aunts,' Benjamin muttered. 'I'm off now. Mum and Dad are home. Bye!'

Charlie and Paton climbed the steps to number nine, but once inside, Paton marched grimly up to his room. Charlie went in to the kitchen to give Maisie and his mother a progress report.

'How did it go?' asked Mrs Bone. 'Any mishaps?'

'It went perfectly,' lied Charlie.

'I'll go with him next time,' said Maisie happily. 'It'll make such a difference to poor Paton if he can go out in the daytime.'

Charlie noticed that Skarpo the sorcerer had disappeared. 'Where's the painting?' he asked.

'Search me,' said his mother. 'Grandma Bone must have taken it to her room.'

Grandma Bone had done no such thing. When Charlie went to bed he found Skarpo on his pillow.

'OK,' he said grimly. 'If they want me to go in, I will, but not until I'm ready, and not until I've decided how you can help me.'

Before he shut the painting in a drawer with his socks, he took a quick look at the sorcerer. The man in black tilted his head towards Charlie and said, 'Welcome, child of the Red King!'

Charlie closed the drawer quickly. He wondered how dangerous it would be to 'go in', as his uncle put it, and ask for Skarpo's help. If Henry Yewbeam was to be rescued before old Ezekiel found him, then a bit of sorcery could come in handy.

'TAKE HIM TO THE DUNGEONS!'

Henry Yewbeam spent the rest of the weekend in Cook's secret rooms.

'If you leave here you'll get snatched,' she warned Henry. 'And then where will we be? Someone in this place wants you got rid of, you know!'

'I bet it's Zeke,' murmured Henry. 'He's never forgiven me for finishing his puzzle.'

'It's Ezekiel, all right,' said Cook. 'There he is, a feeble old man at the end of his life, while the cousin he thought he'd banished forever, has come back as a boy with his whole life in front of him.'

Henry couldn't help grinning. 'He must be in a rage,' he said.

'Yes. And we don't want him to put a stop to the nice long life that lies ahead of you, do we?'

'No.' And yet Henry found it hard to imagine what kind of life it might be.

Cook set about preparing a meal. Mrs Bloor would be joining them later and Henry helped to lay three places

153

on a small round table in the corner.

As Cook worked she began to tell Henry her story. And Henry found himself curling up in the armchair by the stove, and listening to one of the strangest tales he'd ever heard.

Cook and her younger sister, Pearl, had once lived with their parents on an island in the north. Their father, Gregor, was a fisherman. When the girls where five and six, it became apparent that they were like lucky charms. Whenever they watched their father set off in his little boat, he always caught more fish than he could carry. Soon people flocked to the island to buy Gregor's fish. He became very rich and was able to purchase the whole island. He built a grand house with breathtaking views of the ocean, and the sea around his island was always calm. This was because his daughters were endowed with luck and tranquillity, so it was said.

One day, a young man came to the island. 'He was handsome enough,' said Cook, 'but there was something about him that gave Pearl and me the creeps. It turned out that he'd come to marry one of us. It didn't matter which. We were fifteen and sixteen at the time, and my father said, "Be off with you, Grimwald," – that was his name – "Be off with you. My daughters are too young to marry. They want to see the world before they settle down." Grimwald was persistent. "I need one of your daughters now," he said, "while she's still young. I want her for her pure fresh beauty, for her sweetness and tranquillity, and for the luck she will bring me." The young man's attitude annoyed my father. Again he refused him. And then Grimwald began to threaten us.' Cook tasted the stew she'd been cooking. 'More salt,' she murmured.

'Go on,' said Henry eagerly.

Cook continued, 'My father ordered Grimwald to leave the island, and eventually he went, but not before he'd turned his fury on us. "You think you control the oceans, don't you, you little minxes?" he said. "Well, you don't. Very soon you'll find out that my power is far greater than yours. And then you'll come running to me, both of you, mark my words." If only we had believed him,' Cook said sadly.

'A year later, Pearl and I left our island. We travelled all over the world. We dined and danced and met our sweethearts – both sailors, as it happened. We came home to tell our parents and found . . .' At this point Cook gave a terrible sigh and several tears dropped into the sauce she was stirring.

'Found what?' asked Henry.

'Found nothing,' said Cook. 'All gone: island, house, parents – all perished. Drowned by the biggest tidal wave in history. We suspected, but we couldn't be sure, and then when our sweethearts were drowned at sea, we knew. It was Grimwald!'

Henry gasped. 'You mean he could . . .?'

'Oh, yes. He could do anything with water. My sister and I parted. It was safer to travel alone. We were less recognisable. We went underground, took work in secret, shadowy places where *he* couldn't find us. Wherever we went, we tried to improve things, keep children safe. One day I learned that Bloor's Academy needed a cook. I'd heard it was where the Red King once held court, and I thought I could help some of the children who came here. I guessed that, just like Pearl and me, if they were endowed they wouldn't have an easy time of it.' Cook licked the spoon she'd used for stirring, grunted approvingly and put a lid on the saucepan.

Henry would have liked her to continue but, at that moment, Mrs Bloor came through the little door in the corner, and Cook declared their supper was ready.

After supper, Mrs Bloor helped Cook to wash the dishes and then crept away to her lonely room in the west wing.

'Mrs Bloor is a very sad lady,' Henry remarked, as he carefully placed Cook's china plates on the dresser.

'Sad indeed,' sighed Cook. 'If only she could go back to the way she was before her hand was crushed.'

'Perhaps the Time Twister could help?' Henry suggested.

Cook darted a wary look at him. 'People can't go back, you know that, Henry.'

'Yes, but in her case it would only be five years. And she hasn't had a real life here. Who would notice?'

'Hm!' was all Cook said.

Later, as Henry lay in bed, his thoughts kept returning to the Time Twister. Cook had no right to hide it from him. The glowing glass fixed itself in his mind so firmly, Henry couldn't sleep. He got up, threw his blue cape over his pyjamas, and tiptoed out of the tiny room where he slept.

Moonlight, striking through the skylight, lent a pearly glow to the objects in the room beneath. The china on the dresser glimmered softly and Henry, looking up to the top shelf, saw a row of china mugs. They were decorated with bands of gold and silver leaves; two of them were placed closer together than the others, as though someone had moved one of them in haste.

Henry pulled a chair close to the dresser and climbed on to it. He still couldn't reach the top shelf, so he stepped on to the dresser itself. Now he could touch the row of mugs. The first one he picked up was empty. He replaced it and drew the second mug towards him. As he lifted it off the shelf, something rolled out and dropped to the floor.

Henry looked down to see the Time Twister glowing beneath him. He smiled with satisfaction but before he could climb off the dresser, a shadowy form ran towards the glass ball.

'No, Blessed,' said Henry, recognising the dog's dumpy shape.

Blessed took no notice. He scooped up the Time Twister in his mouth and trotted to the door in the corner.

'NO!' Henry said. 'This isn't the time for a game, Blessed.'

They had been playing Chase the Cotton-reel earlier, and now Henry began to wish he hadn't been so enthusiastic.

Blessed nosed open the door and disappeared. Henry leapt from the dresser, knocking over the chair, but by the time he had reached the staircase behind the door, all that could be seen of the dog was his wagging bald tail. Henry tried to grab it and slipped off the first step. Getting to his feet, he leapt up the steps again.

At the top of the staircase, Henry found himself in a dark passage. He could hear the tap of Blessed's claws echoing somewhere beyond him and ran towards the sound.

The passage curved in seemingly endless circles until it eventually led to a low door. The door was locked. Blessed had vanished. How could he have walked through a locked door? Henry stared at the empty passage behind him. He noticed a thin beam of light coming from a wooden panel at the bottom of the wall. Gently, he pushed the panel with his foot. It opened like a cat flap. Or a dog flap? If fat Blessed could get through it, so could Henry.

He knelt down and crawled through the flap. On the other side was a corridor with highly-polished floorboards. Gold-framed paintings hung on the walls and a lamp, with a coloured glass shade, stood on a small round table.

A little further on, Henry could see a dark cupboard. He guessed that it hid the door Mrs Bloor used to visit Cook. As Henry tiptoed down the corridor he could hear a voice. 'Tell me!' it said. 'Speak to me, dog!'

Henry sidled to the end of the corridor and found that it led to the landing above the hall. On the other side of the landing, a small boy in a blue dressing gown was talking to Blessed. He stopped talking and began to grunt and whine like a dog. The boy had white hair and the spectacles he wore made his eyes look like round red lamps.

Henry pressed himself against the wall and watched.

The boy was having no success with his grunting dog language, so he began to use words again.

'Tell me, you stupid dog! Speak! Why won't you tell me where he is? Where's the boy from nowhere?'

Blessed gazed mournfully up at the boy, but he refused to speak.

'What have you got in your mouth?' asked the boy. 'It's that thing, isn't it? The magic marble. Give it to me and I'll take it to Mr Ezekiel.'

At these words, Henry froze. So the boy was working for Ezekiel! He was about to creep away down the corridor when something happened.

'Give it to me, dog!' The white-haired boy suddenly lifted his foot and kicked the old dog in the ribs. Again and again. Blessed groaned and sank to his knees.

As the boy lifted his foot again, Henry cried, 'Don't!'

The boy looked up and smiled as Henry ran towards him.

'You're him, aren't you? The one from nowhere.'

'Leave the dog alone,' said Henry. 'He's old. You're hurting him.'

'He's got the time thing, hasn't he?'

'Maybe,' said Henry. 'Who are you?'

'I'm Billy Raven,' said the boy. 'I talk to dogs. They usually answer me. I don't know what's wrong with silly old Blessed today.'

At that moment, Blessed dropped the Time Twister. It lay between the boys, glowing softly.

'Don't look at it!' Henry warned. He didn't like Billy, but

the white-haired boy was very small, and Henry didn't want him to be twisted into another century.

'It's beautiful,' said Billy. He bent to pick it up but Henry kicked the marble away. It rolled across the landing and dropped through the bannisters. There was a light ping as it hit the flagstones below.

Billy Raven glared at Henry. 'You shouldn't have done that,' he said.

Henry was tempted to run down and find the marble, but the other boy was giving him such an odd, sly look, he hesitated.

All at once, Blessed gave a low rumbling growl.

The warning was too late.

A hand came down on Henry's shoulder and a husky voice said, 'Well, look what the dog dragged in!'

Henry tried to twist away but the hand was strong and held him like a vice. He turned his head and looked into the long, mean face of Manfred Bloor.

'Let me go,' said Henry.

'You're joking,' said Manfred. 'Someone wants to see you, *very* much.' He pushed Henry along the landing. 'Well done, Billy. A little present will be coming your way very soon.'

'Thanks, Manfred!' called Billy.

Manfred shoved Henry into a passage leading off the landing, but Henry continued to struggle. They reached a staircase and, at this point, Henry almost got away, but Manfred shrieked, 'Zelda, where are you?' and a thin, long-

160

nosed girl leapt towards them. She grabbed Henry's arm, almost wrenching it out of its socket.

Henry let out a bloodcurdling yell.

'Shut up!' said Manfred. 'Zelda, hold him still.'

Zelda twisted Henry's arms behind his back, and Manfred tied his wrists together with a length of sticky tape.

'We'll need the torch,' said Manfred. 'Where is it?'

'It's all right,' said Zelda. 'I haven't forgotten it.'

Grunting and struggling, Henry was led up the stairs, along dark passages, down ancient spiralling steps and then up again and into a part of the building he almost recognised; the place where he and James had spent their last miserable Christmas together.

'We're not there yet!' hissed Manfred.

Up they went again. Up and up, into a shadowy world lit by jets of gas, whispering from the wall in their rusty iron brackets. Henry remembered the gaslights, but the walls that had once been covered in richly-patterned paper, were now stained with damp and hung with grey cobwebs.

They reached a door, its black paint scratched and peeling. Manfred knocked.

Henry's mouth felt dry with fear and he could hear his own heart, thumping in his chest.

'Who's there?' The voice was old and slightly hoarse.

'It's Manfred, Grandpa. And guess who else? I've got a lovely surprise for you!' Manfred grinned at Henry.

'What?' There was a delighted shriek from within the room. 'Bring it in! Bring in my lovely surprise!'

Manfred opened the door and shoved Henry into the room.

Henry found himself looking at the oldest man he had ever seen. It was difficult to believe that the wizened creature in a wheelchair had once been his cousin Zeke. And yet there was something familiar about the spiteful hooded eyes and thin cruel mouth.

The air in the room was stifling. Behind the old man, logs burned in a huge fireplace. The floor was padded with many worn carpets and the windows were covered by thick velvet curtains.

'Well,' said the old man. 'Well, I never. If it isn't cousin Henry.'

Henry tried to swallow, but there was a lump in his throat. He couldn't think of anything to say.

'Come closer,' said Ezekiel.

Manfred and Zelda gave Henry another push. He staggered forwards, feeling faint. The old man was draped in rugs. How could he stand the heat?

'My, my! You are young, aren't you?' Ezekiel said resentfully.

Henry tried to clear his throat. 'I'm eleven,' he croaked. 'At least, I was last week.'

Ezekiel scowled. 'Last week? You mean ninety years ago, don't you?'

'Not quite,' said Henry, feeling bolder. 'Not by my reckoning.'

'Ooo! Not by my reckoning,' the old man mimicked.

162

'Always were the clever one, weren't you? Well, you're not so clever now. Got yourself caught, haven't you?'

Henry nodded.

'So where have you been hiding?'

Desperately, Henry tried to think of an answer. He knew he mustn't give Cook away. 'In a cupboard.'

'In a cupboard? Where?'

'In the kitchen,' said Henry. 'No one saw me. I came out at night for food.'

The old man sniggered. 'This time you came out too far, didn't you?'

'Yes,' said Henry meekly.

'What are we going to do with him, Grandpa?' asked Manfred.

'Put him in the attics,' Zelda suggested. 'With the rats and bats.' She cackled gleefully.

The old man stroked his stubbly white chin. 'Hm. Where's the Time Twister?' he demanded.

'I don't know. The dog had it.'

'Did he now? He's a good doggie – bringing his old master another present. He was very scared of that Twister, you know.' Ezekiel's smile was worse than his scowl. He had very few teeth and those that remained were chipped and black.

Henry reckoned that Blessed had just wanted a game but he decided to let Ezekiel think what he wanted.

'So, where's my doggie now?' asked the old man.

'Had a bit of trouble there,' said Manfred. 'Billy Raven

kicked the dog and he dropped the marble.'

'Kicked?' shouted Ezekiel. 'Kicked my dog? The wretch. So why didn't you get the Twister, you nincompoop?'

Manfred sucked his teeth and answered curtly, 'You wanted the boy, so we brought the boy. Billy will find the marble.'

'Tah!' the old man spat into the grate. 'He'd better bring it soon.'

'So is it to be the attics for this one, sir?' asked Zelda. 'Until you can send him off again.'

'No, dammit. There's too much going on up there. Take him to the dungeons.' Ezekiel swung his chair away, turning his back on Henry.

Henry shuddered. 'Couldn't I stay here? I wouldn't be any trouble. I could live with Charlie Bone. He . . .'

'Stay?' screeched Ezekiel. 'Never in a thousand years. Get him away from me. Now! I can't stand the sight of him, all young and hopeful. Get him OUT!'

Henry was tugged away. 'Please!' he cried. 'Don't do this.'

Manfred and Zelda pulled him out into the passage and slammed the door. While Zelda held him still, Manfred covered his mouth with a thick piece of sticky tape, and then Henry was dragged and bundled down to the hall and out into the freezing night. The cold hit him with such force, he gave up struggling and allowed his captors to lead him across the frozen ground.

The icy stars above them gave the world a strange, pale glow, but the moon had disappeared. Zelda's torch threw a narrow path of light across the patches of snow, and although Henry could hardly see a thing in front of him, he knew where they must be heading. It was still a shock, though, when the great walls of the ruined castle loomed before him.

He was pushed through the archway and then into one of the passages leading out of the courtyard. Unlike the passage he had entered yesterday, this one seemed to be leading downwards. The ground was wet with mildew and, every now and again, Henry found himself skidding into Zelda, who led the way.

'Stop that,' she snarled, 'or I'll drag you there on your bottom.'

Where was *there*? Henry wondered.

Deeper they went. Deeper and deeper. The air was so thick and musty, Henry began to choke. The tape over his mouth made it difficult to breathe. Just when he thought he might die of suffocation, they emerged on to a grassy bank. Tall trees reached into the night sky, rustling softly.

'Go on!' said Manfred, giving Henry a shove.

Henry tumbled down the bank while the others ran after him, giggling spitefully.

They hauled him upright and marched him over to a black rock, half-hidden in the undergrowth.

'OK, Zelda. Get to work,' said Manfred.

Zelda gave a crooked smile. She stared at the rock. In the dim torchlight, Henry saw her smile become a terrible grimace as, very slowly, the rock began to move. Zelda was obviously one of the endowed. No ordinary person could have done that. With a rough, grating sound, the rock slid back, revealing a round black pit.

Before Henry knew what had happened, Manfred had pushed him to the edge.

'Go on,' said Manfred. 'Down!'

'Mm, mm!' Henry shook his head.

'Oh, yes you will.' Manfred gave him a thump on the back, and Henry tottered forwards on to a narrow stone step.

'DOWN!' ordered Manfred, this time pushing Henry's head.

Henry bumped and slithered down a flight of steps, desperately groping for something to stop his fall. At last, he touched an iron ring driven into the side of the pit, and clung to it. But even as he started to climb back up the steps, the huge rock crunched across the top of the pit. Henry was plunged into a darkness so deep and dreadful he felt he must be dead.

Roused from sleep by a noise from the next room, Cook had found the empty mug and the upturned chair. She guessed what had happened. The Flame cats were already scratching at her skylight. As soon as she let them in, they sped across the room and up the hidden staircase. They knew when a child was in trouble. But by the time the cats reached the landing, Henry Yewbeam had gone and they found Billy Raven peering over the bannisters. As soon as he saw them he ran back to bed.

The cats found Blessed, lying on his side and breathing heavily. Gently they nudged the old dog to his feet, and then, with soft, encouraging voices, they eased his pain and kept up his spirits until he reached the place he called home. Now he lay at Cook's feet, wrapped in a blanket and half-asleep.

'Poor dog, you paid dearly for keeping my secret, didn't you?' Cook murmured. 'Thanks to you, he'll live,' she told the cats. 'But somewhere in this godforsaken place, there's a poor boy who may not last the night.' She buried her face in her hands. 'Oh Henry, you foolish boy, where are you?'

Aries couldn't bear the sound of weeping. With a gentle miaow, he stood up and patted Cook's knee.

Cook wiped her eyes. 'You're right. This won't help, will it? You'd better go and look for him, my dears.'

She opened the skylight and the three Flames leapt out into the dark. It did her heart good to see their bright forms streak into the night.

'What's become of the Twister, I'd like to know,' Cook said to herself. 'Has that wretched Billy Raven found it?' As she closed the skylight, she heard the distant chimes of the cathedral clock strike midnight.

Billy Raven was fast asleep in bed. Down in the hall, the Time Twister still glimmered in a corner. The door to the west wing stood slightly open, and now a figure emerged. Keeping to the shadows, the dark form slowly circled the hall until it reached the marble. The glowing glass sphere was lifted out of its corner and slipped into a deep pocket.

EZEKIEL'S VISITORS

On Monday morning, Olivia Vertigo's famous film star mother had to be at work very early; so Olivia was dropped off at the academy long before her friends. She was surprised to find the hall full of people. Cleaners with mops and brooms were sweeping in corners; Dr Saltweather and some of the stronger teachers were moving furniture away from the walls; others were peering under the long tapestries and heavy curtains.

'Don't just stand there, girl, do something!' Dr Bloor shouted from his seat in the middle of the hall.

Olivia wasn't sure what she should do. 'Are you looking for something, sir?' she asked.

'Of course we are. A marble. A most particular marble. Get on with it.'

'Yes, sir.' Olivia dumped her bag by the door and wandered round the hall. She kept her eyes trained on the ground but there was hardly a speck of dust to be seen.

After an hour of fruitless searching, Dr Bloor ordered the furniture to be moved back and the hall to be cleared. 'It's not here,' he muttered. 'So who's got it?'

Olivia heard voices in the courtyard behind her and, picking up her bag, ran out to see if she could catch Charlie before he went into assembly. She found him coming up the steps with Fidelio. They were talking about a pets' café.

'Hi, you two!' said Olivia. 'I've got news.'

'Look out, vegetable,' said Damian Smerk, almost knocking her off the steps. Damian was a bit of a bully, particularly where girls were concerned.

Olivia wasn't afraid of him. 'I'd rather have green hair than a face like yours,' she retorted, patting her freshly-dyed spinach-coloured hair.

'Weirdo!' grunted Damian, marching off.

Fidelio pulled a face at Damian's back. 'What's the news then?' he asked.

Olivia told them about the search for the marble. 'It must be that thing that brought your cousin here,' she said to Charlie. 'You know, the Time Twister.'

While the boys stared at her, she took a breath and went on, 'I met him by the way.'

'You met Henry?' said Charlie.

'Yes, in the ruin. Manfred and Asa were looking for him. He said he'd been hiding in the kitchen, so Bindi and I took him back there before those two could catch him.'

'Well done,' said Charlie.

At that moment, Emma Tolly came up the steps and Olivia turned to follow her.

'Emma, stop,' called Olivia. 'I want to . . .'

But Emma had already gone into the hall where talking was forbidden.

'I don't know what's the matter with her,' sighed Olivia. 'She doesn't seem to want to be friends any more.'

'Maybe you're too weird for her,' joked Charlie.

'Look who's talking!' Olivia grinned and bounced up the steps into the hall.

Charlie and Fidelio made their way to the blue cloakroom where they found Gabriel sitting on a bench. He was holding the bag of Asa's old clothes and he looked worried.

'What's up?' asked Fidelio. 'Has Asa been after you?'

'I reckon he has,' muttered Gabriel. 'Something attacked our goats last night.'

Charlie sat beside Gabriel. 'None of them were killed, were they?' he asked gently.

'No, they were just scared, and they wouldn't be milked this morning.' Gabriel sighed. 'I think I ought to give this stuff back, but I don't know how to. Asa might get nasty.'

'Give it to Olivia,' Fidelio suggested. 'She can slip it into the Drama cloakroom in break.'

'OK.' Gabriel pushed the bag under the bench and followed the other two into assembly.

After assembly, Charlie dragged himself off to his music lesson with Mr Paltry – Wind. The old music teacher had decided to let him try the trumpet instead of the recorder, and Charlie liked this much better. His lesson was almost enjoyable.

At break, he found Gabriel and Fidelio wandering round

the field. Gabriel still looked worried. He told Charlie he'd given Asa's clothes to Olivia and, as far as he knew, she had managed to hang the bag on Asa's peg.

'So, everything's OK,' said Charlie.

'Not exactly. When I went for my piano lesson, Mr Pilgrim wasn't there.'

Fidelio reminded Gabriel that Mr Pilgrim had a terrible memory. He was always forgetting things.

'Not lessons,' murmured Gabriel.

Olivia strode up, wearing a big smile. 'Done,' she declared. 'I put the bag on Asa's peg, but guess what?'

'What?' asked the boys.

'Asa came in just a second after I'd done it and he looked a real mess. He's got bandages on his hands and he was limping.'

This didn't surprise the boys. Charlie told Olivia about the Pets' Café, and Asa being chased by a pack of dogs. Olivia found this so funny she had a fit of giggles that turned into hiccoughs.

When Fidelio and Charlie went to English, Olivia, still hiccoughing, went to recitation. Gabriel was supposed to have mathematics but he was feeling rather odd. He wasn't wearing any second-hand clothes so he didn't understand why he had butterflies in his stomach and a tingle creeping up the back of his head. Before he knew it, he was in the west wing and climbing the stairs to the top of the tower. The sound of a piano began to echo down the stairwell. Mr Pilgrim was evidently back in his room.

When Gabriel reached the top of the tower he knocked

on Mr Pilgrim's door. There was no answer. The piano music swelled and bass chords thundered out a finale. In the silence that followed, Gabriel opened the door. Mr Pilgrim stared at him over the gleaming black piano.

'Excuse me, sir,' said Gabriel. 'But you weren't here before, so I . . . um . . . I missed my lesson, and I wondered if I could have it now.'

'Now?' said Mr Pilgrim, looking puzzled.

'Yes. Please, sir.'

'Now. Yes.' Mr Pilgrim moved up the piano stool to make way for Gabriel.

'Thank you, sir.' Gabriel sat next to the piano teacher and, without waiting for instructions, launched himself into his scales.

When the scales were finished, Mr Pilgrim made no comment. He sat patiently listening to Gabriel as he played two complicated Bach fugues.

Towards the end of the second piece, Gabriel felt a strange tension in the room. He came to the end of the piece and rested his hands on his knees, waiting for Mr Pilgrim's remarks. Sometimes the teacher said nothing at all.

From outside came the chimes of the cathedral clock as it began to strike twelve.

'I'd better go, sir,' said Gabriel.

'You played very well today,' said Mr Pilgrim.

'Thank you, sir.'

Gabriel was about to get up when Mr Pilgrim said, 'Gabriel, they have the boy!'

'What boy, sir?'

'The one that was here.'

Gabriel suddenly realised who Mr Pilgrim was talking about. 'D'you mean Henry, sir? Charlie Bone's cousin?'

Mr Pilgrim frowned. 'Henry? They took him, Gabriel. He needs help.'

'Yes, sir.' Gabriel stood up. As he turned away, Mr Pilgrim caught his arm.

'Wait.' The music teacher took something out of his pocket and pressed it into Gabriel's hand.

Gabriel could feel it was a large glass marble. It held a strange glow that cast reflections through his closed fingers.

'Take it,' said Mr Pilgrim. 'You can go now.'

'Yes, sir.' Gabriel left the room. When he was halfway down the stairs, he sat on a step. He wasn't sure what to do. If Mr Pilgrim was right then Henry had been caught. The Bloors were searching for this marble – the Time Twister. Did they mean to send Henry back to a time where he couldn't survive?

Gabriel slowly opened his fist. He glanced at the swirling shapes and colours, and then closed his fingers over the glimmering ball. 'Better not look,' he murmured, remembering what had happened to Henry.

A movement caught his eye and he looked down into the shadowy stairwell. Mrs Bloor's pale face came into view. She smiled up at him. 'You played beautifully today,' she said.

'Thanks.' Gabriel stood and walked down towards her.

He held out his fist. 'I want to give you something.'

'What is it, Gabriel?' Mrs Bloor looked slightly alarmed.

'It's a Time Twister. It can take you back to how you were before.' He took her gloved hand and placed the marble on her palm. 'Don't look at it now,' he said. 'You have to wait until the time is right.'

'I know.' She lowered her voice. 'Cook told me. I thank you, Gabriel, from the bottom of my heart.'

Her slight black figure whisked away so quickly, Gabriel hardly saw where she went. He felt a lot better and ran lightly down to the bottom of the tower.

'You're late,' said Fidelio, as Gabriel put his plate of chips on the canteen table.

Gabriel looked over his shoulder. The noise in the canteen was loud enough to drown his voice, but he had to be sure no one was listening. He sat between Charlie and Fidelio and, leaning forward, said, 'They've got Henry!'

'What!' cried Charlie.

'Sssh!' Gabriel looked round the room. No one was paying them any attention. 'Mr Pilgrim told me. I don't know how he knew.'

'He's so peculiar, he could say anything,' said Fidelio.

'He seemed very sure,' said Gabriel.

'Cook will know.' Charlie stood up. 'I'll take my plate into the kitchen and see if I can find her.'

'Better go now,' advised Fidelio. 'There's still a crowd round the counter, so no one will notice you.'

Charlie walked towards the counter, and then quickly

nipped through the kitchen door.

It was very steamy in the kitchen and he kept walking into busy dinner ladies carrying pans of hot food and piles of plates. 'You shouldn't be in here,' one of them said sharply.

Charlie scuttled to the back of the room where he found Cook. She was sitting with a bowl on her lap, peeling carrots. Her eyes were red and she looked very unhappy. When she saw Charlie, she shook her head.

'Is it true?' Charlie whispered. 'Have they caught Henry?'

'It's true, Charlie,' said Cook. 'They've got him. How did you find out?'

'Mr Pilgrim told Gabriel.'

'Mr Pilgrim?' Cook looked puzzled. 'That's strange. But who knows these days.'

'D'you know where they took him?' asked Charlie.

'I can't be sure. But sometime after midnight, I saw Zelda and Manfred come through the garden door.'

'That means he's in the castle.'

'I wouldn't be surprised.' Cook shook her head again. 'There's some nasty dungeons in that place, but the ruin is so big I wouldn't know where to start looking. Mind you, the cats probably know where he is. They'll take care of him.'

'What can they do if Henry's locked up?' said Charlie. 'I've got to get him out, Cook.'

'Someone has to, that's for sure. You'd better get back now, Charlie. We'll think of something. We mustn't give up hope.'

Charlie had no intention of giving up hope. He sneaked

175

back into the canteen, took a biscuit from the counter, and joined his friends at their table.

'It's true,' Charlie told them. 'Cook thinks he's in the dungeons.'

'Then we'll get him out,' said Fidelio confidently.

'We've got to find him first,' Gabriel reminded them.

'Come on, let's start now,' said Fidelio. 'We've got half an hour before the next lesson.'

They stacked their plates and went out into the garden. The snow had melted and the sun shone down from a bright blue sky. It all looked very promising – until they reached the ruin.

When they went through the great arch, they found Mr Weedon in the courtyard. He was nailing several thick planks across the entrance to one of the five passages.

'Buzz off, Charlie Bone,' said the gardener. 'I'm busy.'

'We won't get in your way,' said Charlie.

'I said buzz off,' shouted Mr Weedon. 'The place is getting dangerous. Why d'you think I'm doing this?'

They had a very good idea why Mr Weedon was blocking an entrance into the ruin. They left the courtyard quickly.

'That's obviously the way to the dungeons,' said Gabriel. 'Now what are we going to do?'

The three friends walked round the field in gloomy silence. Olivia came running up and asked why they looked so miserable. When she heard about Henry, she was stunned.

'That's awful. How are we going to rescue him?'

'We don't know yet,' said Gabriel.

Charlie found it difficult to concentrate on any of his lessons. Teachers shouted at him and badgered him. Twice, he went to the wrong classroom. If Fidelio hadn't kept an eye on him, he would have been sent to the head boy, and that was something he definitely wanted to avoid.

There was a very bad atmosphere in the King's Room that night. Lysander stared gloomily at his books, Bindi had a terrible cold, Emma worked away, silent and studious, and Asa grunted and fussed whenever he had to turn a page with his bandaged hand. Tancred's empty chair seemed to hold a huge emptiness that kept drawing attention to itself, almost as if a ghost were sitting there.

The only happy person in the room was Zelda, who kept whisking everyone's books across the table. When she stared at Tancred's chair, it whizzed round in circles until even Manfred lost his temper.

'Stop doing that,' he snarled at Zelda. 'It's not clever. It's just stupid.'

'It's called telekinesis!' Zelda retorted. 'If you don't mind, darling!'

'I don't care what it is,' barked Manfred. 'It's getting on my nerves. So shove it.'

Zelda made a face and went back to her homework.

Charlie would have found this funny if he hadn't been so worried. The minutes ticked by so slowly, he was sure someone had tampered with the clocks. He looked at the painting of the Red King, hanging above Tancred's chair. What would you have done? thought Charlie.

The mysterious dark eyes gazed out at him. The circlet on the king's head glittered as if it were real gold. Shadows moved in the folds of the deep red cloak. Then, unbelievably, the tall figure began to change shape and colour, until Charlie became convinced he was looking at a red and gold tree. Why can't I hear him? he wondered. He closed his eyes. When he opened them again, the tree had gone. My mind's playing tricks, he thought.

By the time eight o'clock came round, Charlie could hardly contain himself. He rushed out of the King's Room with Gabriel loping behind him.

'Have you thought of something?' Gabriel whispered as they hurried up to the dormitory.

'I haven't got a real plan,' Charlie admitted, 'but I'm going to the ruin tonight, whatever happens.'

'I'll come with you.'

'No,' said Charlie. 'It's best if only one of us goes. You can keep an eye on things in the dormitory.'

'I don't like it,' said Gabriel. 'Anything could happen out there.'

'Asa's injured. He won't be so dangerous.' Charlie sounded a lot more confident than he felt.

When Fidelio heard Charlie's plan, naturally he wanted to go with him.

'No,' said Charlie. 'Two of us will attract attention. I think I should go on my own. Henry's *my* relation.'

Billy Raven came into the dormitory and watched the three boys sitting on Charlie's bed.

'You look as if you're plotting something,' said Billy.

'We're plotting your downfall,' Fidelio told him.

Billy scowled. 'You think you're so clever, Fidelio Gunn.'

The dormitory began to fill up with boys getting ready for bed and the three friends said no more to each other.

When the cathedral clock struck eleven, Charlie put his blue cape over his dressing gown, and slipped on his socks and shoes. Tiptoeing in heavy shoes wasn't easy, but Charlie managed to creep out of the dormitory without making too much noise. He was beginning to feel rather excited about the adventure ahead. He was certain that he would eventually find Henry. And then he turned a corner and walked straight into Lucretia Yewbeam!

'Where are you going?' the matron demanded.

'I think I was sleepwalking,' said Charlie.

'Rubbish. What's that you've got?'

'Nothing.' Charlie held Cook's torch behind his back.

'Give it to me. Now!'

Charlie reluctantly handed over the torch.

'Hm. Interesting.' Lucretia turned the torch over in her hand. 'Where did you get it?'

'I found it at home.'

'Did you now? Well, it's confiscated. Go back to bed.'

'But I can't see without my torch.'

'Then sleepwalk. Go on!'

Charlie turned back and felt his way along the dark passages. He had almost reached his dormitory door when he fell over something and crashed on to the floorboards.

Picking himself up, Charlie groped in the darkness until he found what had tripped him up. A body lay sprawled across the passage!

Whoever it was, lying so still, had a mop of hair like Fidelio's.

'Fidelio,' breathed Charlie. 'Fidelio, wake up!'

Charlie tapped his friend's cold forehead and shook his arm, gently at first and then desperately. 'Wake up! Wake up!'

The body didn't stir.

Charlie ran in to the dormitory and found Gabriel's bed.

'Gabriel,' he whispered harshly. 'Gabriel, help me!'

Gabriel grunted and sat up. 'What's going on?'

'Fidelio's lying in the passage,' said Charlie. 'I can't wake him up.'

Gabriel grabbed his torch, swung his feet to the floor and followed Charlie into the passage. Between them, they managed to lift Fidelio and carry him back to his bed. Fidelio slept on. He was limp and cold and barely breathing. Gabriel shone his torch on Fidelio's face. His eyes were wide open but they stared out with a blank, fixed expression.

'He's been hypnotised,' gasped Charlie. 'We can't leave him like this till morning, he may never wake up.'

Gabriel went to the bathroom and came back with a mug of cold water. 'Sorry about this,' he said under his breath. He poured the water over Fidelio's head.

With a shiver and a moan, Fidelio opened his eyes even wider and looked up at Charlie. 'What happened?' he said.

'You tell us,' said Charlie. 'I found you in the passage.'

'I tried to follow you,' mumbled Fidelio. 'Manfred caught me. He held a torch up to his face. And made me look at him. His eyes were horrible – like coal, black and shiny.'

'You were hypnotised,' said Charlie. 'D'you feel OK now?'

'Sleepy. Got to get some sleep.'

'Me too,' said Gabriel. ''Night, you two.'

Charlie got into bed. He took a long time drifting off to sleep. He was worried. Now even his friends were being watched. Someone was determined to stop him from rescuing Henry.

At the other end of the dormitory, Billy Raven lay wide awake. When he was quite sure that everyone else was asleep, he got out of bed. It was time to see Mr Ezekiel. He knew it was no use waiting for Blessed. The old dog was an enemy now and Billy was a little sorry about this. 'Couldn't be helped,' he muttered, wrapping himself in his new blue dressing gown.

The powerful beam from his new torch helped him to find his way quickly through the building, but once he was in the gaslit passages of the west wing, Billy turned off his torch. Almost as soon as he did this, he tripped over an empty jam jar. Something else lived in Ezekiel's shadowy regions, and occasionally it threw jam jars down the rickety steps that led to the attic. Billy wasn't sure if it was a ghost, or something worse. He ran towards Ezekiel's room, but as he approached it, he heard several angry shouts. Billy put his ear to the door.

181

'Someone's hiding it!' screeched Ezekiel. 'One of those wretched children.'

'The children were all at home,' said a voice, 'except for Billy, of course.'

Billy stiffened. He recognised the voice of Miss Yewbeam, the matron.

'I want it,' growled the old man. 'I must have it.'

'Calm down, Ezekiel. There are other ways of getting rid of the boy.'

'Has Charlie got the painting?'

'Oh, yes,' said the matron. 'We made sure of that.'

'You think he'll be tempted to go in?' Ezekiel's voice had turned sly and eager.

'I'm sure of it. But who knows if he'll fetch the dagger.'

'Of course he will,' said Ezekiel. 'Any boy would choose a dagger; all sharp and shiny.'

'We had a bit of trouble with Paton,' said Lucretia. 'I think he knows more than he should.'

'You'll have to do something about that brother of yours. He reads too much.'

The matron gave a nasty laugh. 'Oh yes, he reads,' she sniggered. 'And that will be his downfall. Leave it to us.'

Miss Yewbeam's laugh was infectious and soon they were both swept into a bout of unrestrained giggling.

Billy chose this moment to knock.

'Who is it?' said Ezekiel, still chuckling.

'Billy Raven, sir,' said Billy.

'Ah, I want a word with you,' said Ezekiel.

Billy entered the room. He was feeling hopeful. Surely he was due for a reward? He was in for a nasty shock.

When the old man saw Billy, he screamed, 'You wretch! You kicked my doggie.'

'But I helped to catch the boy from nowhere,' said Billy, taken aback.

Ezekiel ignored this. 'Why did you kick my Percy?'

'He wouldn't talk to me.' Billy was beginning to lose hope. 'When am I going to get new parents, sir?'

'You don't hurt my doggie. No parents for you. You'll have to do better. Now, get out!'

As Billy turned to go, he saw a look of scorn cross Matron Yewbeam's face. It was quite obvious that she didn't like children one bit.

RUN OVER!

Charlie couldn't remember when he'd had such a horrible week.

It took Fidelio several days to recover from being hypnotised. He wandered along beside Charlie, hardly talking. Sometimes he forgot Charlie's name, and sometimes even his own.

During the day, it was impossible to get into the ruin because Mr Weedon was always there.

'Clear out!' the gardener would shout. 'Go on. Buzz off!'

At night, whenever Charlie tried to leave the dormitory, Lucretia Yewbeam was always lurking round a corner, ready to pounce on him. In the end he just gave up. But Henry was on his mind all the time. Where was he? Was he being starved to death?

It suddenly dawned on Charlie that Henry had no parents to come looking for him. No one would miss him because he shouldn't really exist. There was Cook, of course, and Mrs Bloor. But what could they do, and who would believe poor Mrs Bloor?

'It's up to me,' Charlie murmured.

'What's up to you?' asked Fidelio.

It was Friday afternoon and they were packing their bags, ready to go home.

Charlie looked up. 'Fidelio, that's the first sensible thing you've said all week. Are you feeling better?'

Fidelio nodded. 'It's wearing off. But I've still got a headache. I'd like to give Manfred a taste of his own medicine.'

'One day we'll get our own back,' muttered Gabriel.

Billy Raven came in and Fidelio whispered, 'It's all his fault. He's a spy.'

But Charlie felt almost sorry for Billy, he looked so lonely and fed up.

'Don't be deceived,' Fidelio muttered. 'He's still dangerous.'

The three boys ran down to the hall and out through the great oak doors.

'Another weekend of freedom!' cried Gabriel. 'Gerbils, here I come!'

They leapt on the blue school bus and were soon on the move. Filbert Street was one of the last stops and Charlie could hardly wait to get home. He wanted to ask his uncle what to do about Henry.

As soon as Charlie got off the bus, he saw Benjamin and Runner Bean racing towards him. From the look on Benjamin's face, Charlie knew that something was wrong.

'What's happened?' he asked, when Benjamin stood panting beside him.

'Oh, Charlie, it's awful, your uncle was run over!'

'What?' Charlie dropped his bag. 'When? How? Is he . . .?'

'No, he's not dead.' Benjamin paused to get his breath back. 'He's in hospital. It was up near the cathedral,' Benjamin panted. 'Someone saw your uncle step into the road while he was reading a book. A car came round the corner and went straight into him. It didn't stop, it just sped off.'

'No,' Charlie moaned. 'I was afraid this would happen.'

When they reached number nine, Benjamin didn't come in with Charlie. 'You'll want to be alone with your family,' he said. 'I expect they'll be going to the hospital.'

Maisie opened the door and squeezed Charlie with a violent hug. 'Oh, Charlie,' she cried. 'What a catastrophe. Did Benjamin tell you?'

'Yes.' Charlie twisted himself out of Maisie's arms. 'Is Uncle Paton . . .? Is he OK? I mean, is he talking?'

'He wasn't yesterday,' said Maisie. 'His head was all wrapped up and so were his ribs. Poor Paton. He looked awful.'

'Do they know who did it?'

'Hit and run,' said Maisie grimly. 'There were a couple of witnesses, but they didn't get the number. The car just raced away.'

Maisie led Charlie into the kitchen where his mother was laying three places at the table.

'We're going to see your uncle later,' she said, pecking Charlie's cheek. 'D'you want to come, Charlie?'

'You bet,' said Charlie.

After tea, they took a taxi up to the hospital. It was a large building and they spent a long time looking for the right ward. As they walked down the long aisle between the rows of beds, they recognised two people sitting beside one of the patients: Emma and Miss Ingledew.

'I'd like to give that woman a piece of my mind,' Maisie muttered. 'It's all her fault. She's been horrible to Paton.'

When it came to it, Maisie couldn't say a word because as soon as she saw them, Miss Ingledew jumped up and said, in a tearful voice, 'I'm so, so sorry for what's happened. I blame myself entirely. Paton was coming to see me, and I . . . oh, he shouldn't have put himself at risk like that. I feel so guilty.' She blew her nose very loudly.

'It's not your fault, Julia,' said Amy Bone, putting an arm round her shoulders. 'Paton was just trying out a little experiment. One of us should have been with him, but he just slipped out without our knowing.'

All that could be seen of Paton was his white face. He had a black mask over his eyes and a bandage round his head.

'Is he conscious?' Charlie asked in a whisper.

'Yes,' said a thin voice that was still unmistakably Paton's.

Charlie bent closer to his uncle. 'How d'you feel, Uncle Paton?' he asked. 'You are going to get better, aren't you?'

187

'Of course.' His voice dropped to a whisper. 'It was one of them, Charlie.'

'One of who?'

'My sisters. She was wearing a wig. I can't tell them apart without seeing the hair, but I know.'

Charlie was so shocked he sat down heavily on the side of the bed.

Miss Ingledew got up to leave, but before she went she handed Charlie a small, battered-looking book. 'I found it in the gutter after your uncle's accident,' she said. 'He asked me to give it to you. That's right, isn't it, Paton?'

'Yes,' he said weakly.

'Goodbye Paton, dear. I'll be back tomorrow.'

As Miss Ingledew turned away, Paton gave a very slight smile.

Emma came round to Charlie's side of the bed and said, 'I'm sorry, Charlie. I haven't been very nice just lately. But I want to help.'

'OK,' said Charlie awkwardly.

'I mean, I *will* help.'

'Thanks,' he said. 'See you on Monday.' Emma had a talent that could be useful.

Miss Ingledew and her niece walked away and Maisie began to tell Paton all the news she could remember, both public and personal. While she talked, Charlie looked at the small brown book. The name GEIRIADUR was printed in faded gold on the cover. Inside, there were columns of words in a strange language.

After a while, Paton gave a huge yawn and murmured, 'I'm wearing the mask because of the lights. I told them they hurt my eyes. It could've been nasty.'

'It certainly could,' said Mrs Bone, gazing up at the rows of fluorescent lights.

'Goodnight, everyone,' said Paton with another yawn.

Taking the hint, Mrs Bone and Maisie got up to leave, but leaning closer to his uncle, Charlie said, 'Uncle Paton, the book's in a foreign language.'

'Welsh,' muttered Paton. 'You'll need it for Skarpo.'

'Why?'

Paton didn't answer. He merely said, 'Keep it safe.'

Charlie wanted to ask his uncle's advice about Henry but he didn't see how he could while Paton was so ill.

A nurse appeared with a trolley of pills and, promising to return next day, the three visitors said goodnight to Paton and left the hospital.

At number nine, they found Grandma Bone in the kitchen eating cake.

'You haven't been to see Paton,' Maisie said accusingly.

'I've been busy,' grunted Grandma Bone.

'Grizelda! Your own brother!' Maisie turned away in disgust. 'You've got a heart of stone.'

Grandma Bone ignored her. She took a large bite of cream cake and then noticed the book Charlie was holding.

'What's that you've got?' She stared at Charlie's hand.

'A book,' said Charlie.

'I can see that,' she said irritably. 'What sort of book? Give it here.'

'No. It's private.'

Charlie ran upstairs. He didn't trust Grandma Bone. She was bound to come snooping in his room as soon as she got the chance. He found that the book just fitted into his trouser pocket. He would keep it with him wherever he went. Tomorrow, they would pay another visit to the hospital and he could have a private chat with his uncle.

It was not to be. Next day, when Charlie asked to visit the hospital, Maisie looked glum. 'Grandma Bone and the Yewbeams are going today,' she said. 'And I'm not travelling up there in Eustacia's car. She drives like a maniac.'

'What about Mum?' asked Charlie.

'She can't get away from work until after visiting hours.'

Charlie didn't know what to do. At length he decided he must see his uncle so at three o'clock, when Eustacia's black car pulled up outside number nine, Charlie got in the back with Grandma Bone. Aunt Venetia was in the passenger seat.

'What a treat,' exclaimed Aunt Venetia. 'We're going to have little Charlie with us.'

'Not *little*, if you don't mind,' muttered Charlie.

'Sensitive about our size, are we?' Venetia giggled.

Charlie didn't think there was any point in replying.

As soon as they reached Paton's ward, Charlie realised that any conversation with his uncle would be impossible. When Paton heard his sisters' voices his face took on a blank, shuttered look, and he refused to speak.

'He doesn't appear to be conscious,' said Grandma Bone. She raised her voice, 'PATON, IT'S US. YOUR SISTERS. AREN'T YOU GOING TO TALK TO US?'

Paton's face remained blank.

'We've brought grapes,' said Eustacia, plonking a bag on the bedside table.

'And Charlie's here,' added Venetia.

Paton gave no sign that he'd heard them. Charlie didn't blame him. The three sisters sat round the bed discussing the weather and the national news, as if their brother were not there.

After half an hour, they stood up, and Charlie took his chance. Leaning over his uncle, he whispered, 'See you next weekend, Uncle P.'

'You're on,' murmured Paton.

'He spoke!' cried Venetia. 'Charlie, what did he say?'

'Nothing,' said Charlie. 'He was just breathing.'

They frowned at him suspiciously. On the drive back to Filbert Street, the three sisters ignored Charlie and chattered away to each other. He had never known Grandma Bone to be in such a good mood, but then poor Henry had been caught and was probably locked up in some dark, secret place. No wonder the Yewbeams were happy.

By the time he got home, Charlie was desperate to discuss Henry with someone. He decided to have a talk with his mother.

When Mrs Bone got home, Charlie followed her to

191

her small room at the back of the house.

'I've got a problem, Mum,' he said. 'Can we talk?'

'Charlie, of course.'

Mrs Bone took a bundle of clothes out of the armchair and made Charlie snuggle into it. Then she swung another chair round so that she could sit close to him.

Charlie's mum was a very good listener. She never interrupted or exclaimed, but when she heard the extraordinary story of Henry Yewbeam, her eyes widened and her expression changed from curiosity to amazement, and then horror.

'That poor boy,' she said, when Charlie had told her everything. 'What can we do? And Paton – his own sisters! But I suppose that shouldn't surprise me.'

'Why, Mum?' asked Charlie.

'Because of your father. I know they had something to do with his accident. And Grandma Bone, removing all his photos. As if he didn't exist.'

'One day he *will* exist, Mum,' said Charlie.

She shook her head and smiled sadly. 'I'm afraid not, Charlie. But I've had an idea. Miss Ingledew knows something about the little book. She found it, and she was talking to Paton before we got to the hospital. Why don't you go and see her?'

Charlie thought this was a very good idea. 'I'll take Benjamin,' he said. 'And Runner Bean.' He didn't like to admit it to his mother, but he always felt nervous in the narrow streets round the cathedral.

Benjamin was, as always, very happy to join Charlie on an expedition. So was Runner Bean. On Sunday afternoon, all three set off for Ingledew's Bookshop while Grandma Bone was taking a nap.

Dark clouds hung over the city and there was still a hint of snow in the air. By the time they reached the bookshop, the boys were ready for a hot drink and a bite to eat.

'I hope they're in,' Benjamin muttered as Charlie rang the bell.

They were in luck. Emma answered the door.

'Come in,' she said with a bright smile. 'But excuse the mess.'

She led them into the cosy room behind the shop. A large sketchbook lay on Miss Ingledew's desk. Emma had apparently been working there. The drawing of a huge bird covered both pages of the open book. It looked like a golden eagle and yet there was something far more menacing and powerful about it.

Apart from Miss Ingledew's piles of books, the room seemed to be full of feathers. Black, white, blue and grey, they covered the floor and lay on every table and chair in the room.

'I've been copying them,' said Emma, sweeping a pile of feathers off the sofa. 'Mind where you sit.'

The boys perched on the sofa where there were fewer feathers than anywhere else. Runner Bean was confused. He started hunting for the birds that must surely be hiding somewhere in the room.

'What's that?' asked Charlie, nodding at Emma's drawing.

'A tollroc,' she said.

'Never heard of it,' said Charlie.

'No, you wouldn't have. I invented it.' Emma held up the book. 'It's supposed to be like the roc in Sinbad the Sailor. You know, the giant bird whose egg was fifty paces around.'

'Wow! Some egg!' said Benjamin.

'Some bird!' added Charlie.

'It has to be strong,' said Emma. 'Very strong. And fierce. See its talons! Each one will be the size of my hand.'

'Nasty,' said Benjamin.

It dawned on Charlie that this bird wasn't just a drawing, made for fun. It had a very special purpose. 'Emma,' he said, 'is that how you . . .? I mean, do you have to be a bird before you can – fly?'

'Yes. But I have to think of the bird first. I see it in my mind, and then – it happens.'

The boys stared at her in awe.

'Wow. That must be brilliant,' Benjamin said at last.

'It's a bit scary, actually,' Emma admitted. 'I've only done it three times in my life. When I came to live with Auntie Julia, she didn't even want to talk about it, but now she's got used to it. There are times when I shall just *have* to fly.'

'Hullo, boys!' Miss Ingledew looked into the room. 'How about some hot muffins? It's such a cold day.'

'Yes, please,' said the boys, both rubbing their stomachs.

Miss Ingledew popped out to the kitchen and came back

194

with a tray of muffins and cocoa. Charlie told her about his visit to the hospital.

'I wanted to ask Uncle Paton about the book, but my awful aunts were there and he wouldn't talk.' He handed Miss Ingledew the little brown book. 'He said I would need it for . . .' Charlie hesitated, 'for visiting someone.'

Miss Ingledew darted him a quizzical look. 'I see.' She opened the book and scanned the pages. 'This is a Welsh dictionary, Charlie. Welsh and English, that is. Your uncle has marked some of the words, see?' She showed them the small stars that were scattered throughout the book.

'Why those words?' said Charlie.

'I've noticed that they're all verbs,' said Miss Ingledew, 'or commands. Move, fly, talk, push, listen, look, catch, run, et cetera. And look, he's written the pronunciations at the front of the book.'

'But why?' asked Charlie. 'What can it mean?'

'Welsh is an unusual language. It doesn't always sound the way it looks. I can only think that your uncle wanted you to learn the Welsh for these words. But I've no idea why.'

'When the time comes, you'll know,' said Emma.

Miss Ingledew smiled at her niece. 'What strange children you are,' she said fondly. 'I'm not sure that I would like to be endowed.'

'Me neither,' said Benjamin.

A chilly dusk had begun to steal through the streets as Charlie and Benjamin left the bookshop. Runner Bean made sure they kept up a brisk pace.

As they approached number nine, Benjamin slowed down. 'Who is this person you might be visiting?' he asked Charlie.

Charlie told him about the painting of Skarpo.

'You mean you can go in, *right in*, to the painting? And then what?' Benjamin looked alarmed.

'He's a magician, Ben. A sorcerer. And a bit of magic could help me to rescue Henry.'

'Which bit?' said Benjamin gravely. 'And how?'

'I don't know, do I – until I get in!'

'Suppose you can't get out?'

'Don't be daft, Ben. It's not as if I'll go right into another time, like Henry. It'll be like when I hear voices. I don't go right in to the photos. It's just my mind.'

'Hm,' muttered Benjamin. 'Be careful.' He turned away and crossed the road, with Runner Bean bounding beside him.

Charlie ran up the steps to number nine. He wished he hadn't snapped at Benjamin. To tell the truth, he was a little afraid of what might happen when he went into the sorcerer's room.

Mrs Bone had laid clean clothes on the bed, ready for school. Charlie began to pack his bag. He left the painting until last. Without looking at it, he began to wrap it in a shirt. But as he turned the painting over, he caught sight of the sorcerer's dark figure. Once again, the face turned towards him.

'Soon!' said the sorcerer.

THE TOLLROC

Olivia had made a decision. If it was impossible for Charlie to find Henry, then she would. She wouldn't tell anyone about it. She would just do it.

During the first break on Monday, Olivia wandered round the field by herself. Bindi was still at home with flu and Olivia didn't feel like joining the other girls. They were discussing the new play and Olivia hadn't been given a very good part. Mrs Marlowe, head of Drama, had told her that she must let others have a chance to shine. After all, she'd had a starring role in the Christmas play.

'What's up, Olivia?' called Charlie.

'What? *Brown* hair?' said Fidelio.

The two boys strolled over to her.

'I've been too busy for hair,' said Olivia. 'Anyway, I needed a change. Any news of Henry?'

Charlie shook his head. 'I know he's in the ruin, but I can't get in. I'm still being watched. Look!' He glanced across the field at Zelda Dobinski and her friend, Beth Strong. They were both staring at him. On the other side of the field, Manfred and Asa were pacing beside the wood.

Manfred looked over his shoulder, saw Charlie and looked away.

'Asa's bandages are off,' Olivia remarked.

'That means he's back in business,' said Fidelio grimly.

This was bad news. Olivia gave a nervous shrug. She noticed Lucretia Yewbeam standing beside the garden door. The matron was watching Charlie.

'Your aunt's still on the warpath then,' said Olivia.

Charlie told her about Paton's accident. 'He said they did it; his own sisters tried to run him over.'

'But why?' asked Olivia.

'I'm not sure, but I think it's got something to do with a picture they gave me. It's a painting of a sorcerer called Skarpo. He might be able to help me rescue Henry.'

'How?' asked Fidelio. 'He can't come out of the painting, can he?'

'No, but I can go in.'

Fidelio and Olivia looked dumbstruck.

'But you've got to *find* Henry first,' Olivia murmured.

'I know.' Charlie sighed. 'And I haven't a clue how I'm going to do that.'

Olivia looked up at the slate-grey clouds and gave a mysterious smile. 'Not long now,' she said.

Before Charlie could work out what she meant, the horn sounded for the end of break and Olivia rushed off to her mime lesson.

That evening, when the juniors were getting ready for bed, Olivia prepared herself for the night ahead. She set the

198

alarm on her watch for midnight, kept her tights on under her pyjamas, and placed her outdoor shoes close to the head of her bed.

She needn't have bothered with the alarm. At midnight she was still wide awake. She was both anxious and excited at the prospect of going into the ruin alone, at night.

Quickly slipping out of bed, Olivia put on her shoes and swung her purple cape round her shoulders. She tiptoed across the dormitory and was about to open the door, when a voice whispered, 'Is that you, Olivia?'

'What if it is?'

'Where are you going?' asked Emma Tolly, in a hushed voice.

'Ssh! To the bathroom.'

'You're not. You're going out, aren't you?' There was a creak and, all at once, Emma was standing beside Olivia. 'Let me come with you.'

'No. It's got nothing to do with you. Go back to bed or we'll be caught.' Olivia opened the door and leapt into the passage.

'I want to help,' said Emma, but Olivia closed the door.

Why's Emma being friendly? Olivia wondered as she hurried along the chilly passages. Suspicious, that's what it is.

She became more cautious as she passed the senior girls' dormitories. She didn't want Zelda Dobinski or Beth Strong to leap out and grab her. The assistant matrons always looked so tired, they were bound to be asleep. That only left Matron Yewbeam, and she was probably lurking near Charlie's dormitory.

A cold wind had blown the clouds away and a full moon beamed through the windows that Olivia occasionally passed. There was just enough light in the long passages for her to see her way to the staircase.

The hall looked vast when it was empty, and here Olivia kept close to the panelled walls. As she skirted the great flagstoned room, she kept an anxious eye on the staircase, but no one appeared. She reached the garden door, drew back the bolts and slipped out into the night.

The moon was so bright that every stone and plant, every bush and blade of grass, was silvered with light. Olivia gave in to a sudden urge. She spread her cape out like wings, and rushed across the frozen ground in joyful, leaping strides.

The dark walls of the ruin brought her back to earth. This was the part she'd been dreading. She wrapped her cape tightly round her body and slipped through the entrance.

For a moment, Olivia thought she must be dreaming. A cat sat in the centre of the paved courtyard. It was a bright coppery red and, from the tip of its tail to its sooty black nose, was glowing.

The cat mewed softly, and Olivia realised that she had seen it before, at Miss Ingledew's Christmas party. In the bookshop it had looked unusual, but here, in the dark, it was magical.

'You're Aries, aren't you?' breathed Olivia.

The cat purred, then he turned and ran to one of the

dark tunnels that led into the ruin. It was boarded with thick wooden planks, but the cat stepped neatly through a gap at the bottom.

If he can do it, so can I, thought Olivia. Kneeling on the ground, she squeezed under the planks, just as the cat had done; arms first and then her legs. As soon as she was in the tunnel, Olivia stood up and followed the glowing cat.

The tunnel had a dangerous slope; the ground was slimy and black water dripped from the rocky walls. Olivia kept her eyes on the cat. He was leading her somewhere and she had to trust him.

They emerged at last on to a wooded bank and before Olivia had time to get her bearings the cat was off again, weaving his way down through the trees to a shadowy glade. In the centre of the glade, an orange cat and a yellow cat, stood on a large black rock. Their eyes glittered green and gold in the moonlight.

Using the trees to steady herself, Olivia walked down the steep bank. She crossed the glade and reached the black rock. The three cats, standing so close together, shone like a bonfire.

Olivia looked down to see her heavy black shoes turned to gold by the Flames. And then she noticed a thin gap beside her feet. The rock seemed to be covering a pit. Could it possibly be a dungeon? She knelt in the grass and called, 'Henry! Henry! Are you there?'

A thin voice came floating up to her. 'Hullo. I think it's me, but I'm not sure any more.'

'Well, I'm sure,' said Olivia. 'You're Henry all right. Have they been starving you? I forgot to bring food.'

'Zelda and Manfred push bread through the gap, and bottles of water.'

Olivia heard a scuffling noise and, all at once, two eyes were peering up at her through the gap.

'Hullo, Olivia,' said Henry. 'I'm so glad to see you.'

'It's good to see you too, Henry. But not in that pit. How did they catch you?'

'A boy with white hair tricked me.'

'Billy Raven,' muttered Olivia. 'I didn't think he'd sink that low.'

'Manfred brought me out here, and a girl called Zelda. They put sticky tape on my mouth. It hurt like billy-o when I pulled it off.'

'Ouch!' said Olivia.

'Olivia, I've seen my cousin Zeke,' said Henry. 'He's so old and horrible. He still hates me after all this time. He made them bring me out here. Zelda moved that rock just by looking at it. I can't get out. I've tried and tried. But I can't budge the rock an inch.'

'I'll try,' said Olivia.

She threw her whole weight at the rock, but it didn't move. For the next few minutes, Olivia tried pushing and pulling, kicking and hitting the rock, but it was useless.

'I'm sorry Henry, we'll have to try something else,' she said. 'I'll tell Charlie where you are and we'll work something out, I promise.'

'They're going to move me on Sunday,' Henry said desperately. 'I don't know where I'll be going. I don't think I'll see any of you again – ever.'

'We'll get here on Saturday,' Olivia said firmly. 'Charlie's uncle will help. Will you be all right till then? Is it cold down there?'

'It was at first, but the cats keep me warm. They keep my spirits up. Their light is so cheerful. And then, there's the tree.'

'What tree?'

'It must be very close,' said Henry. 'Whenever I feel really gloomy, I can hear the leaves singing, and it makes me feel better.'

Olivia was mystified. It was winter and the trees were bare. She looked round, and was just in time to see two figures in tartan dressing gowns, rush down the bank. The cats yowled a warning and leapt at the strangers. There were two shrieks as Zelda and Beth tripped over the cats and tumbled to the ground.

Olivia jumped up and ran for the tunnel, but Zelda was on her feet again. She made a grab for Olivia and caught her arm. Olivia swung round and punched Zelda in the stomach.

'Help!' screeched Olivia, although there was no one else around.

The cats were having quite a tussle with big Beth Strong; biting and scratching every part of her body that they could reach. With a loud grunt of fury, Beth threw them off and lunged at Olivia, catching her round the waist.

'Got you!' Beth cried triumphantly.

'You've had it, Olivia Vertigo,' said Zelda. 'We're going to tie you to a tree, and very soon a vicious old beast is going to come prowling round here. You'll be in a very nasty mess by morning.'

'You won't get away with this,' cried Olivia. 'My mum'll . . .'

'Your mum'll be too late,' said Beth. 'Naughty girls shouldn't go out at night.'

Shrieking with laughter, Zelda drew a piece of rope out of her pocket. As she pulled Olivia's wrists behind her back, the moon was suddenly obscured by a huge black cloud. The cloud seemed to be falling to earth; it dropped towards them and now Olivia could see that it was a gigantic bird.

The vast wings drove a rustling wind across the glade and Zelda and Beth gazed up in horror. All at once they were in the air; hooked up by the necks of their dressing gowns, and dangling from the talons of a great feathered foot.

'Kraaak!' called the bird.

Olivia shrank against the bare trees and watched in horrified amazement. Beth and Zelda sailed into the night sky. Beth's head lolled forward in a faint, while Zelda's mouth was open in a silent scream.

Olivia tore up the bank and began to slither along the tunnel. The cats had joined her and filled the tunnel with their bright light. But when Olivia squeezed through the boarded entrance, the cats remained behind.

'Thanks!' whispered Olivia.

She raced across the garden, not daring to look back. The door into the hall was still unlocked. There was no one about. Olivia crept up the stairs. As she entered her dormitory, one of the windows closed with a soft thud. Olivia could see a figure silhouetted against the moonlight.

'Who's that?' she whispered.

'Me,' said Dorcas Loom. 'I was just shutting the window. It was freezing in here. Where've you been?' Dorcas was one of the endowed but Olivia had never seen any evidence of a magical talent.

'I've been to the bathroom,' said Olivia.

'Did you see Emma? She's gone too.'

'Er – yes,' said Olivia.

''Night then.' Dorcas closed the curtains and got into bed.

For several minutes, Olivia sat in the dark wondering about the window. Who had opened it? And where was Emma? They said Emma could fly. Was it possible that she and the bird in the ruin were one and the same? If it were true, then Emma would need a way to come back in.

When she was sure Dorcas was asleep, Olivia tiptoed out of the dormitory and opened one of the windows in the corridor.

'Good luck, Emma!' she murmured.

Next morning, Olivia could barely keep her eyes open. Emma looked exhausted too. The girls went down to breakfast together. They caught up with Charlie and Fidelio, just as they were going in to the dining hall.

'You two look as if you've been awake all night,' said Charlie.

'We have,' said Olivia, grinning at Emma. 'Tell you about it later.'

In the first break, the two girls found Charlie and Fidelio sitting on a pile of logs outside the ruin.

'What's the news then?' asked Charlie.

Olivia told them about her adventure. Charlie looked at Emma. 'The tollroc came to life?' he said.

'Of course,' said Emma.

At that moment, Gabriel came running up. 'Have you heard?' he cried, dropping on to a log. 'Beth and Zelda were found wandering on the Heights in their pyjamas. They're in a state of shock and can't remember how they got there.'

'We know,' said Olivia.

When she told Gabriel about the tollroc, he stared at Emma in disbelief.

'You don't eat gerbils, do you?' he asked gravely.

Emma shook her head and everybody laughed. But as the laughter died, a chilly draught crept down Charlie's neck and he thought of Henry.

'I can't wait until the weekend,' he said. 'Tonight, I may need your help.'

Fidelio stared at Charlie. 'You mean . . .?'

'I'm going to visit Skarpo.'

THE WAND

Charlie decided to use the art room for his visit to the sorcerer. The painting of Skarpo wouldn't look out of place among the other pieces of artwork, and if anyone caught him, he could say Emma had asked him to look at her sketches.

As soon as homework was over, he began to make his way up to the dormitory.

'What's the hurry, Charlie Bone?' asked a voice behind him.

Charlie turned to see Manfred strolling towards him.

'No hurry,' said Charlie, as casually as he could.

'I want a word with you,' said Manfred.

'Now?'

'Yes. Now.' Manfred came up to Charlie and stared at him.

Charlie looked away quickly. He couldn't afford to be hypnotised when he was so close to rescuing Henry.

'Look at me!' Manfred demanded.

'I don't want to,' said Charlie. 'Anyway, you know I can play your mind games.'

'Hm.' Manfred stroked his chin where a few wispy hairs were beginning to sprout.

'You've got a fine beard coming on, Manfred,' said Charlie.

Manfred couldn't decide if Charlie was being rude or flattering him. 'All right. You can go now. But try and keep out of trouble.'

'Yes, Manfred.' Charlie hurried away.

Why had Manfred stopped him? It was almost as if he were trying to slow him down.

As Charlie walked into the dormitory, Billy Raven turned quickly from Charlie's bedside cupboard. He was holding the painting of Skarpo.

'What d'you think you're doing?' said Charlie angrily.

'I was looking for something of mine,' said Billy innocently. 'I thought it might have got into your cupboard by accident. So I looked, and this fell out.'

'It couldn't have. It was right at the back. You've been spying.'

'Why are you always so suspicious?' said Billy resentfully. 'I'm telling the truth.'

'Give it to me!' Charlie demanded.

'OK. OK.' As Billy handed the painting to Charlie, he pointed to a dagger lying on Skarpo's table. 'Look at that dagger. It's so bright. I bet it was as sharp as anything. I bet it killed a few people.'

'I bet,' said Charlie, grabbing the painting. 'Just leave my stuff alone in future.'

'Sorry, Charlie.' Billy smiled. 'I didn't mean to be nosey.'

Charlie hurried out of the dormitory. He waited for a

few seconds, to make sure Billy wouldn't follow him, and then he ran down the passage that led to the art room.

He was surprised to find his friends already waiting for him. Even Lysander had turned up.

'Gabriel told me what you're going to do,' he said. 'I'll stand by the door in case anyone tries to come in while you're . . . out of action.'

'Thanks Lysander,' said Charlie.

They chose an empty space behind one of Mr Boldova's large canvasses. Charlie sat on the floor with the painting in front of him. Olivia and Emma knelt on either side of him, while Gabriel and Fidelio perched on a bench in front of him.

All at once, Charlie began to have doubts. He'd never done this before. How would he get out of the painting? He hadn't really thought it through. But somehow it was too late to stop.

Charlie took a deep breath. 'OK. I'm going in.'

'Hold on, Charlie,' said Gabriel. 'Just so we know – are you going to bring that weird-looking person in to this room?'

'Skarpo? No, I hope not. I'm just going to ask his advice. Maybe I'll borrow something.' Charlie was already beginning to feel slightly dizzy. 'I don't . . .' he began, and then Skarpo looked at him, and he could hear the swish of the sorcerer's robes and the squeak of chalk on stone.

'Enter,' said a voice.

Charlie's friends began to fade. A white mist drifted

round him, obscuring everything except the sorcerer's bony face with its strange golden-yellow eyes.

When the mist cleared, Charlie found himself in a chilly, candlelit room. He could smell burning candle-grease, pine, spices and ancient decaying things. The sorcerer's possessions were no longer merely painted objects. Now they were real; pages were rough and ink-stained, feathers were delicate and velvet smooth, the earthenware bowls were pitted and chipped, and belts and straps had a worn, shiny look.

Charlie's eyes fell on the dagger. It was lying in front of a large open book, right at the edge of the long table. Candlelight made it gleam with life. The blade was so thin it was just a shaft of brilliant light.

'What is it you want, child?'

Charlie jumped. He'd forgotten that the sorcerer could see him too.

'You know what that weapon is? It's magic, boy.' The sorcerer's magnetic eyes glittered.

'You can see me,' breathed Charlie.

'I can see your face. You've been peeping at me for days, you rascal.' The sorcerer's voice had a lilt to it, but it was definitely not Welsh.

'I've come to ask for your help,' Charlie said nervously.

'Is that so?' Skarpo smiled grimly. 'Then it's the dagger you'll be after. It can pierce a heart and leave no mark at all. Not even a pinprick.'

'I don't want to *kill* anyone,' said Charlie.

210

Skarpo ignored this. 'A mere touch and they're gone,' he persisted.

Billy Raven had drawn Charlie's attention to the dagger. But Billy was no friend of Henry's and the dagger was the last thing Charlie would choose.

'I don't want the dagger,' he said. 'I want to rescue a friend.'

'Someone wants it,' muttered the sorcerer. 'Someone wants it very much. They've been trying to reach it but they're not – how can I put it? They're not accomplished magicians.'

Ezekiel Bloor, thought Charlie. He scanned the table. What could be used to get Henry out of his dungeon? How could he possibly know what to choose? Skarpo was being deliberately unhelpful.

'Herbs?' the sorcerer suggested. 'A poisonous potion?'

'No, thank you.'

'Slip one of these fine feathers into your enemy's boot, and he'll be lame for a year.' Skarpo gave a malicious chuckle.

'I don't want to make anyone lame.' Charlie was beginning to lose heart. 'I just want to rescue someone.'

'Rescue? Rescuing is no concern of mine. Destruction is more to my liking. If you want someone maimed, or fatally wounded, poisoned, burned, vanished, shrunk, driven mad . . .?'

'All those things sound very useful,' Charlie thought he ought to be polite, just to keep Skarpo on his side, 'but right

211

now I need something that will . . . move a rock.'

It was then that he saw the wand. It had to be a wand, for it couldn't be anything else. A slim white stick lay behind one of the huge books. It was about half a metre long with a pointed silver tip. Charlie picked it up.

'You can't have that,' said Skarpo sharply. 'It doesn't belong to me.'

'Whose is it then?' asked Charlie. The wand was cool and smooth, and it seemed to fit into his hand as if it belonged there.

'I stole it,' said Skarpo. 'It belonged to a Welsh wizard. It'll be of no use to you at all.'

'But I think it will,' said Charlie excitedly. 'I think it's just what I need.'

'NO!' Skarpo made a grab for the wand.

Charlie ran round the table. 'I'll bring it back. Honest.'

'Give it to me this instant,' roared Skarpo. 'Or I'll turn you into a toad.'

'No, I need it.' Charlie ducked away from the sorcerer's long arm.

'Villain. Thief. You've asked for it!' Skarpo picked up a spear and swung it at Charlie's head. Paper, feathers, and herbs went fluttering off the table.

Charlie rushed for a low door at the back of the room. He twisted the handle but it was stuck fast. As he bobbed out of Skarpo's reach again, he closed his eyes and thought of his friends in the art room. 'I want to be there – NOW!' he said aloud.

It didn't work. He was still in the sorcerer's cell. Skarpo was chanting now, as he raised the spear, ready to hurl it at Charlie. 'Vile, creeping wretch, I'll burn your heart out,' he cried.

Charlie cowered against the wall. There was no escape. Benjamin had warned him about this. Why hadn't he listened? 'Help,' he moaned.

The tip of the spear glowed like a red hot poker, then suddenly burst into flames. As it flew towards him, Charlie bent his head and wrapped his cape round the wand.

The flaming spear never reached him. When Charlie looked up, he saw two hands catch the spear and fling it back at the sorcerer. The hands were brown, with shining gold bracelets at the wrists; beyond the bracelets there was nothing, no sign of a body at all.

The spear struck the wall and then fell at Skarpo's feet. He screamed as the flames caught the hem of his long robe. Charlie didn't see what happened next because invisible arms tightened around him and tugged him away. Back, back through the wreaths of smoke that were filling the room.

'CHARLIE, COME BACK!'

Charlie blinked. His eyes were still smarting from the fire, but the sorcerer's room looked small and far away. He was looking at it, but he wasn't in it. The painting was held by two brown hands. The hands that had saved him. Charlie looked up into Lysander's anxious face.

'You had us worried for a moment there, Charlie,' said Lysander.

'It was your hands,' Charlie murmured. 'You saved me.'

'Not me,' said Lysander. 'I had to call on my spirit ancestors. Good to have you back, Charlie.'

'What happened – out here?' asked Charlie.

'It was amazing.' Olivia poked her head in front of him. 'You were rocking about and shouting, and we kept saying, "Wake up, Charlie! Come out!" '

'But you wouldn't.' Fidelio peered over Olivia. 'So Lysander used his African language to call his ancestors. And then, all of a sudden, you stopped moving and something appeared in your hands. Just like that. Look!'

Charlie found that he was still holding the wand. It lay across his knees, smooth and pale, its silver tip glittering in the bright lights of the art room.

'What is it?' asked Emma.

'A wand,' said Gabriel. 'I bet it's a wand.'

Charlie nodded. 'Skarpo didn't want me to have it. He stole it from a Welsh wizard. I know what I've got to do now! I'll have to use one of the words in my uncle's book.'

'You haven't got long, Charlie,' said Olivia. 'They're moving Henry on Sunday, and then we'll never find him.'

'How are we going to get into the ruin?' Fidelio asked with a sigh. 'They're watching us like hawks.'

'If only Tancred would come back,' Lysander murmured sadly. 'A storm would be a good distraction.'

'A storm would be great, but we can't wait for Tancred,' said Charlie. 'It'll have to be Saturday when we can get help from outside.' He stood up and tried to hide the wand in the

214

sleeve of his cape, but it was too long and stuck out beyond his hand.

'Give it to me,' said Lysander. 'My arms are longer.'

Charlie held out the wand and Lysander fitted it neatly into his sleeve.

'We'd better go now,' said Emma. 'Matron'll be on the warpath.'

Charlie hid the painting under his cape, and the six children filed out of the art room.

As they walked back to their dormitories, Matron came rushing towards them, shouting, 'Where have you children been? It was lights out five minutes ago.'

'Sorry, Matron,' Lysander said with a smile. 'We were looking at Emma's work. And mine, actually.'

Matron had 'detention' written all over her face. The children waited to hear their fates. If they were given detention on Saturday, how could they possibly rescue Henry? Matron smiled triumphantly. 'You'll all . . .' she began.

But a voice behind the little group said, 'It's my fault, Matron. I gave them permission. In fact, I told them to come to the art room. Blame it on me, eh?'

Lucretia Yewbeam's smile of triumph faded as Mr Boldova walked to the front of the group.

'Sorry about this, Matron,' said the art teacher. 'I lost track of time.' He turned back to the children. 'You'd all better run off now. And thank you for your excellent criticisms.'

The six children scattered like dust as Mr Boldova asked

the matron's advice about a very bad bruise he'd received while playing rugby.

'Good old Boldova,' Gabriel whispered as the three boys crept into their dormitory.

'Where've you lot been?' Billy demanded.

'You wouldn't like to know,' said Charlie.

TANCRED AND THE TREE

At the top of Thunder House, Tancred Torsson surveyed the wreck of his bedroom. He kicked a pile of shoes out of his way and sat on the bed, or what was left of it. The mattress lay on the other side of the room, and his covers were in a tangled heap under the fallen wardrobe.

Tancred was wearing his pyjama bottoms and his green cape. Most of his clothes were torn or stained with food. He was tired of being angry, but he couldn't do anything about it. Little waves of fury kept spilling out of him, sending the air into a turmoil.

Mrs Torsson put her head round the door. 'Are you coming down to supper, dear?' she asked nervously.

'D'you trust me?' Tancred stared grimly at the floor.

'Well, it's been a bit quieter today,' said Mrs Torsson.

'Sorry about the headaches, Mum,' said Tancred.

'You can't help it, dear. I know.'

Tancred's mother scuttled downstairs. There were days when she longed to live somewhere else, with a nice ordinary husband and a small, quiet son. But she loved her tempestuous family and, in spite of the headaches, she knew she could never be as happy with anyone else.

Tancred followed his mother downstairs and took his place at the kitchen table. Mr Torsson was already tucking in to a large portion of shepherd's pie.

Mrs Torsson put a plastic plate in front of her son. She'd given up on china for the time being. 'There,' she said, spooning some pie on to Tancred's plate.

'It's about time you calmed down,' Mr Torsson told his son. 'This stormy bout has gone on far too long.'

Tancred's paper cup blew over. Luckily, it was empty. 'I can't help it, Dad,' he said. 'I've tried, but I can't.'

'If you ask me, that hypnotiser's got something to do with it,' boomed Mr Torsson. 'Manfred Bloor. He's put you into a real state, hasn't he?'

'I don't want to talk about it,' said Tancred, as the hood of his cape suddenly blew over his head.

'Control yourself,' thundered Mr Torsson.

The light above the table swung violently from side to side.

'See, you're not much better,' Tancred remarked.

'I can direct the violence,' said Mr Torsson. 'What we have is a very useful talent, but talents have to be focused.'

'Yes, Dad.' Tancred gritted his teeth, but the window behind him blew open with a loud clang. 'Sorry,' he mumbled.

And then, through the window, a curious sound could be heard. It was hardly more than a whisper, but it had a strange effect on Tancred. He found that he was listening to music that was like no other music in the world.

He stood up, straightened his cape, and carefully pushed back his chair.

'What is it, Tancred?' asked Mrs Torsson, surprised by his unusually calm behaviour.

'I have to go,' Tancred said gently.

'Where?' asked his father.

'Out there!' Tancred pointed through the window at the dark trees in the wood. He strode past his startled parents and left the house before they had time to ask any more questions.

The ragged moon threw a thin light through the trees, but Tancred didn't hesitate. He knew which way to go. Deep in the wood, he found what he was looking for; the source of the haunting music.

It was a tree.

The tree was red. The leaves that covered its slender branches seemed to burn with an inner fire, and the glade where Tancred stood was lit by a golden glow. Deep lines scored the bark, where water dripped slowly down the trunk. Looking closer, Tancred saw that the water, too, was red; as red as blood.

As he listened to the tree's hushed song, he felt a great stillness overwhelm him. His storms were there, deep inside, but Tancred knew he could control them. His strange talent had lost its grip on him.

He left the tree but when he was almost out of the wood, he looked back. The fiery light was gone and the song had ended.

'I kept your supper warm,' said Mrs Torsson as Tancred entered the kitchen.

'What happened out there?' asked his father.

'There was a tree, Dad. A red tree; it was kind of singing, but not any sort of song I've ever heard before.'

Mr Torsson frowned. 'I've heard of a red tree,' he said thoughtfully. 'My mother told me a story when I was very young. Damned if I can remember it now. She said it was the Red King.'

'Our ancestor!' said Tancred.

'My headache's gone!' murmured Mrs Torsson.

Tancred smiled. 'I'm going to see my mates tomorrow,' he said.

'About time too,' said Mr Torsson.

After supper, when Tancred was tidying his room, his mother appeared with a pile of clean clothes and sheets. She'd kept them hidden while he was in the grip of his storms, as she put it.

'You look so much better,' she said. 'Even your hair is lying down.'

'I *am* better, Mum,' said Tancred.

He had the best night's sleep he could remember. When he woke up, the mattress was still on his bed, and so were the bedclothes. He dressed quickly and had a very civilised breakfast with his family. Mrs Torsson even served his bacon and eggs on a china plate.

Charlie didn't know Tancred was back until he went to the

King's Room that evening. He had just put his homework on the table, when Gabriel came running in.

'Guess what?' said Gabriel. 'I've seen Tancred!'

Charlie could hardly believe it. 'That's fantastic!' he said happily.

Asa limped into the room. His bandages were off but the scars on his hands were still red and painful. 'What are you two smirking about?' he snarled.

'Just a bit of good news,' said Charlie.

The room began to fill up. Emma took her place next to Charlie, and Billy came hopping in after Manfred. Dorcas was next, and then, at last, Lysander and Tancred arrived.

'Hi, Tanc!' said Gabriel and Charlie.

'Good to see you back,' Emma added quietly.

Before Tancred could reply, Manfred said, 'Shut up and get on with your homework. Tancred and Lysander, you're late!'

'Sorry, mate,' said Tancred, with a grin.

'I'm not your mate,' snapped Manfred.

'OK, Manfred,' Tancred said pleasantly.

This seemed to annoy Manfred even more. He scowled at Tancred, but couldn't think of anything else to say.

Billy Raven gazed sadly at Manfred. 'So sorry to hear your girlfriend's ill,' he said, obviously hoping to earn a few sweets. Unfortunately, it had the opposite effect.

'What?' Manfred glared at Billy.

'Zelda,' said Billy nervously.

'She's not my girlfriend,' barked Manfred. 'And I'd

advise you to mind your own business, Billy Raven.'

'Yes, Manfred.'

Everyone put their heads down and began to work. In spite of the intense concentration in the room, Charlie was aware that, somehow, a weight had been lifted. There was a fresh and hopeful atmosphere. Now there are five of *us*, he thought. And only three of *them*.

Dorcas was a puzzle. No one knew what her endowment was. Even when she was doing homework there was a smile on her face. Charlie liked to think that she was neither on one side nor the other, but placed firmly in the middle.

He looked up at the painting of the Red King. Would the tree appear again? And could he go into this painting? Would he hear the Red King speak?

Manfred's voice cut into Charlie's thoughts. 'Daydreaming won't get you anywhere, Bone. Get on with your work!'

'Yes, Manfred.' Charlie was about to look away from the painting when he noticed a shadow fall behind the figure of the king. Gradually, the shadow took shape. It became a face beneath a dark hood. And Charlie became convinced that this dark figure was blocking him. It would never let him hear the king's voice, or step any closer.

'D'you want detention, Bone?' shouted Manfred.

'No . . . no. Sorry, Manfred. I was just thinking. My homework's a bit difficult today.' Charlie fumbled with his books.

'Just get on with it,' grunted Manfred.

Charlie kept his head down until the clock struck eight, and they were all released.

Tancred and Lysander caught up with him as he hurried away from the King's Room.

'Sander's put me in the picture,' Tancred told Charlie. 'I hope I can help with your cousin's problem.'

'You bet you can,' said Charlie. 'Somehow, I've got to get into the ruin. It must be on Saturday, when I'm not being watched.'

'That means you'll have to get in from the other side.' Lysander looked doubtful. 'It's very dangerous, Charlie. There's a deep gorge with a river at the bottom. You'll have to scale the cliffs and they're almost sheer.'

Charlie didn't like the sound of it. 'Maybe I could get in through a window in one of the towers, if there was a distraction.' He looked at Tancred.

'A storm?' asked Tancred.

'That would be great.'

'D'you want me to keep the wand, Charlie?' Lysander made a sweeping movement in the air.

'I think it would be safer with you,' said Charlie.

'What are you three doing?' Dr Bloor came marching up to them. 'You shouldn't be lurking about here. Hurry along now.'

'Yes, sir,' said the three boys.

They dared not say anything more to each other. With a quick grin, Charlie left the older boys and walked up to his dormitory.

That night, Charlie found it difficult to sleep. He was haunted by thoughts of falling down steep cliffs and drowning in fast-flowing rivers. Next morning, he was so preoccupied he nearly went down to breakfast in his pyjamas. Luckily, Fidelio was waiting for him.

'You'll be in trouble if you go down like that.'

'I can't think properly. I keep wondering what'll happen to Henry if we don't get him out.'

'We *will* get him out,' said Fidelio, though he sounded much less confident than usual.

Later that day, something happened that changed their mood entirely. When they went to the canteen for lunch, they were surprised to see Cook behind the counter.

As Charlie came up to get his portion, Cook bent her head over a pan of macaroni and said in an undertone, 'I've had a message from Mr Onimous. You're to go to the Pets' Café at two o'clock on Saturday.'

'Why?' said Charlie.

'Move up, Charlie,' Billy Raven whined from the queue. 'We're hungry.'

Fidelio stepped back on to his foot.

'Ouch!' yelled Billy.

'So sorry, Billy,' said Fidelio in a loud voice.

Taking advantage of the noise, Cook murmured quickly, 'It's going to be all right. Mr Onimous has the answer.' She raised her voice and said, 'Here you are, Charlie. Macaroni without the peas.'

'Yippee!' said Fidelio, joining Charlie at his table.

'Something for veggies, at last.' He lowered his voice. 'I heard what Cook said, so cheer up, Charlie! All will be revealed on Saturday.'

The next day was Friday. During the first break, Charlie and Fidelio managed to pass on Cook's message to Tancred and Lysander. Gabriel had already been told, and he passed the news on to Emma and Olivia. After all, it was *they* who had found Henry.

'You'll have to bring a pet,' Gabriel warned the girls. 'I can lend you a gerbil each; I've got plenty to spare.'

'Actually,' said Olivia, 'I've got some very nice rabbits.'

Emma accepted the offer of a gerbil.

That evening, Charlie wrapped the painting of Skarpo in his pyjamas. He put it carefully at the bottom of his bag and then piled the rest of his clothes on top.

Billy Raven sat on his bed watching Charlie pack. The others had already left and the two boys were alone.

'Why are you taking that painting home again?' asked Billy.

'Because I want to,' said Charlie. He used to feel sorry for Billy, all on his own in the creepy academy every weekend. But he was sure that spying had brought the orphan a great many rewards; bars of chocolate, late-night cocoa, fur-lined boots and powerful torches, to name but a few.

'I'll be off then,' said Charlie, zipping up his bag. 'Have a good weekend, Billy.'

'I don't think *you* will,' said Billy.

What did he mean? Charlie was too distracted by his

225

own plans to worry about Billy's spiteful little digs. He rushed down to the hall where Fidelio was waiting for him. The two boys were the last to leave.

On Friday afternoons, Dr Bloor and Manfred always waited in the hall until the last pupil left the building. As Charlie and Fidelio walked towards the tall double doors, Dr Bloor stepped in front of them.

'I want to see what's in your bag,' the headmaster said to Charlie.

'My bag, sir?' Charlie was very glad he'd given Skarpo's wand to Lysander.

'Your bag, Bone. Empty it!'

'Here, sir?'

'Right here!'

'He'll miss the bus, sir,' said Fidelio.

'This is none of your business, Gunn,' barked Dr Bloor. 'Run along.'

Fidelio didn't move. 'I'll wait for Charlie, sir,' he said.

Charlie opened his bag and turned it upside down. Clothes, shoes and books lay in a pile on the floor. Manfred bent down and shook out every item of clothing and every book. Even Charlie's trainers were investigated. As the head boy picked up Charlie's pyjamas, the painting fell out.

'There's only this!' Manfred held the painting out to Dr Bloor.

'Ah. A very fine work,' said Dr Bloor. 'Nothing else? Look in the bag, Manfred!'

Manfred felt inside Charlie's bag. He ran his hands along

the lining, shook the pockets, and lifted the board at the bottom.

'Please, sir. We're going to miss the bus,' Fidelio said bravely.

'Then you'll have to walk, won't you?' snapped Manfred. 'Nothing here, Dad.' He threw the bag at Charlie. 'All right, you two. Get out of here.'

The two boys just managed to catch their bus, but as it travelled round the city, Charlie suddenly began to have doubts about his uncle. Suppose he were still in hospital? Suppose his sisters had done something even worse? Paton had looked so ill when Charlie last saw him. How could he possibly recover in time to help Henry?

Charlie ran down Filbert Street, dreading more bad news. When his mother opened the door of number nine, Charlie's worst fears were confirmed. Mrs Bone never came home this early.

'What's happened?' breathed Charlie.

'Nothing, love.' His mother kissed his cheek. 'I just took the day off. Had some shopping to do.'

Charlie stepped into the hall. 'Is Uncle Paton . . .?'

'He's up in his room. A bit sore, but nothing serious.'

'Wow!' Charlie dropped his bag and rushed upstairs.

For the first time in his life he burst into his uncle's room without knocking. Paton was sitting at his desk.

'Hullo, Charlie!' said Paton.

For a moment, Charlie didn't know what to say. He was so relieved, so overjoyed, in fact, to see his uncle. A hug would have been appropriate, he thought, but Uncle Paton might be embarrassed.

'I'm so, *so* glad you're better,' said Charlie at last.

'Me too. You should see my bruises. They're very impressive.'

Charlie could see a cut and a large bruise on his uncle's forehead where the bandage had been. 'Your head looks very, er, colourful.'

Paton laughed. 'That's nothing. The others are works of art!' He patted the arm of his rather shabby velvet jacket. Lowering his voice, he added, 'They didn't finish me off though.'

'D'you think they really meant to?' asked Charlie.

Paton shrugged. 'Who knows? With sisters like mine, anything is possible.'

'Uncle Paton, I've got a lot to tell you,' Charlie said gravely.

'I'll bet you have. Run along and have your tea and then we'll *discuss*!'

Charlie went down to the huge Friday spread Maisie provided to make up for the academy's meagre rations.

'Doesn't your uncle look grand – considering?' said Maisie.

'Did they find out who did it?' Charlie asked tentatively. 'I mean, will they be sent to prison?'

'It was a hired car,' Amy Bone told him. 'And the driver was a blonde in dark glasses. That's all they know.'

A wig, thought Charlie. Uncle Paton *knows*, but he can't prove a thing.

He bolted his enormous tea as fast as he could and ran up to see his uncle again. Paton had actually cleared a space on his bed for Charlie to sit down. He had never been invited to sit in his uncle's room before. The candles had been lit and the oil lamp gave the room a cosy glow.

Charlie told his uncle everything; from the moment he'd discovered Henry's capture, to his escape from the sorcerer. Paton did not interrupt, though he gave a low whistle when Charlie described Olivia's night with the giant tollroc.

'I knew you'd find the wand,' said Paton. 'So, a friend of yours now has it?'

'Lysander,' said Charlie. 'I trust him. He saved me from Skarpo.'

'But you have the book? You'll have to use Welsh to command that wand, you know. It's the only language it will understand.'

Charlie nodded. He'd already learned some words, and repeated them to his uncle. 'Symuda'r gareg yma!'

'Move that rock.' Uncle Paton nodded approvingly. 'But it's pronounced like this, Charlie. Summidar gareg umma!'

'I'll practise,' said Charlie. 'It's lucky that Miss Ingledew found the Welsh dictionary. It was lying in the gutter after your accident.'

'It was very lucky. She's a remarkable woman, Miss Ingledew.'

'Are you . . . friends again?' Charlie asked tentatively.

Paton went slightly pink. 'I believe so.' Then he gave a light cough and asked, 'So what's your next plan?'

'Tomorrow, me and my friends are meeting at the Pets' Café. Mr Onimous sent a message. He says he has the answer. But I don't know what that means. How can *he* rescue Henry?'

'The Pets' Café,' Paton murmured. 'The Pets' Café.' He rubbed his chin thoughtfully. 'Aha! I should have remembered.' He gave a delighted chuckle. 'There's an old passage, long forgotten. It's mentioned in one of these.' He tapped a pile of books on his desk. 'It leads underground, from somewhere in the old city walls, right into the centre of the ruined castle. No one knows where it starts, but I'll bet you anything Mr Onimous knows. He has a wonderful, underground, burrowing look about him.'

'It's in the Pets' Café!' Charlie exclaimed.

'Without a doubt,' said Paton. 'Charlie, get a bag packed. Tell your mother you're coming to the coast with me on Saturday night.'

'I don't understand,' said Charlie.

'Tomorrow, you're going to get Henry out of that pit. You'll take him back to the Pets' Café, and there he'll have to stay until nightfall. You'll come back here and tell me that all is well, and together we'll drive to the café and collect our poor lost relation.'

'And where will we take him?'

'Ah – you'll have to wait and see.'

AMBUSHED!

On Saturday morning, Benjamin Brown crossed Filbert Street to number nine. He had done this every Saturday for as long as he could remember. Runner Bean, as usual, raced across the road in front of him.

When Benjamin rang the bell, he had to wait at least a minute before Charlie opened the door.

'Oh!' said Charlie, when he saw Benjamin. 'It's you!'

'Of course it's me,' said Benjamin. 'Why are you so surprised?'

Charlie felt guilty. He had completely forgotten about Benjamin.

'Come upstairs,' he whispered. 'I've got a lot to tell you.'

Benjamin stepped inside. 'Where's your grandma? She'll be cross about Runner.'

'It's OK. She's gone out. She had a plotting look on her face. I dread to think what she's up to.'

It took Charlie a long time to tell Benjamin everything that had happened. Benjamin sat motionless on the bed with his mouth open and his eyes getting wider and wider.

'Phew!' he said, when Charlie had finished. 'You *are*

going to let me come to the Pets' Café, aren't you?'

Charlie didn't see how he could leave Benjamin out. 'Course. And Runner Bean might be useful.'

'Mum wants you to come to our place for lunch. We can sneak out the back afterwards. And then your grandma won't know where you are.'

Charlie thought this an excellent idea. His mother was at work, so he ran down to tell Maisie where he was going, and then the two boys walked over to number twelve.

That afternoon, everything went according to plan until they reached Frog Street. Runner Bean gave a low growl and Benjamin saw a woman in red boots disappear round a corner. The High Street was full of shoppers, so he didn't get a clear view, but the figure looked very familiar.

'I reckon your auntie's been following us,' said Benjamin, 'the one with the red boots.'

'Venetia!' said Charlie.

Before walking down Frog Street, he scanned the crowds for a glimpse of the Yewbeam aunts. There was a chilly wind and a lot of people were wearing hats and head-scarves. He couldn't see any of his aunts, or his grandmother.

'We'll have to risk it,' he told Benjamin.

They dashed down Frog Street with Runner Bean bounding ahead of them.

'Welcome, Charlie Bone,' said Norton, the bouncer, as the two boys entered the café. 'It's all right, your friend over there is looking after your pet for you.'

Charlie had forgotten about bringing a pet. He was glad

to see Gabriel waving at him from a dark corner.

As he made his way towards Gabriel, he saw that all the others had reached the café before him. They were sitting round one of the largest tables. Olivia had a white rabbit on her lap, and its mate was sitting on Tancred. Gabriel had his usual assortment of gerbils, one of which was sitting on Emma's shoulder. Lysander had brought a parrot in a cage and Fidelio was holding a startled-looking cat.

'She's deaf,' Fidelio explained. 'On account of the noise in our house, but her eyesight's terrific.'

The cat bristled when it saw Runner Bean, but the big dog ignored her and ran over to a group of dogs by the window.

Tancred's yellow hair began to crackle. 'Who's this?' he asked, frowning at Benjamin.

'Benjamin,' said Charlie. 'He lives in my road and I've known him forever.'

'OK.' Tancred's hair subsided. 'Sorry, I'm just a bit edgy.'

'Who isn't?' said Gabriel.

'We're not, are we?' Olivia grinned at Emma.

'Not a bit,' said Emma, pulling a gerbil from under her collar.

'Hi there, Benjamin,' said Lysander with a huge smile. 'Don't you take any notice of us. We're Charlie's school friends. I'm Lysander. He's Tancred. You just sit down and tuck in now.'

'Thanks.' Benjamin eyed the plates of food on the table and sat down beside Charlie. They both helped

233

themselves to a large portion of chocolate cake.

'We didn't have to pay for anything today,' Gabriel told them. 'Mr Onimous said it was a special occasion and to take as much as we wanted.'

'I suppose it will be special – if everything works out,' said Charlie, remembering why he was there.

'It will!' Mr Onimous had suddenly appeared at Charlie's side. 'We'd better make a start, Charlie my lad,' he said. 'Are you coming alone, or d'you want to bring a friend?'

Charlie looked round the group of expectant faces. He didn't want to disappoint anyone.

'I don't want it to be me, if you don't mind,' Benjamin said helpfully.

'Is he going into the ruin?' asked Gabriel, lowering his voice.

'He is,' said Mr Onimous.

'Then we'll be more use here,' Gabriel looked at Lysander and Tancred.

'Fidelio, will you come?' asked Charlie.

Fidelio jumped to his feet. 'You bet!'

Olivia gave a huge sigh. 'I suppose I've done my bit.'

'It's not over yet,' Emma reminded her.

With a furtive look around the café, Lysander slid the wand out of his sleeve and handed it to Charlie. 'Good luck,' he murmured.

'Thanks.' Charlie tucked the wand under his jacket.

Fidelio passed his cat to Gabriel and then he and Charlie followed Mr Onimous to the back of the counter. They walked through a tinkling bead screen and into the kitchen.

Mr Onimous showed them to a small door at the back of the kitchen, and then they were in a long passage lined with shelves of disgusting-looking pet food.

'Come along,' urged Mr Onimous as the boys gazed around them.

The shelves came to an end and the passage narrowed. They were now walking on a rough stone floor and this very soon became a path of hard earth. As Mr Onimous scurried along, he seemed more and more to take on the appearance of a mole or some other burrowing creature.

Charlie realised that the ceiling was now so low he could rest the flat of his hand on its damp surface. It was getting darker. When the light had almost petered out, they stepped into a small round cavern. It was lit by a single lantern hanging from the ceiling, and all round the walls, huge tea chests stood shoulder to shoulder with plastic sacks and wooden crates. There seemed to be no way out except the way they had come.

'Now what?' Fidelio whispered to Charlie.

Mr Onimous had ears as sharp as a rabbit's. 'Aha!' he said, making both boys jump nervously. 'You're wondering where it is, aren't you? You think Mr Onimous has led you into a nasty trap, don't you?'

Charlie gulped, 'Course not.'

Fidelio asked, 'Where what is?'

Mr Onimous beamed and then, with amazing speed, he spun a crate away from the wall. And there it was!

A very, very small and ancient door. The little man's smile disappeared. His next words were spoken in such a solemn tone, Charlie would never forget them. 'Before you go in, I want you boys to swear never to tell a soul about this door.'

'I swear,' said Charlie.

'I swear,' Fidelio repeated gravely.

Mr Onimous nodded. 'Good.' He reached inside his woolly shirt and pulled out a small key on a gold chain. Putting a paw-like hand on the door, he fitted the key into the lock and gently turned it. With a light creak, the door swung open.

'The cats are there,' said Mr Onimous. 'They'll take you. Off you go now. I'm going to lock the door behind you. We can't take any chances.'

Charlie peered into the gloom behind the door. He could just make out the huge stones that formed the walls of a tunnel. A distant glowing light began to draw nearer and Charlie breathed, 'I see them.'

He stepped into the tunnel. Fidelio was right behind him. They walked in single file, treading softly on a smooth cobbled floor. Charlie had expected a rough, earthy burrow, but the tunnel had been carefully built. The large red stones fitted neatly together, even in the low ceiling.

'It's very old.' Fidelio's hushed voice echoed down the tunnel. 'I wonder who used it?'

'Soldiers, perhaps,' said Charlie. 'It would have been a secret way out, if the castle was under siege.'

'And children,' said Fidelio. 'Now it's Henry's way out.'

They could see the cats clearly now, but before the boys could reach them, the three animals turned and began to hurry along the tunnel ahead of them.

Charlie and Fidelio began to run. The tunnel was far from straight and they had to make several turns before they could see a welcome speck of daylight in the distance. Instead of making for the light, however, the cats swerved away from the main passage and disappeared into a long fissure. The boys hesitated and then squeezed themselves into a tunnel that was so narrow they had to walk sideways. At the end of a very nasty journey, they inched themselves past a pillar and stepped into an astonishing room.

The ground was paved with tiny squares of colour. On a white background, lines of red, orange, and yellow radiated from a huge red circle. The walls were covered in frescoes; golden domes blazed beneath blue skies and tall robed figures paced through leafy arbours. The vaulted roof echoed the pattern on the floor, only here the central circle was open to the sky.

'It's the sun,' murmured Charlie. 'See, the pattern is like the rays of the sun.'

'There's so much light.' Fidelio gazed up at the tiny circle in the roof. 'It must be a trick – or magic.'

'It was on his shield,' said Charlie. 'The Red King's shield was like a burning sun. It's *his* room. His own, special place. I don't think anyone's been here since he left.'

'Not ever?' asked Fidelio.

Charlie shook his head. 'I don't think so.'

At that moment, neither boy could have explained his feelings. The place affected them in very different ways. While Fidelio was uneasy and eager to move on, Charlie felt at home and deeply comforted.

'The cats have gone,' Fidelio observed. 'Now what?'

Charlie noticed a red-gold leaf beside his foot. How did it get there? Through the roof? He studied the ten pillars surrounding the courtyard. They were made of the same deep red rock as the rest of the castle, and there was only the space the width of a finger between the pillars and the wall. Except for two standing opposite to each other. They had entered the courtyard by a narrow opening behind one of these pillars. Charlie walked over to investigate the other.

Screened by the pillar, a small round window led on to a dark wood. Squinting through the window, Charlie could see a green glade beyond the trees. In the centre of the glade there was a black rock. The three cats were sitting on top of it.

'It's here!' cried Charlie. 'Fidelio, it's here.'

Fidelio ran over to Charlie. 'What is?'

'The dungeon. There's a rock, just like Olivia said. See? Where the cats are sitting.'

Fidelio gave a low whistle. 'You first, Charlie. I'll be right behind you.'

They scrambled through the round hole and dropped to the ground. When they looked back, all they could see was a wall of ivy. No one would have guessed what lay behind it.

Charlie led the way. The cats yowled encouragement as

he knelt in the grass and called, 'Henry? Henry, are you there? It's me, Charlie!'

'Charlie?' From a narrow gap beside the rock there came a sound of shuffling footsteps. And then Charlie was looking into a pair of large grey eyes. 'Good to see you, Charlie,' said Henry.

'Great to see you, Henry. Sorry it's taken so long. But we're going to get you out of there, right now.'

'How?' The grey eyes looked anxious.

'Well, I've got something powerful here.' Charlie drew the wand out of his jacket and held it above the eyes. 'Can you see it?'

'But it's just a stick.' Henry sounded disappointed. 'That won't do it, Charlie.'

Fidelio peered over Charlie's shoulder. 'Actually, Henry, it's a wand,' he said, 'and wands can do anything.'

'Oh! Who's this?' Henry asked.

'My friend, Fidelio,' said Charlie. 'He's great in a crisis. Never panics. I think you'd better get away from there now, Henry. Just in case the rock moves the wrong way.'

'I won't be able to breathe if it does that,' Henry said in a scared voice.

'Don't worry. It'll work,' Fidelio said confidently.

'If you say so.'

The eyes disappeared and they heard Henry shuffle down into his dungeon.

Charlie stepped away from the rock. He held out the wand. 'Suppose it doesn't work?' he muttered.

'Of course it'll work,' said Fidelio. 'Think where it came from, Charlie. Believe in yourself.'

Encouraged, Charlie flourished the wand in the air and then, pointing it at the rock, he chanted, 'SUMMIDAR GARREG UMMA!'

The three cats leapt off the rock, but nothing else happened.

'Things like this never work the first time,' said Fidelio. 'Like our car. It always needs two goes.'

Charlie repeated the Welsh words, pronouncing them exactly as his uncle had told him. The rock didn't move. A cold, panicky feeling clutched his stomach. Perhaps Skarpo had tricked him. He shouldn't have chosen the wand. It was useless.

'Useless, useless,' Charlie muttered. 'What are we going to do, Fido?'

'Try again,' said Fidelio. 'Only this time, use a different kind of voice. You sound like someone pretending to be a wizard. A bit false. And too bossy. I bet a real wizard treats his wand like a friend. Try and sound more friendly, and more polite.'

'OK.' Charlie cleared his throat. Once again, he pointed the wand at the black rock, and when he spoke the words, he tried to imagine that he was speaking to his Uncle Paton; polite but friendly.

'SUMMIDAR GARREG UMMA!'

This time, as soon as Charlie had spoken, the wand became warm in his hand. It felt as if it were turning through his fingers. A red glow spread through the wood and its silver tip sparkled like a firework. With a sudden explosion of light, the wand flew out of Charlie's hand and landed on the rock.

All round the glade, birds fluttered into the sky, calling anxiously. Fidelio and the cats rushed to Charlie's side as the rock gave a thunderous groan. There was a deep underground boom, a crushing rumble, and the rock slowly rolled backwards.

The boys were so amazed they stood rooted to the spot, and then Henry's head emerged from a dark hole beside the rock.

'Hurrah!' he said. 'I'm out. Well done, Charlie!'

They were shocked by his appearance. Never had they seen a boy so drained of life. His face was white and pinched, and the circles round his eyes made him look like an exhausted owl.

Fidelio and Charlie took an arm each and helped Henry to climb the rest of the way out of the pit. He was a bit unsteady but so happy to be alive and free, he couldn't stop himself from doing a skip and a jump as soon as he was out.

Charlie looked down into the pit. It was hard to imagine how it must have felt to be trapped in that awful place for two whole weeks.

The wand had lost its strange glow and was once again a pale stick with a silver tip. Henry gazed at it in awe, as Charlie slipped it under his jacket.

'I'll tell you how I got it,' Charlie said, 'but not here.

Let's go before someone comes snooping round.'

They hurried across the glade and through the wood, but when they reached the ivy-clad wall, the round window seemed to have disappeared. Fidelio eventually found it by clambering up the thick vines and pulling aside a long curtain of leaves.

One by one, they wriggled through the window, and then dropped into the domed room. Henry gazed at the painted walls in amazement. 'It's like the world in the Time Twister,' he murmured, 'the world of the Red King.' He would have liked to stay longer but the others hurried him across the room. They squeezed past the pillar and entered the tunnel. The cats had followed them every step of the way and now lit the darkness with their bright coats.

As they made their way along the tunnel, Charlie told Henry about Skarpo the sorcerer, and the stolen Welsh wand. Henry found all this rather hard to take in, so soon after his escape. It was easier for him to understand Fidelio's description of the Pets' Café and, after two weeks on little more than bread and water, he began to look forwards to the delicious cakes that he would find there.

They had almost reached the end of the tunnel, when the small door into the café was flung open and a tall figure appeared. The boys stopped. It was difficult to see the stranger's face. And then, Mrs Onimous ran towards them, frantically waving her hands.

'Oh, boys,' she cried. 'It's no use. A dreadful thing has occurred. It's an ambush!'

'What?' said Charlie. 'What's happened?'

'Dr Bloor and one of your aunts are in the café. They're watching every move we make.'

This was very bad news.

'Maybe we could sneak Henry out while they're eating,' Charlie suggested.

'Not a chance, dear.' She peered down at Henry. 'So you're the young traveller. What a thrill to meet you, dear. I'm Mrs Onimous.'

'How d'you do?' Henry shook her hand. 'I've been looking forward to one of your cakes,' he said.

Mrs Onimous beamed. 'Then you shall have one very soon, dear. But you'll have to stay here for a bit, nice and quiet, mind, while your friends come back with me.'

'We can't leave Henry *here*!' said Charlie.

'You'll have to, dear. They saw you both come in to the café. Your aunt has been asking where you were. I told her you were helping in the kitchen, but who knows if she believed me. She'll be behind the counter and nosing in the kitchens before we know where we are.'

Mrs Onimous took Charlie and Fidelio by the arm and drew them up the tunnel and into the storeroom. The last thing Charlie saw before she closed the door was Henry's pale, stricken face.

'I'm sorry, Henry,' Charlie whispered. 'You won't have to stay there for long. There'll be a storm, but you mustn't worry. It's to protect you. Wait for Mr Onimous. He'll tell you when it's safe to come out.'

'Goodbye, Charlie,' said Henry.

Charlie shivered when Mrs Onimous locked the door. Henry's words had sounded so sad and final.

'I didn't think I'd have to leave him in the dark again,' he muttered, as Mrs Onimous led the way back to the kitchen.

'It won't be for long,' said Fidelio.

Charlie wasn't sure. How long would his aunts be watching the café? Who knew what could happen in the next few hours? When darkness fell, the beast would be about.

When the two boys walked back into the café they found Lucretia Yewbeam staring at them from a table in the centre of the room. Dr Bloor sat opposite her. Lucretia gave a nod and the headmaster turned in their direction. As the boys made their way over to their friends, they could feel two pairs of eyes watching them.

'We were getting worried,' said Olivia. 'Did you . . .?'

'Yes,' said Charlie.

'Sssh!' said Gabriel. 'Let's get out of here. I've got a feeling there are spies everywhere.'

The eight children filed past Dr Bloor's table. Dr Bloor gave them a curt nod and Lysander said, 'Afternoon, Dr Bloor!'

Lucretia Yewbeam glared at Charlie and said, 'Earning pocket money, Charlie? I hope you'll be putting it towards your school fees.'

'What?' Charlie's jaw dropped. He couldn't think what his aunt was talking about.

Fidelio came to the rescue. 'They pay us very well, Matron,' he said. 'We do the washing up and sometimes they let us make the sandwiches.'

'Do they now?' said the matron. 'Pity you don't do more of that at home, Charlie. It seems that children won't do anything these days, unless they're paid for it.'

Dr Bloor was about to agree when there was a loud yelp from the floor. Charlie had stepped on a hairless tail beside Dr Bloor's foot.

'Look where you're going, boy!' barked the headmaster.

'Sorry, sir!' Charlie realised that Blessed must have been dragged along to the café as Dr Bloor's pet companion.

Aunt Lucretia had brought something in a cage, though it was impossible to guess what it was. The cage was made of thick wire mesh and all that could be seen was a large blue blob.

'Snake!' whispered Fidelio.

Charlie hurried on.

As they stepped out into Frog Street, someone in red boots leapt out of sight round the corner.

'Aunt Venetia again,' Charlie muttered grimly.

Lysander and Tancred sprinted up to the High Street, but the red boots had vanished in a crowd of busy shoppers. However, when Charlie caught up with his friends, he saw someone else. There, sitting on a bench, was Grandma Bone.

Charlie marched up to his grandmother. 'What are you doing here, Grandma?' he asked.

'Why does one usually sit beside a bus stop?' she said

245

coolly. 'One is waiting for a bus, of course. You're very popular today, Charlie. Lots of friends, I see.'

'Yes,' said Charlie. He walked on.

When they were some distance from Grandma Bone, Olivia's curiosity couldn't be contained any longer. 'How did you get Henry out?' she begged. 'Did the wand work?'

Charlie told them everything that had happened in the castle.

'So he's stuck in the tunnel,' groaned Olivia. 'Now what?'

'The rest is up to my Uncle Paton,' said Charlie.

They had reached the traffic lights and Gabriel spotted his mother, waiting in her Land Rover on the other side of the road. She had promised to give Lysander and Tancred a lift back to the Heights.

Before he crossed the road, Tancred turned to Charlie and said, 'I think we're due for a storm. It'll get a few of these busybodies off the streets.'

Charlie had just caught sight of Aunt Eustacia, watching them from the doorway of a chemist's shop. 'A storm would be great,' he said.

'You're on,' said Tancred.

As the three older boys crossed the road, Tancred's hair stood up in stiff tufts and a cold breeze blew into Charlie's face.

Raindrops began to spatter the pavement.

'Good old Tancred,' said Fidelio. 'Let's get home before the storm gets going.'

Charlie agreed to let everyone know when Henry was

246

safe and then, as thunder rumbled in the distance, Emma and Olivia headed off to Ingledew's Bookshop. Fidelio hurried away through a sea of umbrellas, and Charlie, Benjamin and his dog rushed back to Filbert Street.

'I'll come over after tea,' Benjamin called as Charlie leapt up the steps to number nine.

'See you!' Charlie let himself in and ran straight up to his uncle's room.

Paton was waiting for him. 'Did it all go according to plan?' he asked.

'Almost,' said Charlie. 'But I had to leave Henry in the tunnel. Dr Bloor was in the café, and the aunts were *everywhere*. Even Grandma Bone was watching us.'

'Calm down, Charlie,' said his uncle. 'They'll have to give up soon. There's a fine old storm brewing out there, and my sisters hate getting wet. Mr Onimous will take care of Henry. All we've got to do is wait.'

'But for how long?'

'We should be safe by ten o'clock,' said Paton. 'I'll phone the Pets' Café to make sure all is well, and then we'll pop along and collect our Henry. It's going to be quite a night, Charlie.'

Uncle Paton's dark eyes shone with confidence, so why did Charlie feel so uneasy?

'We shouldn't have left him in the tunnel,' he murmured.

THE TIME TWISTER

Henry had fallen asleep. A crack of thunder woke him up and he scrambled to his feet. Charlie had warned him that there would be a storm, but he didn't expect it to sound like this. Another boom echoed down the tunnel, and something scurried through the dark behind him. One of the cats pounced. There was a squeal and the crunch of bones.

This was worse than being in the pit. Henry thought of the room where a red sun sent bright rays across the floor. It was a cheerful place and he longed to be there again.

'Why shouldn't I?' he said to himself. 'They'll come and find me when it's time.'

He set off towards the comfort of the bright room. Immediately he moved away from the café door, the cats leapt round him mewing loudly. They seemed disturbed to find him walking in the wrong direction.

'I'm not going far,' Henry told the cats. 'Just to the sun room.'

They followed him down the dark tunnels and into the room. When he spread his cape on the red sun and lay down, they relaxed and sat close to him, washing themselves vigorously.

Light from the hole in the domed roof began to fade. Soon the sky was inky black. The storm raged on, and lightning lit the patterned walls with sudden fierce flashes.

Undisturbed by thunder or lightning, the three cats curled up and went to sleep.

Who knows what made Henry do what he did next? Perhaps it was the sound that came from the round window? Some might have thought it was the wind, or raindrops falling through the branches. Henry thought he heard someone sobbing. It reminded him of James. He could never hear that sound without wanting to do something about it.

The cats slept on as Henry tiptoed to the round window and climbed out. He had only taken a few steps through the wood when there was a deep snarl behind him.

Henry ran. He tore round the glade where the dark pit gaped beside the rock. He mounted the wooded bank beyond the rock, while the beast stalked him through the trees, grunting hungrily.

Henry searched desperately for a way out of the glade. His fingers tore at dry rock, walls of ivy, and branches of thorn. All at once, a flash of lightning showed him a stone archway and he leapt through it. He found himself in a dark, damp passage where the ground was covered in thick, slippery moss. Stumbling blindly up a steep incline, Henry made his way towards the streaks of lightning that lit the far end of the passage.

The grunts and snarls of the beast echoed behind him as he crawled through a network of planks and then fell on to the flagstones of a large courtyard. Without looking back, Henry got to his feet and rushed through the huge arch that led into the garden.

As he tore across the wet grass, the noise of the storm intensified. A howling wind swept rain across the garden in torrents and, by the time Henry reached the academy, he was soaked to the skin.

The garden door was unlocked and Henry thankfully leapt inside, slamming the door behind him. At the top of the stairs, on the other side of the hall, Billy Raven stood staring at him. The white-haired boy didn't say a word, he just watched impassively as Henry rushed for the nearest door: the door into the west wing. He hadn't got long to hide. Billy wouldn't waste any time. In a few minutes, the Bloors would know their prisoner had escaped and they would be searching the building.

Henry began to climb the stairs up to the music room. He had been safe there before. The music teacher was a strange man, but Henry knew he could trust him. The storm was now at its height. The whole tower rocked under deafening thunder, and lightning flashed continuously through every window.

Henry had almost reached the top of the spiralling stairs when there was a shout from below.

'He came in here!'

Two pairs of footsteps could be heard running up the

tower steps. Henry leapt forwards, missed a step and tumbled back on to the floor.

'Hear that? He's up there!' shouted Manfred.

Henry picked himself up. He began to wonder if there was any point in trying to escape. They would find him in the end. He gazed hopelessly up the narrow stairs, and gave a sigh of despair. The next moment, his arm was touched by a slim, gloved hand.

Mrs Bloor was standing beside him. An utterly changed Mrs Bloor. Gone were her dark clothes. Now she wore a red coat and a brightly-patterned scarf. She had a violin case tucked under her arm and in her free hand she carried a small leather bag. Her hair shone and her eyes were sparkling.

'It's time to go, Henry,' she said, uncurling her crippled hand. 'Look!'

Henry saw the Time Twister glowing against her dark glove. He looked away quickly.

'We'll go together,' said Mrs Bloor. 'Take my arm and come this way.'

Without thinking, Henry grasped Mrs Bloor's left arm as she hurried through the door behind her. It led into one of the long, dark corridors in the west wing.

Mrs Bloor began to run. 'The time is perfect,' she said. 'There was a storm, you see, the night they broke my fingers. I can go back now, to the way I was. I can leave before they catch me.' She put on a sudden spurt and Henry almost tripped as he tried to keep up with her.

251

'Suppose . . .' he said breathlessly. 'Suppose you go back to the wrong place?'

'I won't, Henry. I've been thinking so hard about where I want to be. I trust this ancient marble. I'll be five minutes ahead of them. This time, I'll be through the doors and hailing a taxi before anyone knows I've gone.'

'I don't think I can come with you,' Henry panted.

'But you must.'

A voice bellowed down the corridor, 'Dorothy, STOP!'

'Faster, Henry!' cried Mrs Bloor.

Henry felt as though his lungs were being crushed by an elephant. He couldn't keep running. He'd never breathe again.

'MANFRED, GET THEM!' roared Dr Bloor.

As Manfred came bounding after the runaways, a short fat shape ambled across the corridor. There was a loud yell and Manfred tripped over Blessed. He fell headlong on to the floorboards, groaning and swearing.

'Blasted, wretched, hateful . . .'

While Manfred cursed the old dog, Mrs Bloor swerved round a corner and under a low arch. Beyond the arch, a flight of stone steps ascended to a narrow window.

'Bother,' Mrs Bloor panted as she mounted the steps. 'I didn't mean to come this way, but there's no help for it. Come along, Henry.'

Henry had, by now, let go of Mrs Bloor's arm. He was in two minds whether to follow her, but he didn't seem to have a choice.

'Come on, come on,' she urged.

When she reached the top of the steps, Mrs Bloor unlatched the window and appeared to leap into the air. Henry froze as a bolt of lightning lit the sky. Had his companion fallen to her death, or was she already twisting back through time? He scrambled up the steps and looked out.

Mrs Bloor was standing in a wide passage between the roof and a long parapet. From the top of the parapet, strange stone beasts looked out over the garden and the dark, far away trees.

'Come on, dear,' said Mrs Bloor. 'Don't be afraid.' She was gazing at the Time Twister, and the glowing glass ball threw dazzling colours out into the night sky.

Henry couldn't help himself. He stepped towards her. Behind him came the thud of heavy footsteps.

Without taking her eyes from the Time Twister, Mrs Bloor hitched the strap of her bag over her shoulder and grabbed a corner of Henry's cape. 'A few more seconds,' she breathed. 'I can feel it, Henry. Soon we'll be gone.'

She ran beside the parapet, tugging Henry with her, and laughing happily. Henry wondered what would happen when they reached the end of the roof. But they never got that far. Mrs Bloor's red coat began to shiver under the fierce white lightning. Her pale hair sparkled and scattered in a burst of starlight.

'Henry,' came a soft, disembodied voice. 'There was something I meant to tell Charlie. I know where his father . . . but now it's too late . . . he'll never . . . oh, Henry, we're going!'

But Henry didn't want to go out there, to another world he didn't know. He'd only just got used to this one. Slipping out of his cape, he flung himself behind one of the massive chimneys that rose above the roof. From the chimney's deep shadow, he watched Mrs Bloor twist into a bolt of rainbow colours – and disappear. There was a gentle floating laugh – and then nothing.

The wind died and the thunder rolled away, but in a last brilliant shaft of lightning, Henry saw Manfred Bloor standing by the parapet. He was looking up into the sky and calling out. It was a faint, strangled cry and Henry could have been mistaken, but it sounded very like the word 'Mummy!'

'Has she gone then?' Dr Bloor shouted from the window.

'They've both gone,' said Manfred, blowing his nose. He picked up Henry's blue cape. 'The boy left this behind. I dare say he won't be needing it where he's gone.'

'Wherever that is,' muttered Dr Bloor.

'Great-grandpa will be disappointed,' said Manfred as he walked away from Henry's hiding place. 'He wanted to have a bit more fun with the little beast.'

Henry shuddered. What sort of fun, he wondered?

Manfred stepped through the window and closed it with a bang.

A wan moon peeped through the rolling clouds. Henry moved out from the shadows and looked down into the garden. He had no idea how he was going to get away without being seen. The Bloors were bound to catch him before he reached the ruin. And even if he got that far, the beast would be waiting for him.

He ran to the window and found that it was locked. Cold and hungry, Henry thought of the Pets' Café and the cakes Mrs Onimous had promised him.

'It just wasn't to be,' he sighed.

He had almost decided to risk breaking the window when something swept through the air above him. A huge bird landed on the parapet, its great wings glistening with raindrops. Henry had never seen such a gigantic bird. Its beak had a cruel curve and each of its massive talons was like a shining scimitar. And yet Henry wasn't afraid. He sensed something friendly about the great creature, something almost kindly.

As he approached the bird, it bent its head. Henry put his arms around the long feathered neck and closed his eyes.

At seven o'clock Benjamin went to see Charlie.

'I want to know what's happening about Henry,' said Benjamin.

'I'm going to get Uncle Paton to ring Mr Onimous soon,' Charlie said. 'It's horrible just waiting and waiting and not knowing what's going on.'

Benjamin and Runner Bean followed Charlie up to his room. Grandma Bone hadn't come home and this was worrying Charlie. Was she still waiting outside the Pets' Café?

Would she be lurking there when Uncle Paton drove round to collect Henry? And what of the Yewbeam aunts? Was Henry still safe in the tunnel? That was another worrying question.

After a while, Charlie couldn't stand it any longer. He went to his uncle's room and knocked on the door. 'It's me,' said Charlie. 'Uncle Paton, d'you think you could ring Mr Onimous? I'm worried about Henry.'

'Very well,' sighed Paton. 'If I can find my phone.'

At that moment, the front door slammed and someone marched across the hall. Charlie recognised Grandma Bone's footsteps and ran back to his room.

A few minutes later, Uncle Paton's troubled face looked round Charlie's door.

'I found the phone,' said Paton. 'I rang Mr Onimous. Henry's gone!'

'What!' Charlie stared at his uncle in horror. 'But how? Did Mr Onimous look?'

'He told me he went right to the end of the tunnel and out into the ruin. There was no sign of Henry. The poor little man is very distressed.'

'Henry went into the room with the sun,' Charlie murmured. 'He'd feel safe there. But why didn't he come back?'

'We'll have to wait,' said Paton. 'That's all we can do. Wait and hope. My father will be waiting too.'

'You mean . . .' Charlie suddenly realised what Paton meant.

'Yes, I've told him about Henry. That's where I was hoping to take him, to live with his brother by the sea.'

Waiting and hoping is a hard thing to do when you've already been waiting and hoping for almost as long as you can bear it. Terrible images kept springing into Charlie's mind: Henry being chased through the ruin, captured, eaten alive!

Benjamin stayed as long as he could, but after another half hour, he told Charlie he'd have to go home or his mum would start to worry.

'OK,' Charlie said gloomily.

As Benjamin turned to go, Runner Bean rushed to the window and barked.

'Sssssh!' said Benjamin.

The big dog barked again. He stood on his hind legs and pawed the curtains.

'Shut up, Runner,' said Benjamin. 'Grandma Bone'll catch us.'

Runner Bean looked at his master and whined mournfully.

'We don't go out through the window,' Benjamin said impatiently. 'Come on, Runner, this way.'

'Ben!' Charlie jumped up. 'I think there's something out there.' He went to the window and drew back the curtains.

There was a large chestnut tree outside Charlie's window. Sitting on a wide branch was Henry Yewbeam. He waved at Charlie and mouthed the word, 'Hullo!'

Charlie dashed downstairs and out of the front door. He waited anxiously while Henry swung from a branch and dropped to the ground, then the two boys ran into the house.

'Upstairs,' Charlie whispered as he closed the front door.

Henry quickly mounted the stairs, but before he reached the top, Grandma Bone came out of the sitting-room.

'Who's that boy?' she demanded.

'Benjamin.' Charlie was halfway up the staircase.

'Oh?' She looked suspicious. 'I hope that dog's not in your room.'

'Course not, Grandma.'

Charlie followed Henry up to the landing, while Grandma Bone walked across to the kitchen.

'In here,' said Charlie, quickly drawing Henry into his bedroom.

'Hullo! I'm Henry.' While Charlie closed the door, Henry shook Benjamin's hand and then the paw that Runner Bean was eagerly holding up to him. 'I'm very pleased to meet you both,' he said. 'Please don't be alarmed.'

Benjamin realised he was staring at Henry with his mouth open. 'I'm Benjamin,' he said. 'You look quite normal.'

'He *is* normal,' said Charlie. 'He's just . . .'

'Out of time,' said Henry. He sat on the bed and announced, 'I'm free. I'm safe. The Bloors think I've gone back, so they won't be looking for me.'

'I don't understand,' said Charlie. 'How did you get here?'

'It's a long story,' said Henry and he began to describe his extraordinary adventure.

'You say a *bird* rescued you!' Benjamin exclaimed.

'It must have been Emma!' said Charlie.

Benjamin and Henry looked baffled, so Charlie explained.

'I'd like to thank all your friends,' said Henry, 'the ones that helped me.'

Charlie told him there wouldn't be time to meet his friends. 'Tonight Uncle Paton's taking us to a place where you'll be safe,' he said. 'We have to go before Grandma Bone finds out that you're in the house.'

'Where will I go?' Henry looked worried.

'You're going home. To the house by the sea. And I'm coming with you. Just for the day. It'll be the very first time I've seen my great-grandpa.'

Henry frowned. 'And who's he?'

'He's your brother, James.'

'James?' cried Henry. 'Little Jamie? He's still alive?'

If it hadn't been for Runner Bean, Henry might never have seen his brother again. With a low, rumbling growl the dog stared at the door. Charlie pushed a startled Henry under the bed, and the door opened.

Grandma Bone stood on the threshold, glaring at Runner Bean. 'You're a liar, Charlie Bone,' she said coldly. 'You *did* have a dog in here. Get it out. Now!' She looked round the room, her long nose wrinkling like a pug's. 'Who else are you hiding? What's been going on?'

'Nothing, Mrs Bone,' said Benjamin. 'My dog's scared of storms so I brought him over here to take his mind off it.'

'Storm's gone!' bellowed Grandma Bone. 'Hadn't you noticed? Now, go home.'

'Yes, Mrs Bone.' Benjamin shuffled meekly past the tall woman in the doorway. Runner Bean bared his teeth and directed one of his best growls at Grandma Bone's skinny ankles.

'Aaaah!' she shrieked, backing out of the door. 'Get him away from me.'

When Benjamin and his dog were safely out of the house, Grandma Bone looked in on Charlie and told him to get ready for bed.

'Yes, Grandma.' He closed the door and ran to the window. Benjamin had just reached the other side of the road when Charlie looked out.

'Ben!' he called. 'Pass on the news, will you? Tell the others what happened!'

Grandma Bone gave up wondering about all the creaking and whispering that went on in the house that night. As far as she was concerned, Henry Yewbeam had disappeared into the past – or the future – so whatever was going on, it was all childish nonsense and she couldn't be bothered with it. She drank a stiff whisky and went to sleep.

A JOURNEY TO THE SEA

Charlie told the rest of the household about Henry's arrival and, one by one, they began to visit the boy from the past.

Paton came first. He stood in the doorway for a second, blinking speechlessly, and then he strode up to Henry exclaiming, 'My dear, dear fellow, I can't believe it. This is just too wonderful for words.' He shook Henry's hand vigorously. 'I've heard so much about you. My father idolised you, you know.'

'Did he?' said Henry. 'I suppose I'm your uncle.'

While Paton was still chuckling over this, Amy Bone looked in.

'This is my mum,' Charlie told Henry.

'And you're Henry.' Mrs Bone gazed at Henry as if she couldn't quite believe her eyes. 'All that way,' she murmured. 'All those years, I should say. So it really can happen.'

Was she thinking of his father? Charlie wondered. Was she wishing that he, too, might come twisting through time to be with her again?

As Henry and Mrs Bone solemnly shook hands, Henry said, 'Mrs Bloor told me she knew . . .' and then he seemed to change his mind.

There was no time to ask Henry what Mrs Bloor knew because, at that moment, Maisie arrived on the scene.

'He looks a bit like Charlie, doesn't he?' she said.

'Mm. Just a little,' said Amy.

Wherever Henry had come from, it didn't matter to Maisie; he was a boy in trouble and therefore in need of a hug. 'You poor, poor mite,' she cried, almost squeezing the life out of him. 'You look half-starved. Come to the kitchen this minute and I'll cook up a feast.'

'I don't think that'd be a good idea,' said Charlie. 'Grandma Bone might come down.'

'Drat Grandma Bone,' said Maisie. 'What's she up to now? If she so much as lays a finger on this poor boy, I'll give her a good wallop.'

'Maisie, dear, please lower your voice,' said Paton in a quiet, but commanding tone. 'If you want to help, you can bring a snack up to Charlie's room. And we shall need food and rugs for a long journey to the coast. I did mention it before.'

'Yes, Paton,' Maisie said patiently. 'I hadn't forgotten.'

'Come on, Mum, we've got work to do,' said Amy.

The two women went downstairs to prepare a hamper, while Henry chose some of Charlie's clothes to wear in his new life.

'It'll be so strange,' he said to Charlie. 'I was always the oldest. I took care of James. What's he going to make of it all?'

'I can't wait to find out,' said Charlie.

At ten minutes to twelve, Charlie and Henry climbed into Uncle Paton's midnight blue car. They were followed by a pile of rugs and cushions, and a huge hamper of food.

'You help yourselves whenever you're peckish,' said Maisie, as she stuffed cushions behind their heads and tucked rugs around their legs.

Paton was already in the driver's seat glancing impatiently at his watch. He was a man of habit and he liked to leave for the coast on the stroke of midnight. As the great cathedral clock began to ring out across the city, he said, 'Snuggle down, boys! We'll have breakfast by the sea.'

The car doors were slammed and Mrs Bone and Maisie waved and blew kisses from the kerb, as Paton drove slowly up Filbert Street. In case of lamp accidents, he liked to keep to the side roads, and after driving down several badly-lit alleys, they were suddenly deep in the countryside. Here there were no lights at all, except for the odd twinkle from a cowshed or a porch lantern.

Charlie was beginning to drift off to sleep when a question popped into his head. 'You told my mum Mrs Bloor knew something,' he said to Henry. 'What did she know?'

Henry yawned. 'It was about your father,' he mumbled sleepily. 'Just before she disappeared, she said there was something she meant to tell you. I think she knew where your father was.'

Charlie sat bolt upright, throwing his cushion to the floor. 'Didn't she tell you?' he demanded.

'No,' Henry murmured. 'She just vanished.'

'What did she say *exactly*?' Charlie asked frantically.

There was no answer. Henry had fallen asleep, and Charlie didn't have the heart to wake him.

'Did you hear that, Uncle Paton?' said Charlie. 'Mrs Bloor knew where my father was – or is.'

'I heard, Charlie. Perhaps it means that he isn't very far away. We'll find him one day. That's a promise.'

Charlie thought he would never sleep after this amazing piece of news, but before he knew it, his eyes were closed.

Whether he was awake or dreaming, Charlie could never be sure, but at some time during their long journey to the sea, his uncle began to talk about the Red King. Perhaps Charlie had mentioned the vanishing tree he had seen in the snow, or the strange red tree that had appeared in the king's portrait, but Paton's words remained very clear in his head.

'*I believe he is a tree, Charlie. That's what my books seem to tell me. When the king lived in the great forests with only the trees and his leopards for company, he became a part of the forest himself. Can trees move, you might ask? Who can say? Who is to know if a tree standing in a field at dawn, cannot later be seen in a castle ruin, or in the shadows of a great park? Perhaps, one day, you'll find out.*'

When Charlie opened his eyes again, he saw a great sweep of grey sea. They were travelling along a narrow cliff road and light was beginning to fill the sky. He nudged Henry, who was still asleep beside him. Henry stirred and rubbed his eyes.

'Look!' said Charlie. 'The sea!'

Henry looked out of the window. 'I know this place,' he cried. 'We're nearly home.'

'There's a few miles to go yet,' said Paton. 'Let's have breakfast.'

There was a shout of agreement from the boys and soon they were enjoying Maisie's feast. A cold wind was howling outside, and so they ate in the car, watching huge foamy breakers crashing on to the shore below.

When breakfast was over, they set off again. The road ran beside the sea almost the whole way and Charlie never tired of watching the waves, the tumbling cliffs, and the misty islands far out in the water. And then they turned a corner and Henry cried, 'We're here.'

Ahead of them was a small bay where the sea was calm and blue. As they drove down towards the beach, sunlight spilled over the horizon and the water became a sheet of sparkling glass. It was like entering another country. Gone were the dark clouds and the winter wind. Gone were the wild waves pounding the shingle.

'What's happened?' said Charlie. 'Everything's gone calm.'

'Like a spell,' breathed Henry.

They parked on a patch of grass beside the beach. On the other side of the road, Charlie could see a white house perched on top of a steep cliff.

'Is that it?' he asked Henry.

Henry just nodded.

They crossed the road and climbed two flights of

whitewashed steps set into the cliff. Uncle Paton went first with Charlie following. But Henry hung back. He seemed to be afraid of what he might find in the house at the top of the steps.

There was a porch with a blue painted door at the side of the house. Paton let himself in and Charlie stepped in after him. They went through another door and into a room that seemed to be full of sunlight.

An old man came towards them. His hair was white and his eyes were grey, and although he was obviously very old, his face looked young, somehow, as though all his wrinkles had come from smiling and sea weather.

'I saw you arrive,' said the old man, giving Paton a big hug. 'So this is Charlie. Well, well, well! At last we meet!'

'At last,' said Charlie, while his great-grandfather clutched him to his chest.

Henry was standing just inside the door. He was staring at the old man. And then the old man saw him, and they just gazed at each other, without saying a word.

At last Henry said, 'Jamie!' as if somewhere under all those wrinkles, he'd suddenly seen his little brother; the boy he'd left behind when he went to play his last game of marbles.

James Yewbeam still couldn't speak. His eyes had a glittery, tearful look, and Paton took Charlie aside while the two brothers hugged each other.

It was almost too much for the old man. He sank into an armchair and shook his head, over and over again.

'I can't believe it,' he said. 'It's really you!' He reached into his pocket and brought out a small leather bag. 'Look, Henry. I've still got the marbles.'

Henry sat on the arm of his chair. 'I'll teach you how to play Ring Taw,' he said.

'About time too,' said James with a laugh.

And then, another extraordinary thing happened. A door opened and Cook walked into the room. Or was it Cook?

'Cook?' said Charlie.

'Not Cook,' said the woman. 'I'm Cook's sister, Pearl.'

'So that's why the sea was so calm,' Henry murmured.

Pearl nodded and gave him a big smile. It turned out that Pearl had been James Yewbeam's housekeeper for twenty years.

They all began to talk about Henry's future. How he would go to the local school beyond the bay.

'It's small and friendly,' said Pearl. 'Henry will fit in perfectly. He can start in the summer term, when Charlie's filled him in a bit about all these new-fangled things, like mobile phones and videos and what-not.'

It was decided that Charlie would come to see Henry once a month, every time that Paton visited his father.

'And in the holidays too,' said Henry. 'Charlie *must* come here in the holidays.'

'Of course,' said Paton.

Charlie had never had a holiday by the sea. It was something he'd always dreamed about, but he'd never really believed it would happen. He looked through the window at the sparkling water and the sandy beach.

He didn't have to wait long to visit the beach. Old James Yewbeam had been awake all night and now, after all the excitement, he fell fast asleep in his chair. Paton went upstairs for a snooze before his long drive back to the city, and Pearl began to prepare a meal.

'You two should go down to the shore,' she told the boys. 'You both look as if you could do with some fresh air.'

They didn't need any more encouragement. Charlie and Henry spent the rest of the day on the beach. They skimmed pebbles across the water, jumped over rock-pools, and explored the caves that Henry knew so well.

All too soon, night clouds began to roll in across the water, and Uncle Paton was calling the boys to supper.

They sat round a table in the bay window, where they could watch the moonlit water. There were candles on the table but the rest of the room was in darkness. Old Mr Yewbeam always removed the light bulbs on Paton's visits. As Charlie tucked into the delicious supper that Pearl had prepared, he couldn't help thinking of Cook in her little underground rooms, far away from the sea and the sun.

'I wish Cook could find a place like this to live,' he said.

Pearl told him that Cook was very happy where she was. She loved keeping an eye on the children at Bloor's Academy. 'We talk on the phone for hours,' said Pearl. 'And Treasure – that's her name – Treasure tells me everything that's been going on with you children of the Red King, and sometimes I think it's me who's missing out.'

'But now you've got Henry,' said Charlie.

'Now I've got Henry.' Pearl's eyes twinkled. 'And I can see that he's going to be quite a handful.'

They all laughed at this, and then Uncle Paton stood up, saying, 'Come on, Charlie. We've got to get you home, or you'll never be awake in time for school tomorrow.'

'School,' sighed Charlie. He wished he could have stayed a little longer.

The two brothers – one so old and the other still young – stood at the top of the cliff steps and waved goodbye as Paton and Charlie climbed into the midnight blue car. Charlie snuggled down in the seat beside his uncle and the car roared into life.

'I think Henry's going to be OK, don't you?' he said.

'OK?' said Paton. 'He's going to be absolutely splendid. Well done, Charlie!'

PATON HAS A PARTY

Every year, on Uncle Paton's birthday, Grandma Bone and her sisters took a short holiday. They hated having to buy presents or indulge in 'nonsensical celebrations', as Grandma Bone put it.

This year, Paton's birthday was on the first day of half-term. Maisie decided that before Charlie and his uncle set off for the coast, Paton should have a real party for a change.

'We've never had a proper party here before,' she said. 'But Charlie's new friends have got such *interesting* parents, we really ought to get to know them.'

Invitations were sent out and, surprisingly, everyone accepted. Even the judge.

The party was kept secret from Grandma Bone in case she tried to put a stop to it. Maisie managed to hide the champagne under a sack in the larder, and the birthday cake was put in a crate marked CAULIFLOWER. Grandma Bone hated cauliflower so she kept well away from it.

On the morning before the party, Charlie carried his grandmother's suitcase down the stairs. Grandma Bone was right behind him when he crossed the hall to the front door.

There was a bang and the sound of breaking glass. Charlie dropped the case and looked round.

'Oh dear,' said Grandma Bone. 'That picture's broken again, and Paton's just had new glass put in it.'

The photo of Henry and his family lay on the floor; the glass in the frame had smashed into a thousand pieces. Had Grandma Bone knocked it down on purpose? She had a nasty smile on her face.

'Well, its good riddance to *him*,' she said, pushing the frame with the toe of her boot.

Charlie didn't say a word. If only she knew the truth, he thought.

Once she was out of the house, everyone breathed a sigh of relief.

'To work,' cried Maisie. 'Let's make this old house as smart as a palace!'

At seven o'clock, their work complete, Maisie and Paton, Charlie and his mother, waited for their guests to arrive.

Tancred and his parents came first. As soon as the Torssons walked through the front door, all the candles flickered violently. A few went out.

'Sorry!' boomed Mr Torsson. 'We'll try and keep the breezes to ourselves.'

Maisie was delighted. 'How clever,' she said. 'We could do with a bit of fresh air in here.'

Benjamin and the detectives came next, and they were quickly followed by Fidelio and the singing Gunns, and Gabriel and his parents. Mr Silk wrote murder mysteries

271

and when he heard that Mr and Mrs Brown were private detectives, he whipped out his notebook and was soon deep in conversation with Mr Brown.

The Onimouses, the Flame cats and the Vertigos arrived at the same time. Olivia's father was a famous film director and immediately wanted to know if Mr Onimous had considered a career in the movies. 'I'm casting for *The Wind in the Willows* right now,' he said.

'I'll consider it,' said Mr Onimous.

By eight o'clock, the party was in full swing. Charlie thought everyone had arrived, but Paton told him that there was just one more guest to come. A few minutes later, the bell rang. Charlie opened the front door and found Cook on the doorstep.

'Pearl's told me everything,' she said. 'It's a happy ending for Henry, after all.'

'And Mrs Bloor,' said Charlie.

He took Cook into the kitchen where Gabriel Silk was helping to serve the drinks.

'There's just one thing I'd like to know,' said Cook, sipping her glass of wine. 'Where did Dorothy find that marble?'

'I gave it to her,' said Gabriel.

Charlie was surprised to hear this.

'Well, well,' said Cook, 'and where did *you* find it?'

'Mr Pilgrim gave it to me,' said Gabriel. 'I think he knew I would give it to Mrs Bloor. She was always in the tower, listening to his music.'

'Of course.' Cook nodded slowly. 'Mr Pilgrim *is* a mysterious man.'

'Where d'you think Mrs Bloor is now?' asked Charlie.

'She'll be in Paris, just as she always intended. She'll have got herself a nice little apartment and soon she'll be giving violin lessons. Maybe she'll join an orchestra. Who knows? She'll be playing her violin again, that's all she ever wanted. And she'll be safe.' Cook looked at Gabriel. 'Thank you, Gabriel.'

There was a sudden loud bang on the front door. It came again. Someone wasn't even bothering to ring the bell.

BANG! BANG! BANG!

'Whoever . . .?' said Paton.

Charlie followed his uncle to the front door.

Grandma Bone stood on the top step with her three sisters behind her.

'What's going on?' she demanded.

'We're having a party,' said Paton coolly. 'What are *you* doing here?'

'I forgot my keys,' snapped Grandma Bone. 'How dare you have a party in my house. Stop it this minute!'

'Stop it!' said Lucretia.

'Everybody out!' said Eustacia.

'You can't have a party without our permission,' said Venetia.

'SHUT UP!' said Paton. 'I *can* have a party. In case you've forgotten, it's half my house.'

'What's the trouble, Paton?' Mr Torsson had come to see what the fuss was about.

'No trouble,' said Paton. 'Nothing I can't handle.'

Whether Paton could handle it or not was beside the point. Mr Torsson took one look at the four angry sisters, puffed up his cheeks, and blew them down the steps and clean across the street.

Grandma Bone narrowly missed being hit by a bus.

Charlie watched in awe and astonishment as the Yewbeam sisters picked themselves up, patted their hair, brushed their muddy clothes, and shook their fists at Paton and Mr Torsson.

A loud thundercrack and a sudden cloudburst sent them scurrying away down the street, shrieking and cursing.

'We'll pay for that,' Paton murmured.

'But not tonight,' said Charlie.

As soon as the four sisters were well and truly gone, Olivia Vertigo said, 'Let's dance!'

'Yes, a dance!' cried Fidelio.

Before anyone could stop them, they had moved the table in the dining room and rolled up the rug. Emma put some music on the CD player and all three of them began to dance round the room.

The other boys hung back at first, but then Maisie grabbed the judge round the waist and whirled him on to the dance floor. After that, no one else could resist the music. Soon, the usually cold and cheerless room was full of swaying, bobbing figures. Uncle Paton even managed to persuade Miss Ingledew on to the floor. The room was so crowded they had to dance very close. Charlie noted that

Miss Ingledew didn't seem to mind a bit.

He couldn't see his mother in the room and so he went to find her. She was sitting in the kitchen staring through the window. Little flakes of snow were drifting down from the sky, but Charlie knew his mother didn't see them.

'Dad *will* come back,' said Charlie quietly.

When Mrs Bone turned to him, she didn't look sad at all, in fact she was smiling.

'You know, Charlie, I'm beginning to believe you,' she said. 'After what happened to Henry, I can believe almost anything.'

TO BE CONTINUED . . .

Read about Charlie's next adventure in:

CHARLiE BONE
AND THE BLUE BOA